Y0-BBX-319

Mullins the Munificent

Mullins the Munificent

with
Some Episodes from the
Lush Life at the Turf

By
Jacob Kraft

ᑯᑭ

Aventine Press

Copyright © 2004 Jacob Kraft
First Edition

Without limiting the rights under copyright reserved above, no part of this
publication may be reproduced, stored in or introduced into a retrieval
system, or transmitted, in any form or by any means(electronic, mechanical,
photocopying, recording, or otherwise), without the prior written permission
of both the copyright owner and the publisher of this book.

Published by Aventine Press
1023 4th Ave #204
San Diego CA, 92101
www.aventinepress.com

ISBN: 1-59330-206-1

Printed in the United States of America

ALL RIGHTS RESERVED

To my family, and to my other family.

A special thanks to Amin, Ian, Tyler, Robin, and of course, Jayon for their invaluable advice.

"Therefore I will not restrain my mouth; I will speak in the anguish of my spirit, I will complain in the bitterness of my soul."

Job 7:11

Preface

I've never done drugs, and I haven't been beaten or broke. I've never hit somebody in the face, slept a night on the street, or had my wallet stolen. I haven't been divorced or married, fought a war, or had to pay my children's college tuition. I don't even have kids. I have enough trouble paying my own bills.

Last year though, I saw some real trouble for the first time. It wasn't me suffering, but I felt it all the same, and I can still feel it now. I'm writing this story to remember what I learned, but also to remind myself that life's nasty troughs aren't everything. Things smooth out eventually, because everything changes, and because even the biggest mountains look small from far away.

* * *

Chapter One

"I don't get it—of all people, why do I get kicked in the ass?" That's what Mullins whispered to me before he passed out in the hospital. That was the last thing he said that night. But it's not the only thing I remember.

I remember a Mullins who was brash and brilliant. I remember a Mullins who was shameless and subtle. And I remember a Mullins who put himself on the line just to make other people laugh. Sometimes I remember him as an unsuspecting martyr. But I always remember him as a friend.

Mullins was childish too. He had a lot of expectations for himself, and he complained whenever something didn't work out. Most of the time, he ignored the facts of his life, preferring to create his own fantasy world. And even when it sent him to the hospital, he swore he was innocent.

* * *

When I met him in the fall, Mullins had just arrived in Philadelphia after spending the summer in Spain. I didn't know anything about him beforehand, except what I could glean from a letter he had sent to my roommate Prateek. We were renting a room in our apartment because one of our roommates had

decided to study abroad in Buenos Aires. Prateek sent Mullins'
letter on to me, a wrinkled yellow paper, and I still have it:

```
                                    July 18th
                                    Madrid

        Prateek,

           I'm Matthew Mullins and I'm interested
        in renting the room. I'm not a student or a
        member of a "larger intellectual enterprise"
        like you advertised for, but I do know how
        to bake.
           You asked for a self-description. I'm
        a Franklin grad, and currently without a
        career, but this is my last year off after
        college. I'm moving to Philadelphia so I
        can find out how to join the freight train of
        the real world. I don't have a girlfriend at
        the moment, and I'm quiet when I'm asleep.
           What else can I tell you? I'm pretty
        clean. I pay on time. And I drink green
        tea. Fresh tea, you know, loose tea.

        Cheers.
        MULLINS

           PS Everyone except my Mom calls me
        Mullins.
```

Who was this guy? He was slightly older, and we knew he
had traveled in Europe. But would he be a good roommate? I
typed his name into the internet and to my surprise, found his
resume on a website of job applicants in Philadelphia. Mullins,
it seemed, had been the valedictorian of the Asian Languages
students at Franklin, and president of two volunteer organizations
for the Philadelphia homeless. He had been on the Ivy League
Council, a co-captain of the debating team, and vice-president
of the baking society.

His resume was impressive. But that didn't tell us what kind of roommate he would be. And as he was traveling in Spain, we couldn't interview him in person. Prateek was worried about that. He wrote to me and said: "you can't trust what people tell you about themselves because even if they're honest, they miss things." But I wrote back to Prateek, and to our other roommate Ellen saying we should choose Mullins anyway. He was the only person who had written us a note on real paper. I liked that. He was the only applicant who showed us some character. I liked that. And he was the only one of our applicants who I thought could challenge us in the ways we liked best. Prateek and Ellen agreed with me. So without more thought, without an interview, and without any idea what we were getting into, we invited Mullins to join the Turf.

                            *   *   *

I arrived in Philadelphia at 10:14 am on a scorching September day. The air-conditioning in the train was broken, and I had been sweating through my shirt since Washington DC. I disembarked at 30th Street Station, and being cheap, I carried my bags and contrabass all the way across the Market Street Bridge to the Moorhead Apartment Building on 18th St. and Moravian. I barely made it. But when I got there, I forgot about my sunburn, sweaty cloths, and sore muscles. It was exciting to walk past the Moorhead's fake marble columns, where various tenants and streetwalkers had carved their names. And it was exciting to get back in that rickety cage "elevator" where you had to open the door with both your hands because it was always stuck, and where there was a big sign on the inside which said "IN CASE OF FIRE, DON'T USE ELEVATOR. USE WATER." The elevator had recently been repainted grey, but it still had strange pipes sticking out of its metal walls and oil dripping out of random spots in the caged roof. I'm not complaining though.

That elevator was fickle, and took more time-off then the French, but it never failed me when it showed up.

I rode up four floors and managed to get my bags and bass out of the cage. Then I put my key in the door and took a deep breath. I was about to start my last year of school and my last year at the Turf. I would be with the people I knew best, in the best city I knew, and I couldn't wait.

The apartment door wasn't locked. In fact, it never was. So when I turned the key and pushed with all my excitement, I opened it much too hard, tripped over my bag, and fell right into a huge pile of garbage. As I put my hands out to block my fall, I let go of a terra cotta wine jug I had been carrying and it smashed into a million pieces on the kitchen floor. Luckily, I didn't hurt myself, or more importantly, my bass. Not that my roommates worried. They came out of their rooms laughing like I'd won a grand prize.

"Aaron!" My closest friends, Ellen Chung and Prateek Singh admired me in the garbage. After a moment, they helped me get up. Ellen wiped the dirt off my back and Prateek went to get my bags from the hall. I gave Ellen a hug, and shook Prateek's hand when he returned.

"Aaron Richards," Ellen beamed at me, as we picked up the pieces of the wine jug, "Our bard is back."

They asked about my trip, and I told them everything had been fine, except that the train had been hot and delayed by a nuclear waste spill in Delaware.

"The corporate cheats finally take it in the ass!" Prateek grinned. He had spent his summer researching business ethnics and knew quite a bit about Delaware.

"Take a load off," Ellen said. "Do you want some of these fresh scones that I just made?"

I did, and I ate two. Then I ate six more. Nuclear waste makes you hungry.

Ellen smiled and asked if I wanted any more. I did, but then I remembered it was almost lunch time, so I decided instead to move in and unpack. My roommates helped me shuffle my bass, suitcase, and duffle-bag from the kitchen into my room. When I walked inside, the first thing I noticed was a huge scratch in the middle of the wooden floor, and I swear to you that it was there I when I arrived. Do you hear me any readers associated with the landlord-- I did NOT scratch that floor. I did NOT install those permanent shelving units with a very small and annoying screwdriver. I did NOT ruin the drawers in the desk by kicking them closed with a steel-toed boot. I did NOT ruin the bed springs on the left-top corner by trying to dive into my bed from the desk chair when drunk. Nor is the bedspring-like mark on my shoulder related to that event. Oh yeah, and I did NOT ruin one of the outlets by pulling out an extension cord from down the hall. You know what I did though: I put on D'Angelo's *Brown Sugar* and got ready to unpack. Opening the window, I realized that my room, and my year, were fresh with possibilities.

*   *   *

We spent the next few days getting the apartment in shape. Our first task was to pick up all of Prateek's books from the post-office and put them in the living room. This would have been easy if Prateek had maintained a normal or even large library. But Prateek wasn't interested in libraries; he had created what he called a "literary enterprise." What did that mean? That meant that I had to spend an entire morning loading boxes and boxes of books into cabs at the 30th Street Post Office and then unloading them and carting them up to the apartment. We're talking about thousands of books, more than most people could afford to buy in their lifetime, much less ship around the country.

Ellen and I did a lot of cleaning those first few days. We trashed the old house-plants, the extra VCRs, and the random garbage around the apartment. We hung our paintings. We bought new plants. We bought spices and kitchen equipment. We cleaned the floor. (Well, we put floor cleaner on the floor and left it there. We figured it would take about a year for the floor cleaner to eat through all that dirt. We would mop it up, we said, at the end of the year.) We set up our liquor cabinet. We bought liquor. We bought candles. I bought some black paint and did NOT use it on half of one of my walls.

Prateek vacuumed. He vacuumed everywhere. You weren't safe when he was vacuuming. He didn't make allowances for feet, or any other limbs that happened to be on the floor. He didn't make allowances for sheet music either, so I spent part of an afternoon taking apart the vacuum cleaner.

When we finished cleaning the common rooms, I polished my bass. Ellen hung blankets she had bought in India on her walls and every other bare wall that didn't talk back. Prateek cleaned his room to absolute sterility. You were safer to eat on his floor than on the kitchen table. But we ate on the kitchen table anyway. Principles, we had principles.

Four tireless house-work days later, we were slouching on the living room couch listening to Buena Vista Social Club, and trying to avoid organizing the piles of magazines on the floor. For one reason or another (laziness), we had kept every New Yorker, Economist, Men's Health, GQ, Atlantic Monthly, New York Review of Books, and Playboy (for the "articles" of course) that we received during our two years at the Turf. In the middle of the pile was a huge volume of Gore Vidal's essays. I have no idea why it was there; nobody read Gore Vidal.

I was about to ask Prateek where the book came from when the front door burst open. Two seconds later, we saw someone fall through the doorway and into the latest pile of garbage.

"I told you guys that was dangerous," I nagged.

"Ridiculous!" Prateek responded.

"Guys!" Ellen scolded.

We got up to see who had fallen into our clutches. A young man picked himself up off the floor, replaced his glasses, and wiped his hands on his jeans. Then he extended his hand.

"I hope you hope you don't mind," he said, "but I've taken the liberty of compacting your garbage."

Everyone laughed and we introduced ourselves to Mr. Matthew Mullins. I helped him move his bags into his room while Ellen made some green tea and Prateek vacuumed around the kitchen.

Tea cups in hand, we escorted Mullins around the Turf. We pointed out the Fire Escape NEVER to be used, the Smoke Detector NEVER to be attached, and the bathrooms NEVER to be cleaned. Well, we didn't actually say the bathrooms were never cleaned. That was obvious.

After our tour, we went in the living room to chat. I put on some Glenn Gould and sank into the couch next to Ellen. Prateek sat in his leather wing-back chair, which left Mullins the white recliner.

"Tell us about yourself," Prateek asked our new roommate, and leaned back with his hands folded on his lap.

"How much time do you have?!" Mullins responded enthusiastically.

Prateek looked pleased. The point of this query, he had once explained to me, was to see how a person would immediately respond. Confident laughter? Embarrassed laugher? Arrogance? Charm? I don't know what he got from Mullins' response, but he smirked as if he'd had an insight.

"Well, where are you from exactly" Ellen asked.

"All over the place. I moved around a lot growing up."

"Army brat?" she asked

"No. My Dad's a businessman. He follows the green."

"Uh huh. So what made you come back to Philly?"

Mullins smiled. "Nostalgia I guess. I went to college here you know, and since I didn't figure out what I wanted to do with myself then, I decided to come back and finish the job."

"Did you work before this?" Prateek inquired.

"I had job before this, and a job before that. Before that I had a job too. Jobs and me though…I don't know, but I really haven't found the right one yet. I got fired from my last job because I was 'distracting the other employees too much.'" Mullins made quotation marks with his fingers "So I went to Spain for the summer." He laughed and repeated 'distracting the other employees,' in a croaking voice.

I asked Mullins what he planned to do in Philadelphia.

"Oh, I'll find something." He spoke confidently. "But mainly I'm planning to have a damn good time."

That sounded like that right attitude to me. Certainly it was the way we lived in the Turf.

"You never know," he continued, "I could find the perfect career. Or meet the love of my life."

"Well, you never know with this place," Ellen said. "Something will definitely happen."

"That's right," Prateek added helpfully. "Remember that time, Aaron, during the party that your ex-girlfriend showed up with her lesbian lover? Ha ha ha," he laughed.

I glared at Prateek and asked him if it was *absolutely necessary* to invoke that moment at least every three days. Our new roommate, I said slowly, might get annoyed after a while.

"Come on Aaron, it's funny and you know it."

Well, I guess it was. Sort of.

*   *   *

The first day I met Mullins, he was a roommate. It was only about halfway through the year that he became one of my closest friends, someone who put himself on the line for me, and someone whose bigger story would intertwine with my own.

The day of my mid-year recital was a disaster. I had cracked the neck on my bass that morning, stubbed my left-hand index finger opening the front door that afternoon, and cut my right-hand thumb with a paring knife while making my dinner. I had also received two rejection letters denying me the chance audition for symphonies, and I had lost two critical pages of my music that I hadn't yet memorized.

I managed to pull myself together though, borrowed a friend's bass, got a copy of my music, and taped my fingers the best I could. But with all the stress and the injuries, I wasn't prepared to perform that night.

At 8:30, I walked onto the stage with my bass, and sat on the lone stool. My roommates, friends, and fellow students were in the audience, as well as my teachers, and my parents. Mullins, by chance, was the Emcee. He was working for Philadelphia's biggest audio company, who were in charge of amplifying and organizing the Bok Conservatory's student performances. He had arranged to work this job so he could get in his hours and attend my concert.

After I arranged myself to play, Mullins came on stage in his tuxedo and announced my name and the pieces I was going to perform. Then he walked off the stage and sat at the soundboard in the wings.

I took a deep breath, and prepared to play, but I realized that I had forgotten the first notes of my piece. I started to sweat. How did it start? These were the pages I hadn't learned well, and I couldn't remember them. I started to panic. What was I going to do? I couldn't play. I couldn't walk off the stage. I looked at the audience in desperation, and then I looked at Mullins. He squinted back at me from the wings. I started to feel nauseous, and I looked at Mullins again.

Suddenly, there was a high pitched squeal in the hall speakers, like a terrible feedback, magnified to a painful volume. After a few seconds the squeal stopped, but then started again. Mullins ran onto the stage.

"Ladies and Gentlemen," he said. "I'm sorry about the disturbance, but we're having some technical problems with the sound equipment. Could you please give us five minutes to identify the problem, and then we will return to Mr. Richards' performance."

Incredibly relieved, I left my bass on the stage and walked toward the wings. When I got there, Mullins told me: "Wait here a minute." He ran off and returned with my bass teacher and my music. I don't how he found them.

"Your teacher will help you," Mullins said "You guys can go over the music. Just relax now." My bass teacher smiled understandingly, and I started to feel better.

"But I need more time," I implored, "two more minutes isn't enough."

"No problem," Mullins replied. He grabbed the cordless microphone and walked onto the stage.

"Ladies and Gentlemen," he began, "while the sound technicians are working their magic, I'd like to tell you a story about a similar situation that happened a few years ago at the White House..."

With that, my teacher and I left for the green room, and I didn't hear the rest of the tale. While we talked through the music, I could faintly hear the audience laughing, and clapping, and what I thought might have been cheering. Ten minutes later I was ready to go, and I signaled Mullins from the wings. He smiled, told the audience that the problem was fixed, that they would get the rest after intermission, and they clapped him off the stage.

"I think they're ready for you," he whispered to me.

I walked back to my bass, and pulled together a descent performance of my music. It wasn't inspiring, but it was respectable, and soon enough, it was over.

*   *   *

After the concert, Mullins and I walked slowly back to the Turf via Walnut Street.

"I don't know how to thank you," I said.

"Don't worry about it," he assured me, "You know I love telling stories, and tonight, at least, the audience really ate it up."

"Ate it up? Did you make up the whole thing?"

"You bet. And I had them convinced too! They really believed I had worked the audio in the White House and got musically seduced by the Press Secretary in the West Wing bathroom…"

"You didn't say that!"

"I did! Defamed our national leadership I did, and even gave them a solid impression of that ridiculous woman singing Puccini! It was a little hard to put the Italian through her Mississippi accent, but they went for it."

"I can't believe this, Mullins. Did you know that there was a Philadelphia Inquirer reporter there because the mayor was supposed to be in the audience?"

"Hmm, that does explain why those jokes about City Hall flopped…No, I'm kidding, I knew."

"But what about the reporter? What if that gets printed in the paper?"

"Listen," Mullins said, "those people in the White House have to pay a price for getting their stories told all the time, and that price is that they have to live with what the stories say, even if they don't like them."

"But why should they have to live with stories that are untrue?"

"They live with the stories that are told," he insisted, "And that's history."

I shook my head. "Have you always been telling these crazy stories? They haven't gotten you in trouble before?"

Mullins laughed. "Actually, I only started story-telling mid-way through college," he admitted. "My freshman and sophomore years, I didn't have many friends. Even though I was in a fraternity, and I knew some people from my classes, I didn't really know how to talk to people. Most of the time, I found conversations stupid, or I couldn't relate, so I ate take-out food alone in my room. Because I was afraid of going out, I spent a lot of time watching movies, reading, and chatting online. I didn't even like going to the dining hall because I knew I would have to sit by myself and feel awkward while the people around me talked. Sometimes I hated myself for being so anti-social and even for doing well in school, but I couldn't see a way out that I felt good about."

"Were you shy or what?"

"Not really. But I critiqued myself for being too judgmental and intellectual, and decided that was why I couldn't get close to anyone."

"So what happened?"

"Well, at the beginning of my junior year, I went to the dining hall to eat, and saw a guy at the table next to me telling a story. The story itself was ludicrous, about how he had tripped down the stairs of his apartment building or something, but the guy had the rapt attention of everyone at his table. I decided that every one of my awkward moments could also be a great story. So that's what I did. I started turning my life into stories, finding awkward moments and transforming them into pure entertainment. I practiced accents and perfected my gestures."

"Wow," I remarked. "That's a story in itself." We reached our apartment building and Mullins unlocked the door.

"The thing I realized," he concluded, "is that making people laugh always made me feel liked, and confident. At the end of this summer I also realized that the best way to do it harmlessly is to make fun of yourself." And that, he argued, was the true mark of his twenty-four year-old maturity.

*   *   *

After that night, I began to see Mullins as the storyteller that he was, and the storyteller he wanted to be. It wasn't difficult; he was always ready to entertain. Just the next day for example, I heard about his "story geometry."

"So, you want the story of story geometry?" We were drinking at the Blue Fog bar, and sitting next to a shapely Eurotrash dame named Frenchie. Frenchie was a thin-faced regular at the Blue

Fog. She wore a lot of leather and a lot of make-up, and she never smiled. This was part of her cool European aura, along with her extremely expensive sunglasses and the ever-present cigarette dangling from her lips. Frenchie kept her European ties strong: she spent alternate weekends in Milan shopping, and had been given a pink Mercedes convertible wrapped in a massive bow tie for her recent 20th birthday. Sadly, she did not know how to drive. Nor did she care to learn. But she did like drinking in cafés, all day long, and that's where we often found her.

"Most stories," Mullins said, "are what I call the Coital-Jazz shape." Mullins had no inhibitions with profanity, especially when he thought it would color a phrase. In this particular case, he had probably used the term since I was also a jazz musician, and because he wanted to tickle Frenchie, who claimed to like jazz (but, we surmised, liked sex a lot more). He continued, leaning in to whisper, but maintaining the intensity of his words:

"The Coital-Jazz shape takes the form of traditional jazz solos or of good coitus." His leaned in further and deepened his voice. "It starts slow, slow, slow. Then it starts to build; slowly at first, keeping the tension, the friction." Mullins sat back in his chair and smiled. "As the momentum increases, the listeners think they see the end coming. That's when there is a momentary drop-off in the plot, an Indian summer if you will. There are humorous moments, asides, perhaps even a slight lull." He sat up straight and looked at me and then Frenchie straight in the eyes. "But everybody knows where it's going; *it's* no joke." Frenchie tossed her hair and took a deep drag. Mullins watched her and then drew in the air with his hands, talking like a scientist. "From a distance, the graph would look like a single diagonal line going up; in close, there are bumps. But as the line increases its length, it starts to bend, going faster, like a fat parabola."

He paused, smiled, and then whispered: "Or maybe I should say it goes deeper, richer."

"Eventually," he said loudly, after a quick swig of beer, "there is an apex." He raised his glass to toast us. "You come to an apex.

You climax. An orgasm is reached, dramatic, intense!" Mullins was practically yelling now, and he had breached even my flexible sense of social-etiquette. I looked around to see who was there. Luckily, no one I knew. Frenchie, by contrast, didn't worry. Wearing sunglasses indoors, she considered herself incognito.

"The listener forgets himself," Mullins continued, ignoring me. "He forgets the story. His eyes don't see past his eyeballs. All he sees is himself in the moment, his own emotions, his own reactions, his being. He realizes that he IS!"

Mullins snorted and finished his beer. Frenchie sighed and lit another cigarette. The storyteller waited for her to finish and then continued calmly: "Unfortunately, the climax is usually brief—a matter of seconds. Eventually the reader remembers it's a story. Then it's over. That's the form. And most stories fit into that form, just like most people fit into one-size-fits-all aprons. Of course, it's gotten me into trouble once or twice. When I was teaching English …"

Mullins told us about the time he had been teaching English to some Japanese businessmen and had mistakenly made light of the slavish working conditions in their home country. As a sad but amusing consequence, he had apparently lost his job and been forced to apologize to everyone for his inappropriate behavior. But that story isn't important, and neither is Mullins' understanding of geometry. The point is that the Coital-Jazz shape was a story in itself, one that Mullins hoped both Frenchie and I could relate to. As for Frenchie, she left the Blue Fog that day with a Columbian guy named Tomas, and we never saw her again.

*   *   *

Although it had taken several months before I considered Mullins a storyteller, the stories themselves began immediately on his arrival.

Mullins had left Europe, he told us, because "a ham-eating cock-tease had dropped him for a fat Spaniard with a sweating condition." It was his first afternoon at the Turf, and we were lying on the apartment couches in food coma. We had just devoured a hot and greasy special from Tim's Chinese food truck, our "high tea," so to speak. To help us digest, I put on "Jazz from the Lincoln Center," and got out some scotch.

During his summer abroad, Mullins reported, he had "given himself" to a local girl. This misguided lady, however, had taken another man under his very nose. "Can you imagine?" he exclaimed. "A sweating condition! Right under my nose!" He was heartbroken, he told us, victimized, and he swore then to never, ever date another Spanish girl unless he had "absolutely no other choice." She had seduced him, abused his body, and abandoned him in a moment of great passion.

"Abused your body? What did this girl do to you?" asked Prateek.

"You see," Mullins recounted, "She gave me skin-tight jeans which cut off all the circulation in my legs. She told me I had to wear them into a hot shower and let them shrink-dry on my body. It was the pants baptism from hell! Then, barely able to walk, I had to wear them to a nightclub where I was forced to dance and drink all night long. I don't like dancing. I don't like smoky clubs. I don't like Spanish dance music. And I hated spending all that money on liquor that burned my throat and my stomach." He cleared his throat as if to remove any remaining liquid. "By the next morning, my legs must have been as blue as my pants," he continued, "but somehow we made it back to her place, and that's where it ended."

Mullins poured himself another dram of scotch and signed. "In all honesty, I couldn't really communicate with her anyway. All I know in Spanish are some restaurant words, 'where is the bathroom', and numbers up to nineteen. But you know, since we were dating, I figured we didn't need to discuss other things in detail."

"Dating?" asked Ellen. "How long did you know her? She must have spoken English, right?"

"Not really," Mullins answered. "She would point and say something like "Este hombre es cuidado, no?" and I would translate that as: "The bathroom please tip is seventeen, no?"

Ellen raised her eyebrows.

"So how long exactly did you know this bird?" asked Prateek. "And how exactly did you think you were dating her?"

"Dating someone isn't about chatter!" declared Mullins. Then he sat back in his chair. "Or that's what I thought, anyway. Actually, I had met her a few weeks before that, since she worked in my hostel, so it seemed pretty clear."

"Did it occur to you," asked Ellen, "that whatever happened might have been due to miscommunication?"

"Well, no," he responded, "but I don't think it was…I mean, I had already bought her lunch twice, and when she invited me out to the club, she offered to lend me some of her brother's jeans. She even brought me to his house, and that's where they made me take a shower with the…"

I got up to change the music. It was time for Silvio Rodriguez and Mariposas.

"All right, all right…so what happened? What did she do?" Ellen inquired.

Mullins sipped his scotch. "Well, she had brought a bunch of friends back with her from the club. After we arrived at her house, she whispered something to me in Spanish and led me down a hallway to a strange room with bookcases in front of the windows. There was almost no light at all, but I could make out a world map on the ceiling, drooping above a huge bed. She pushed me forward, and I tripped on what I think was a basketball and fell into the bed. I noticed the sheets were silk…"

"You remember the details pretty well," Prateek interrupted, regarding Mullins suspiciously.

"Yeah," Mullins responded quickly. "So," he continued, "I was on the bed, and she came over to me. This is IT! I thought.

My heart started pounding. She unbuttoned my shirt, and then unbuckled my belt…"

"Uh," Ellen butted-in, "I'm not so sure we need to know *all* the details."

"Don't worry," Mullins assured her, "that's as dirty as it gets. After she undid my belt, and the first button of my pants, I smiled at her. But instead of continuing, she said something Spanish in my ear and leapt off the bed. Then she went through another door and shut it.

"So I waited. I thought she was probably going to the bathroom. Girls are always going to the bathroom. No offence Ellen, you can't be blamed for a genetic deficiency."

"Thanks Mullins, that's nice of you."

He smiled. "I waited five minutes, then ten minutes, then twenty minutes. 'Where the hell is she?' I thought. 'Did she get sick or something?' So I got up and buckled my belt. Then I knocked on the door. Mullins snorted. "No answer," he said. "So I said, 'fuck it,' to myself and I opened the door. It was a short hallway, pitch black. I couldn't find the light-switch, so I wandered down the hall until I got to another door. I stopped and heard some noises. So I knocked on that door. "Si?" I heard. It was her. What the fuck was she doing? I wondered, so I pushed on the door.

"As the door swung open, I saw that the room was dark. I moved in a little bit and then I heard a scream, and some kind of wet cloth fell into my face. I tried to move forward, backward, wherever, but my feet were caught in something and I tripped again and fell on the floor.

"The next thing I remember is that I passed out. I totally lost it," he said. "But not before I saw a fat, sweating, naked Spaniard leaning over me, and the double-crosser behind him with a sheet around her. You can only imagine how I felt. And for some reason, I couldn't breath, so I just gave up and passed out."

"Why did you pass out? What happened?"

Mullins looked at me. "I don't know. I woke up a few hours later, back in that big bed. She was dressed now and standing next to me with her man. She had her hand in his shirt and was whispering something about "mi hombre de Cro-Magnon." I couldn't understand it. I pulled my head up and croaked: "What the hell, get me out of here!" but she shushed me and the fatty, hair coming out of every part of his shirt collar, snickered. God he smelled horrible. I can't believe she dropped me for him."

"Did you leave?"

"Hell yeah, I did," he said. "I got up and walked right out the door, and I'll tell you what:" He glared at us defiantly. "On the way out, I took a stuffed owl from the kitchen counter, and it's right here!" He went into his room for a moment and returned with the animal. It was about five inches tall and wearing a mortarboard, glasses, and a bowtie.

"Cute," Ellen commented, "What's its name?"

"I don't know," Mullins answered, "but I'm renaming it the Watch Owl and putting on my shelf to watch over us this year. As long as the Watch Owl is here, we won't even have to watch over ourselves. And it's a good thing too, because when you fall for someone, you can become totally blind to their treachery, as I experienced so painfully."

"I'm not so sure what you missed was treachery," Prateek remarked. "You're telling me this is a girl who you could barely communicate with at two lunches, who invited you out to dance once, and you think she was dating you?"

"Woman's opinion?" Mullins asked Ellen. "She lent me pants!"

"I don't believe in dating people who aren't friends," said Ellen, "but anyway, maybe Spanish people just like to dance? Or maybe she just enjoyed your company?"

"Pfaw!" said Mullins, "You don't invite someone to go dancing in a place where you can't hear yourself think just to enjoy their company."

We sat silently for a moment, pondering this point. Then Prateek glanced at his watch. "You know, I would really like to go for a run today. You want to come?" he asked Ellen.

"Yeah," she said. "Mullins? Aaron?"

"No thanks," I declined.

"Why not," Mullins answered. "And I'll tell you about visiting this double-crosser's cousin the next week in Seville, what a woman…"

Shortly afterwards, they left for their run. I cleaned up all the dirty plates in the living room and went to the Blue Fog to read the papers.

Chapter Two

Down the street from our apartment was our second apartment, a bar, restaurant, and lounge called The Blue Fog. There was nothing blue or foggy about it—the name came from its previous life as a hippy love-shack. Apparently, a group of wealthy students had bought the row-house together in the 1960s as a place to have parties and smoke weed. On the day of their events, the owners would signal their friends with blinking blue lights in the front windows. But like all planned utopias, it couldn't last forever. In 1972 one of the owners led a hostile takeover of the property and converted the house into a bar and restaurant.

The Blue Fog had six or seven public rooms, each with a different collection of ancient carpets, un-matching furniture, and faux French wallpaper. Each of the rooms also had some sort of 'social-mission' theme, a relic of its hippy past. There was, for example, a room where the window-sills were full of Salvation Army charity cans, a room decorated with Chinese-made Tibetan protest signs, and a room with poorly-framed black-and-white photographs of starving African children and work-worn West Virginia coal miners.

The hippy artifacts didn't activate my social consciousness. But they had their own kind of authenticity, the quaint inspiration of naïve do-gooding and old-fashioned signage. When you were drinking, the rest didn't really matter.

The piano room was our favorite of the Blue Fog's non-eating spots, and perhaps the coziest bar in all of Philadelphia. The uneven wooden floor was covered by a faded Persian rug, on which sat mostly maroon tables and mostly olive-green chairs. Across from the small bar in the corner was an old piano missing most of its outsides. But its nakedness was barely illuminated by the brass chandeliers hanging from the fifteen foot ceiling. In fact, it was always seemed to be night-time in the piano room, no matter what time of day it was. For the same reason, you could barely see the Matisse-inspired wall-paper or Chagall-inspired painting on the ceiling. And the curtains, perennially closed, kept the room so dark that you couldn't make out their color at all. I guess there's no question that archeologists would be confused if they dug up the piano room of the Blue Fog. But I can be proud of the fact that they'd find me, or at least the telling imprint of my rear-end, permanently formed into several of the comfy chairs.

The Blue Fog beverage specials were heavily-limed gin and tonics and in cold weather, hot toddies with whipped cream (God's plan for apple juice before some ingrate invented sobriety). When you ordered from your table, you were assured that your drinks would arrive within at least one hour. Thus it was a safer bet to walk across the room yourself and slap down some money on the bar. Usually that would awaken the narcoleptic bartender, who would sleepily fill your order before returning to the Sandman.

As you waited or drank you were entertained by one of two piano players. "Ringus Dingus" Mattieu Pingus, a wrinkled old German with a bow-tie, played war-time classics—Gershwin, Berlin, Rodgers and Hart, and the rest from 3 pm to 2 am every Monday, Wednesday and Friday. The other days you had Roberto Warshasky, a middle-aged rocker from Georgia with long grey hair. He played blues and southern rock standards. I liked them both—neither played too loud, and you could always hear people talking over the music, or if you wanted to, you could sit back and talk to yourself.

To the songs in the piano room my comrades and I had toasted such things "the end of all war!" and "recycling everyday!" But we drank to ignoring our work, to Hemingway, and to drinking. Don't get me wrong—we didn't get drunk, very drunk. No, we just liked to hover in our happy place. The place where I could only smile, where Prateek forgot about his investments, and where Ellen made outlandish claims about all of our futures. It was also the place where we solved the world's problems, and where we were all the most seductive versions of ourselves—the place where we convinced ourselves that we were everything we thought, and that we could be everything more.

*   *   *

"They're just kids, they're just fucking kids. They don't know what they're doing." That was Drew, telling me about his nights.

"Most of the people I talk to are babies. I try to help 'em, but it's not easy. Most of 'em don't have any of their own ideas, and the ones that do just want to do the same fucking thing they've already been doing. So even if I help them, you know, they just continue their nonsense."

Drew was a former Catholic priest and current late night radio-show host who helped people with their problems. He was especially popular with the university kids in Philly for his career advice, because he had strong cynical opinions about universities and professors.

I used to see Drew at the Blue Fog. He often drank there with a lady I assumed was his wife. That afternoon however, she didn't show up and he was drinking alone at the bar in the piano room. I sat next to him, ordered a tea, and read for a while. As I took sips, I noticed him finishing one drink after another. After about five or six, he turned to me and spoke:

"You wouldn't believe the bull-shitters who teach around here," he said. "What they get away with…"

Clearly, I was not going to read anymore. It didn't really matter; I was tired of squinting at the papers.

"What's wrong with them?" I asked.

"Professors," he grunted. "Worthless. Don't help the kids at all."

"Professors are out for knowledge. Making the world make sense," I responded. I didn't tell him, but it seemed like a respectable career for me, and the best option if being a musician didn't work out.

"Aca-dummies?" he said. "You mean wanna-be artists without spines? Humanities, I'm talking about. Well, some of them are all right. But most of them have got no spine. They just bicker about bullshit; they've never been outside in the real world, and they don't have any idea how things really work. They don't care about teaching either." Drew slumped on his stool, and ran his hand through his gray hair. He shook his head, and smirked to himself.

"Wait a minute," I said, "Isn't that a little unfair?"

"Listen, he growled, "most teachers in college don't even know their students' names. Isn't that the ultimate disrespect? How can you engage somebody like a human being when you don't even know their name? It's patronizing, and it's pathetic."

Drew thought he knew something. But did *he* know people's names? I asked him.

"Hell yeah I do. I was a priest for twenty years, goddamit, and I delivered mail before that. I knew everybody's name— everyone—their names, and their problems. I talk to people like they're people, even if they don't know what they're doing. Especially if they don't know what they're doing."

"Uh huh. But what's your bone with professors?"

"Listen, they're babies. But it's not that. Babies are ok; they're cute you know, easy to love. The problem is it's babies in charge of other people, and they treat the other people like babies too. So the students end up being babies, just like the teachers."

"What are you…" I began to ask.

"The whole system is corrupt!" Drew interrupted. He sat up straight and banged his glass on the bar to wake up the bartender. "The classes—where some guy prattles on about nothing and ignores the students; the tests—that measure how well you puke; the grades—that give you a superiority or inferiority complex; the bills—that put your parents in the poor house and keep the poor at home—what's the point? These kids talk to me and they don't know anything about themselves or have any perspective their lives. What do these professors teach? Nothing!"

"Listen, I agree with you about the cost of school and about some of the classes. But you have to test people, and grade, to show if they learned something, right?"

"I didn't say you couldn't test people. Fuck. But ranking people like some are better than others is destructive. It's just a fake way for spineless teachers to avoid teaching."

"So, how do *you* teach then?"

"Teaching is about learning people's names and helping them tell their stories. It's just…it's about being with people and helping them grow as people. So they don't turn into shit." He gestured at himself and chuckled sadly. Then he drained his drink, and stretched out his back. "My kidney is killing me," he said to his drink. He looked at me. "When people come into your class, you don't wanna tell them what to do. I know I'm an radio-host life-advisor, but that's not about advice. I just want to spend some time with other human beings."

I didn't know what to say so I didn't say anything. Drew paid his tab, stuffed a couple of bucks in Warshasky's jar, and left.

*   *   *

On the way back to the Turf, I ran into Mullins, who had finished his run and was exploring the neighborhood.

"Nice place," he told me. "I liked the nut shop and all these book stores. Where do you guys hang out?"

I pointed him to the Blue Fog.

"Good place to meet girls?" he asked.

"Certain kinds," I told him. "But in this part of the woods, as Prateek likes to say, you have to watch out for the yuppies, the guppies, and the crazies."

"Rubbish!" Mullins exclaimed. "Nothing dangerous can get past my forward sensors and invisible shields. Not after that Spaniard."

"They have a way," I insisted. "You may not even see it until it's too late."

"So be it," said Mullins, "But you know, I always figure more experience with the ladies is a good thing. Experience is what I need."

"Well, stick around," I told him, "If you hang out in this street late enough with your jogging cloths on, I'm sure you'll get some kind of proposition or another."

*   *   *

When I got home, I decided to check my email. But before I could get typing, Prateek knocked and, without waiting for a response, came in. A bony Bengali with a growing paunch, he worked hard to make you wonder when you should take him seriously or not. In reality, I'm not sure he knew himself.

Despite his Indian heritage, Prateek considered himself a sort of Roman senator, and made sure to remind you of it at every occasion. His normal laugh, for example, was literally "ha ha ha," and sounded so haughty that you couldn't help but laugh along. And when I first met him, Prateek wore only the most WASPy Ralph Lauren clothes with a brown patent leather belt and matching patent leather loafers (without socks, even in winter). These he complimented with a gold chain and a gold

Omega watch. He always left his shirt collar as open as possible, and was always carefully groomed and perfumed.

Prateek accepted no criticisms of his dandy appearance, even from his friends. When questioned, he asserted seriously that his was the only respectable way to dress. He would then instruct us, in his slightly Indian accent, how we could improve ourselves. Out of respect, we would listen graciously as he mixed up his w's and v's and then we would solemnly agree with his point. But if he was a character with idiosyncrasies, Prateek was still someone who made sense to me. He grew up in Wisconsin, and coming from a Hindu background, he learned pretty well how to worship the American gods (of business acumen), as well as the British gods (of *classic* style), the Greco-Roman gods (of literature and oratory) and many others.

I had met Senator Singh two years ago in a psychology class, which even students of the conservatory were forced to take. Actually the class wasn't all bad, since I never went and never read the book. In fact, taking psychology that semester actually added time to my schedule, time I would not have had were I taking an interesting, demanding, or meaningful class. Good work, school administrators!

You might be suspicious, but I promise I didn't avoid psychology because I was lazy or unwilling to explore a subject outside my direct field of interest. No, it just seemed to me that most psychology was pseudo-science, and that the good stuff required all kinds of biology and anatomy and other classes I would never take. I gave the professor three chances to change my mind, which I thought was more than fair. Life is short, and you can't waste it on other people's priorities. But the teacher, I'm afraid, failed his own test, and I cancelled the class. I was not the only one to do so. Prateek also skipped psychology. But he didn't fail the teacher, he had a different justification, one that I would learn was typical from Prateek: he claimed, in so many words, that he already knew everything about it worth knowing.

"You just have to learn how to measure things," he told me. During our normal class-time, we recognized each other in the Blue Fog and decided to have a drink together.

"It's all an enterprise; it's all about creating value," he said. "The psychology which creates value teaches us how to understand and manipulate people. That's what's important to understand. But all of that you can learn better in a marketing class."

"Right," I said.

Prateek glanced at me and took out a pipe, which he tried unsuccessfully to light. After a minute I realized that Prateek did not know how to use the pipe at all, and that he had never smoked it before. It took him eight or nine matches and two pinches of tobacco before he was able to produce some smoke. But as he fumbled on in front of me, he kept a straight face, as if he had done it a million times. Finally he got the pipe lit and placed it in his mouth. He had, however, forgotten about the lit-match in his other finger, which began to burn his hand. He quickly took the pipe out of his mouth and blew as hard as he could to put out the flame. He was successful, but with his vigor, he also managed to blow the cream from his mocha-latte onto the hair of the lady at the table beside ours. She didn't notice, and he shrugged, nonplussed, and continued.

"Unlike psychology, business gets things right." He finally took a drag on his pipe, but his face turned red and he began coughing smoke. He got up and ran over to the bar to get some water while I sat shaking my head. After a moment, he returned to the table, and sat down as if nothing had happened. He continued his thought:

"When your very existence depends on your theory of how the world works, you get it right. Or you perish. That's the enterprise."

I heard many more of Prateek's philosophies during ditched psychology classes at the Blue Fog. For Prateek, I learned, everything was an enterprise. And though I would often be thinking about a girl, or maybe some music I was trying to write, I would nod my head at him in agreement. Some of it was nonsense of course, but some of it was interesting. And more importantly, I enjoyed what Prateek had to say much more than the psychology professor, who was both literally and figuratively a world expert in the creation of attention deficit.

During that semester of half-listening, I learned a lot from Prateek. I never gave him any satisfaction by admitting it, but I don't regret it. I don't think he needed any assurances that he had the answers.

As we got to know each other, skipping classes on all the wonderful aspects of psychology, I began to see what you could call Prateek's "humane enterprise": his enthusiasm for reading history and literature, his interest in world affairs and debating them, and his refined taste in alcoholic beverages. It's terrible to say it, but all of these are rare distinctions among university students. Prateek, however, knew all about the old ways, and the most sophisticated arts and culture, and though he really belonged in another century, he was one of the few people I knew who saw beyond the wretched television culture and self-sustained stereotypes of college life. Of course, he had his own ridiculous ideas, but at least he had chosen them. Besides, he knew a lot, and you could always depend on him to surprise you. He was driven, but he was almost never stressed. No, he always considered himself to be on top of things.

Now, in our last year at school, we were close. And though I had not changed his mind on many things, I'm happy to report that he had taken up wearing socks and had given up the patent leather for Dock Martins. He claimed, of course, that it was entirely his idea.

"Listen" he had said to me, "they're the original. Don't forget that your dress and manner are the flag markers of your class and your education." He straightened himself and raised one eyebrow. "Your shirts should always be ironed, and you should never, ever, write with a ball-point pen." Little did he know that I had never, ever, written with anything else.

"What we're here to learn," he continued, "is not in books. We come here to learn the dance of the elite, all the steps. That's why I'm the manager of the Cask and Pig comedy troupe."

"Oh?"

"Absolutely. It's an elite group. The point is, anyway, that at Franklin University, and the rest of the Ivies, we're learning how to suck oysters, drink wine, talk wine, and be exclusive."

Prateek didn't know at that point that I was not actually in his Ivy League-school, but at the Bok Institute studying classical and jazz bass-playing. Or maybe he knew but considered me one of the elite anyway. After all, I was one of the few people our age who owned a tux (for gigs) and who had read a Hemingway book besides The Old Man and the Sea. In any case, Prateek was a good lad. He was one of the few friends I had who when you least expected it, would apologize eloquently. He was modest about his own accomplishments, intellectual and otherwise, and he never worried about grades, or the little bullshit which tripped up so many intense and strong-minded people. Besides, when you heard that laugh, "ha ha ha," you couldn't help but dismiss all of Prateek's apparent haughtiness as the biggest joke of all.

*   *   *

SMASH! "Direct hit! Direct hit! I've sunk your battleship."

"Prateek, was that really necessary?"

"Ha ha ha. At least I didn't snap your stick."

After entering my room without permission, Prateek decided to experiment with the aerodynamics of my conducting baton. He launched it like a missile, and though he missed the primary target (me), he successfully knocked my water glass onto the floor.

"Oops" he said, with no emotion. Nonchalantly, he picked up the glass pieces from my rug. He seemed unconcerned that breaking a glass might have been a mistake. Or else he was, but had dismissed his mistake as fast as he made it. Either way, Prateek had an impressive ability to restrain his responses in situations when others would be sheepish or flustered, and I didn't know whether to smack him or applaud his self-control.

While Prateek was picking up the pieces of my glass, he asked what I wanted to do for dinner.

"I have a craving," I said, "for The Banana Leaf."

He nodded. The Banana Leaf was an apartment favorite, the only Malaysian restaurant in the city. Besides the food, we loved the speed and the staff of the place. We had seen the waiters and waitresses perform amazing feats, such as noticing a dropped fork from across a crowded room and replacing it within three seconds. But even more amazing were the prices. Now if I were running a restaurant of that quality, I would charge, say, $25 for a plate of curried chicken with rice and noodles, a meal that was highly delicious and big enough to be two meals. But the Banana Leaf charged a mere $6, a truly student price, a price that showed they valued eating, and a price that was enough motivation for us to walk down to 11th Street several times a week. I told Prateek to alert the proper dinner companions. He nodded again, and carefully placed the shards of glass on my pillow. Then he left the room.

I yelled after him to get me a new water glass. He didn't of course. So I went out to get one myself. On my way to the sink, I saw Mullins sitting at his computer in his room. Knocking quickly, I walked in and asked what was up.

"Just writing the final letter to my ex," said Mullins. "She won't leave me alone."

"This is the Spanish girl?" I inquired.

"Oh God no. This one was much worse. Well, here's the first draft. What do you think?" Mullins read aloud what he had written:

My Dear X,

    I'm sorry to hear that you've gone
nuts. But still, that's no excuse to be so
melodramatic, or to use such trite imagery
in your letters. "Razed the fortress of
your love"? If anything, Captain Liszt,
you've been at siege on me, not the other
way round...

"Hmmm," Mullins interrupted himself. "Not too nice,
probably a bad idea if I want her to stop bugging me. And
besides, I don't want to get caught up with those metaphors.
They're ugly. Here, let me try again." He erased what he had
and typed quickly. Then he read me his next version.

My X,

    Your histrionics are not eloquent or
even amusing. Please refer to the letters of
John Keats before you write any more about
your eternally bruised heart. And while you
are doing your research, find yourself a new
boyfriend...

"No, that isn't much better," he commented. "I don't want to
be a total ass to her. Just a pain in her ass. Perhaps a humorous
approach..." He typed some more and read it.

Dear My X,

    I could tell from your letter that you
were upset about something, but I am not
sure what. Did it have to do with me? And
what's this about your heart? Are you still
eating that fatty cream cheese I told you
to avoid? Listen, you better get some
aerobic exercise, otherwise your arteries
are going to be falling apart as fast as
these 'forts' you mention...

"Funny to me. Aaron?"

I didn't have time to respond. Ellen had walked through the door behind us and yelled "Foul!"

"Voyeur!" I responded. "You have no part in this manly business."

"What?" she asked. She came into Mullins' room and sat down cross-legged on the floor in front of his bed.

I shook my head in mock disgust, and she flashed me her teeth and her dimples. Ellen's smile was dangerous, and not just in the sense of libidinal provocation. This was a smile that made you change your mind, a smile that made you say what you had planned to keep absolutely secret, and a smile that wiped your mind of sourness and discouragement. Although Ellen often wore it with an air of innocence, she knew that her smile opened doors, loosened tongues, and produced wallets. And she used it that way, on occasion justifiably. Having now known Ellen for three years, I had given up resisting the smile, or I should say, attempting to, and I was only glad to see it as much as I did.

This is not to say, either, that I now saw her as unattractive. Oh no. In fact, she was very much not unattractive. That double negative is my solution for expressing insights that violate the laws of roommate-cest. These laws had been violated in the Turf before, and caused a minor civil war, but that is not appropriate for this story. So, as a platonic friend and roommate completely unbiased by Ellen's non-unattractiveness, I will describe her in full objective detail.

Ellen spoke with a sweet southern accent. Her parents had emigrated from Hong Kong to South Carolina when she was nine. They were in some sort of computer business, but like so many first-generation immigrant parents, they had decided early on that Ellen would be a doctor-scientist-engineer. Ellen, however, was less interested in medicine or engineering than in the crap she rubbed out of her eyes in the morning, and she decided her job was to save the world.

How does one save the world, you wonder? Well, everyone has their own way I suppose. Ironically, Ellen had taken a scientific approach to figuring it out, perhaps as a tribute to her forlorn parents. That was how she approached most things, with theories and experiments. So what did she do? How did she figure out the best way of saving the world? Well, she scoured several national newspapers every morning for three weeks, and made a list of the world's biggest problems, and a list next to them of ideas on how they could be solved.

After creating a number of lists and sub-lists, and then comparing the sub-lists and lists with a master list, a list of her own abilities, a timeframe list, and a placebo list, she discovered, she said, that most of the world's problems stemmed from bad education. Her lists dictated that she had to reform our national, then international education systems. Her lists said that she should start researching education immediately and form theories about the best way to fix public schools.

You might find it funny that teaching was not a necessary experience for an education-reformer—it made none of her lists. In fact, Ellen didn't believe in "teaching" at all.

"People have a natural enthusiasm for learning," she would tell anyone, "and that's what our oppressive schools and their know-it-all authorities destroy."

"So you're getting rid of teachers at your schools?" anyone might inquire.

"We'll have guides. Or something else, I don't know. The students can appeal for help when they need it. People learn best when they are personally motivated to study something."

"But who's going to tell them if they're wrong?"

"An independent committee of students, guides, and parents, selected democratically by the entire student body."

"Five year olds?"

"The *entire* student body."

"I see. And who's going to organize the curriculum?"

"No curriculum."

"So how do you make sure the kids learn everything?"

"Learn what?"

"You know, math, reading, that sort of thing."

"They'll learn it if they want to. Kids are observant about the world. If they see that they need such skills they'll go after them on their own."

"But won't people be lazy and do nothing all day?"

"Of course not. Kids only do that now to rebel against the prison-school. They're human beings. Why should teachers keep them in small uncomfortable rooms all day and tell them what to do? It's horrible. I'm surprised more kids aren't delinquents."

"Why aren't they, if schools are so bad? Why don't more people complain about schools if they're really prisons?"

"Because they're brainwashed and because they can't. Adults who went through the system are afraid that to throw it away is to throw away their own authority. And what's more, there's habit. Who would question something this big, this widespread, even if it was designed by a few well-meaning but idiotic individuals? Most people are so accustomed to it that they don't even realize how bad it is."

"So how do you know it's that bad?"

"Because you can see it everywhere else. All the music, all the culture, all the war and destructive behavior, all the unhappiness, all the depression, all the hatred, all the feelings about being stuck or unable to change. All the people who are robots or TV-addicts or racists or xenophobes or ego-maniacs or the people who have dead senses—the people who don't notice what they eat, what they look at, or even how they're feeling. The people who don't notice all the amazing pleasure of life and realize they can take part in everything…"

"And you're going to fix those people with new schools?"

"You bet."

It's funny though, with all of those looks, smarts, and opinions, Ellen was still shy. I had never taken a course with her, but I'd heard from Prateek and others that she rarely participated in class discussions. When I asked her about it, she told me she preferred to watch the other students, and that's why she was majoring in anthropology (the education program, she said, was a joke). She was shy at dinners too, and she was perfectly content to observe a conversation between two people next to her from start to finish. Underneath I think, she had a strong personality, and I figured when she got to be more adult, she would be a presence you could feel before you even saw her.

*   *   *

Mullins took a break from his emails and asked how we'd met. I told him I'd made Ellen's acquaintance in the Franklin freshmen penitentiary. I mean, dorms. She lived with hundreds of other inmates in an apartment-style dorm called Von Smelt Manor, which let me tell you, did not look like a manor, nor smelt like one.

"Which dorm was that?" Mullins asked.

Ellen explained: "It was a fascist concrete monstrosity, a row of pointed brown boxes highlighted with two or three rows of brown bricks. Inside, there were four floors of long, straight, silent, white concrete-block hallways. These were lit by white neon lights, and lined with a series of identical brown doors. The doors led into identical box rooms with identical shit-colored carpets and identical prison furniture. They had identical square living rooms, with identical low-ceilings, and identical bars on identical small square windows. Since the bars were thick and plenty, the windows provided almost no light. Luckily, the rooms were also lit by unshielded neon lights. Also, it's lucky that these lights covered the spectrum from yellow to blue, and were almost blinding, since any other lamps were forbidden as a fire hazard. Unluckily, doors on individual rooms did not lock. Also, walls within apartments were paper thin. Only one poster and three postcards were permitted per student, and these had to be installed by the maintenance man Joe, who was mentally retarded and worked on a three-week time delay."

"Talent," said Mullins. "But I don't think I ever went there."

"Don't forget the basement," I reminded her.

"Oh yeah," she remembered. "Below the ground floor was a dark dirty basement with exercise equipment that looked like it had been stolen from a Bronx parking lot in 1983. You had to get tetanus shots before you could use it. Well, tetanus shots were recommended if you wanted to use it and live." She made a sour face and said she had to call her parents. After she left, I continued the story of our meeting to Mullins, and I will recount it again now for the reader.

One night I was visiting Von Smelt to attend some festivities, or whatever they call it in prison. As I admired the scenery, and thanked the gods I didn't have to admire it everyday, I heard classical music echoing loudly at the end of the corridor. I decided to investigate; it isn't often that you hear Schubert's Piano Sonata in A Major in a penitentiary (and a juvenile one at that). When I got to the end of the hall, I found the door propped open and I peeked in.

There was young Ellen, in a tight white apron, struggling to open a bottle of Chateauneuf De Papes. She was slightly bent over in front of an elegant (and illegal) candlelight dinner, which was marred only by the rusted-iron table bolted to the floor. She must have heard me breathing because she looked up. That's when I saw her lovely face, her perfect skin, and the irresistible dimples in her cheeks. Again, I'm talking from a historical perspective here. Think male college freshman. And count yourself lucky I'm not giving you an in-depth description of her cleavage.

Ellen was wearing a short black dress under the apron, which did not hide her figure. Her straight and shiny black hair was tied back in pony tail with a bow, except for a few strands which had managed to escape and were hanging in her face. After a rather long moment, I realized that she was trying to wrench the cork out of a wine bottle between her muscular thighs.

Now, being the gentleman that I am, I couldn't help but offer my services to a lady who was clearly in distress. How was she going to open this bottle, and who was going to eat this delicious looking dinner if I did not volunteer? The poor girl, I thought, all alone, no dinner guest, no one to enjoy the Schubert with, or to help her drink the wine. Who would compliment the young lady on her appearance, or rather on her fine ideas about life? Yes, indeed, I had been sent from God.

I cleared my throat, drew myself to my full height, and in my most debonair voice, asked 'Might I be of some assistance?'" I then smiled with all my teeth. Ellen looked up at me for an instant, expressionless, and then went back to tugging at the cork.

"Recapitulation," she muttered.

I repeated my offer, with less flair and more volume, hoping for a different reaction. But all I got was the same brief glance, and the same strange muttering.

I thought to myself: damn, this is a strange one. This girl really wants to open the wine-bottle herself. She tugged again, and squeaked, but to no avail.

"What the hell," I thought, and I walked in the room. She looked up at me, stood up, shrugged, gave me the bottle, and put her hands on her hips. She didn't have shoes on, and I saw that she was tall for an Asian woman, about 5'4".

"Open it," she taunted. "If you can."

At this point, I was in a predicament. I could not fail. I had to open this wine-bottle with my superior masculine strength, showing this fine lady why I was indeed a gift of the gods.

I pulled. Hard. It was stuck. Harder. Damn, I muttered under my breath. Then I growled, closed my eyes, and yanked the cork with all my hormonal strength, and...BAM!

The cork was no longer in the bottle! Schwing! Before I even opened my eyes, I knew had succeeded in proving my strength!

But don't celebrate yet. You see, it turns out that I had not only succeeded in removing most of the cork from the wine bottle; I had also managed to remove most of the wine from the wine bottle.

When I opened my eyes, I saw that wine had ended up all over me, the walls, the curtains, the furniture the carpet, as well as Ellen's apron, dress, dinner, and stereo. I had even managed to extinguish her candles, saving her from violating a Von Smelt policy.

But I didn't realize this positive contribution to Ellen's dinner until later. At the time I stood absolutely still, horrified. We were both completely soaked in wine. Neither one of us moved. Then we heard a flushing sound from down the hall, and the opening of a door. I slowly turned my head in that direction and saw a large man appear. He was much larger than me, larger than my bass, larger perhaps than me and my bass. This large man was not happy. He was large and unhappy. His unhappiness was large. And big angry man said, in a large loud angry voice:

"Who are you…what happened to the…What the fuck have you done to my apartment! FUCK!"

Clearly, big angry man was not in favor of scarlet curtains. And I have to admit, scarlet didn't go to well with the brown bars on the windows. Anyway, big angry man, who we shall call "Assholio" turned his brutal gaze to me. I could see that he had declared me guilty and was preparing my sentence. He muscles began to bulge, and I could begin to make out the veins in his neck.

As his hands became fists, I went for the only chance I had. I quickly dipped my finger in a pool of wine on the table, stuck it in my mouth, and then spoke, as calmly as I could:

"Quite full-bodied," I said, nodding to him "and with a healthy hint of French oak. Nice choice!" Either he would laugh, I figured, or totally lose control and kill me instantly. Unfortunately, I figured wrong. His response was to raise his fists in the air and yell:

"YOU SHITS!"

Then I realized he was going to beat me to death, and it occurred to me that I had forgotten to update my will. My music collection was still going to my X. That was a shame. She would never appreciate my 20th century classical music. In fact, she would probably throw it all away. What a waste.

But it was not to be. Behind me, Ellen dipped her pinky into a plate covered with wine and then stuck it in her mouth.

"A little tannic though," she commented, sounding slightly disappointed and distracting Assholio from smashing me into a bloody pulp.

I turned around and looked at her gratefully. She wasn't going to let me be killed! I owed this beautiful woman my life, and perhaps even my body! However, we could work that out later, in my nice dry apartment.

I looked back at Assholio and he growled.

"I'll clean it up!" I said. "Right now. I'll be right back!"

With that, I put the bottle on the table, ran out the room, down the hall, and down Spruce Street. I dashed straight to the BABA quickie-mart where I bought some paper towels and bleach spray, and then I ran back to offer them meekly to my unfortunate hosts.

But when I returned, Assholio had decided that either he couldn't stand Ellen, or a room full of wine, and he had left.

What an idiot, to leave Ellen like that. It wasn't her fault. But frankly, his idiocy was my triumph. Still, I felt terrible about the mess, and about ruining the date. I offered to clean up the whole thing myself and to pay for them to go out to dinner. Strangely enough though, Ellen didn't seem to be that upset. She sat down on the wine-covered chair, crossed her legs, and started to eat from her wine-soaked plate. Then she asked me what I thought of the Schubert sonata. Surprised but not completely unnerved, I also sat down, soaked in Chateauneuf, on a Chateauneuf chair, and started eating what I believe was honey-seared salmon (in a sauce of Chateauneuf de Papes). I replied that I liked the piece, but thought the particular performance was a little bit, well, messy. We both began to laugh, and laugh and laugh, and we didn't stop until I almost choked to death on a piece of salmon. After recovering, we cleaned up the mess, I got Ellen's email address and promised her a new dinner. Still soaked in wine, I walked back down Walnut Street, whistling first, then singing some old Gershwin tunes. I didn't know what I had found then, but it turned out to be one of my closest friends, and a true companion in the art of life.

The next week I took Ellen to the Blue Fog for dinner, and the connection was immediate. We got joint season tickets to the symphony, we spent nights at jazz clubs, and took Sunday morning jogs to the art museum. Was it romantic? I guess I wanted it to be. At first. I mean, when you relate to someone that well, and you think they're beautiful, well, let's say it's tough not to think those thoughts. And the city didn't help. There was winter time, when we used to walk through Rittenhouse Square, lit up in multihued globes. There were the nights when I helped her put her coat on after meal in one of the tiny bistros of South Philly. There were the times at First Friday, going to art galleries in Old City. And of course, there were the times when I was alone late at night and didn't have anyone else. I wanted her then, you can't imagine how much. But right or wrong, I decided after two weeks that I wasn't going to risk our friendship for something unpredictable or even destructive.

Ok, that's a total lie. The truth is that in my immature, foolish way, I tried to put the moves on her. She had probably given me hints to indicate she wasn't interested, which I completely missed (or selectively ignored), and I kept on trying to convey my feelings in ways so obvious that all of West Philly must have been gagging. She didn't let me get too far though. After some good dining and drinking at the Blue Fog one night, I put my hand on her knee and rubbed her thigh. She didn't flinch. Slowly, she removed my hand, smiled, and asked me what girls I was currently after.

I didn't know what to say. At that moment, I was after her. But it was clear that she wasn't after me. So I did what I had never been able to do before, and have rarely been able to do since. I let go of my romantic feelings, and focused on friendship.

Actually, that's another lie. It had nothing to do with me. The next evening I went to dinner with a girl from my composition class not expecting anything, and ended up at her apartment afterwards. I dated this composer through the next year, and I didn't have much time to think about my sexual attraction for Ellen. Instead Ellen and I developed a close friendship. That was what kept me going when my girlfriend left me suddenly for a sleek British guy named Madhan.

Over the last three years Ellen and I had spent a lot of time together. I think we both liked to get away from the dorks at our respective schools, and we both had developed similar tastes in how spent our free time, and how we ate.

*   *   *

"The Banana Leaf?" she asked, coming back into Mullins' room as I finished my story. She pulled her legs into lotus position. A little Buddha. Mullins told her he was happy to go whenever, but that he really wanted to finish this letter to his X first.

That got her started. Have I mentioned that Ellen liked nothing better than to analyze relationships and people? Before we knew it, she had laid out her entire theory on ex-girlfriends, which also dictated exactly, to the line, how he had to write this email.

I laughed at her.

"I have experience being an ex-girlfriend" she told Mullins seriously, "and besides, I've done experiments."

"What kind of experiments?"

"Oh, many experiments," she giggled. I wasn't surprised. She was always performing tests and experiments when you weren't looking, and she recorded the results in one of her many

notebooks on one of her many lists. In this case, apparently, the
theory dictated that he was to be:

1. Soft but firm in his rebuttal
2. Compassionate, but not descriptive
3. Concise

"Wait a minute," I objected, "how is that going to get the
message across to this foolish woman?" In response, Ellen smiled,
and Mullins typed:

```
Dear X,

    I'm sorry to hear you still feel hurt. I
don't mean to cause you pain, I just think
we're not the best match for each other and
I can't continue with you. Please call me
or come over if you want to talk about it.

    Mullins

    PS: YOU SUCK.
```

After removing the postscript, Ellen let him send the letter.
She couldn't vouch for his X's response, she told me, but at least
he wasn't exacerbating his problems.

Chapter Three

"Where's Mullins?" Prateek asked me. "Did you invite him to dinner?"

"I did," I said. "But he disappeared a few hours ago."

The Beatles were on the stereo in the living room and Prateek was reading "Takeover Quarterly".

"Ok," I said, "well, why don't we wait for him for a few minutes, and if he doesn't show up, we'll just go."

I walked around the apartment to see how the cleaning was going. Actually "going," was not the proper word. But in our defense, it's very difficult to concentrate on cleaning in such an apartment. Every object, even the walls of the apartment were so full of stories that you couldn't walk around without falling into a story yourself. And if you weren't careful, you did.

*   *   *

We lived on 18th Street and Moravian, near Rittenhouse Square, in a wood-floored, high-ceilinged, bay-windowed, 100-year-old apartment building that used to be a whorehouse. It was the Turf, and it was mythic.

When Ellen, Prateek and I moved in our sophomore year, we realized there was a lot to say about the apartment, even before we said a single word. For one thing, people, people beside the previous tenants, beside our friends, actually referred to it as "the Turf" like they might refer to a bar or their country estate. When we had a party, you would hear whispers of "are you going to the Turf tonight?" all over Philadelphia. The apartment had no limits; it had only friends. And family.

When I first arrived, I wasn't sure how to size the place up. This was a legitimate difficulty considering the apartment was knee-deep in a flood of book-boxes, kitchen appliances, (ab)used furniture, and other sundries. But living among the ruble (Prateek's room excepted), I learned how to respect it. Eventually, I saw that each object had its job and its place, even if that place was just to be tripped over.

You entered the Turf through a large wooden door on the fourth floor of the Moorhead Apartment building. You may wonder why it was called the Turf when it was just a regular apartment in a seven-story Italianate building. Well, we told our guests that when the building was still a place of business, so to speak, several of the working ladies had broken off from the group to form a more sophisticated enterprise. They, we explained, had developed a taste for refined living, and wanted clientele who could both appreciate and finance it. So they took over their own Turf in the building, and established a highly urbane lifestyle. They filled the apartment with books and art, and insisted on speaking and thinking of only the highest matters.

Underneath, they were still whores of course. But they preferred to think of themselves as revolutionaries in the entertainment world, who had discovered the perfect proportions of all the sensory delights.

Something similar brought our current group together. During our freshman year, we had all rejected the college lifestyles of the jocks, the greeks, the preps, the druggies, the religious kids, the computer dorks, the intellectuals, the pre-professionals, and the academics. To find ourselves, we had to create a new type of community and a new type of lifestyle with a new set of values. And that's what we did. Little by little each of us submitted ideas for something new, or different. Much of the time, the ideas weren't new at all, but what we found in history. Still, we liked to think we were writing our own history, and we announced creations such as our play-reading group and our extreme dinner parties as if we had invented them.

Not everyone in our building was like this. Our neighbors across the hall, for example, lived in an apartment called 402. We didn't hang out with them much, as they were a group of quiet Norwegians who, as far as we knew, only studied and played endless games of pinochle. Their names were Sirhc, Nura, Atims, Det, and Laz. Frankly, I could be spelling those names completely backwards; what you get is a bad phonetic attempt by a bad pinochler. Anyway, since our main encounters with our neighbors were frequent borrowings of their water filter, DVD player, blender, microwave, TV, broom, frying pans, mop, plastic-ware, paper towels, notebooks, notebook paper, textbooks, and pinochle cards (for poker night), I won't worry too much about them here.

When you walked through the wooden door marked "The Turf," you (either fell on your face, or) entered the kitchen. In the kitchen, both the oak-planked table and floor were covered with such a thick layer of grime that they seemed to be growing towards each other. The table, which was perpendicular to the door, was surrounded by a motley arrangement of chairs, some with four legs, and was faced by Fredrick the Fridge. Fredrick the Fridge was dressed with pictures and maps of all kinds including but not limited to the Alhambra, the Forbidden City, and a photo-edited mug shot of Kissinger looking like Pinochet (courtesy of Prateek). Also, as Fredrick the Fridge was highly ticklish, he was only cleaned when he was so rancid that it was painful to enter the apartment.

By contrast, the bathrooms were never cleaned. But you have to understand--we were hygienically talented. We didn't clean the fridge because we were sentimental about food. We didn't clean the bathrooms because we didn't pee on the floor.

To the right of the kitchen table was Ken the counter. Ken the counter was filled with all sorts of absurd devices: flame-throwing coffee-makers, tomato-sauce throwing saucepans, rice-throwing rice cookers, bizarre explosive bean cans, and brownish-blue wrinkled baggies. Ken also featured baskets full of food-like items, and metal objects of unknown origin and no obvious use.

The kitchen was the locale for many late night discussions, news deliveries, brainstorming sessions, non-stop laughter, morning embarrassments, and sometimes, much much hotter things. (Food, of course. Hot food. What were you expecting?) Walking through the kitchen into the living room, you moved from Brooklyn dive to Manhattan loft. The centerpiece was a huge black leather couch which we had bargained away from a lazy MBA student downstairs and got into the apartment at the mere cost of paying to have half the building's stairwell repainted.

When you sat on the couch, you sank down approximately ten feet. And if it was past ten o'clock or you were drunk, you didn't try to get up. The couch matched with a large black two-level coffee-table, which was covered with the subscriptions of the fake Turf Endocrinologist's office, Dr. Turf, an institution we had strategically created to receive every magazine we wanted, cheap. On the right side of the coffee-table were Prateek's leather wing-chair and our white recliner, occasionally stained, sometimes permanently. Behind the chairs was an impressive group bay windows which looked out on 18th street.

The view wasn't amazing—you can't see much from the fourth floor. But it was beautiful to look out and see the city buildings and cars blinking in the night. Or the colored globes in Rittenhouse Square. You had to lean really far to see them, and only one person could see it at a time, which was not very romantic. But it was still good enough to tell potential dates that our apartment overlooked Rittenhouse Square.

We had three enormous bookshelves packed with classics from every genre and era, owned and organized as such by Prateek. Two of the bookshelves were opposite the couch and set up around the TV, which was never used for TV. Instead, we used it to watch movies with one of the seven VCRs piled next to it, whichever was working at the time, or else with the neighbors' DVD machine. Television, however, was not accepted nor allowed as a form of entertainment. We told guests that a Turf roommate in the 80s had tried to watch the TV and had been electro-shocked by the zapper. It was better not to tempt fate.

Our living room, lit by candlelight, scented by who knows what (from the kitchen usually) and ambianced by Miles Davis, served as the salon for stories, sleek dinner parties, foreign film-screenings, passionate poetry readings, polemic political discussions, white and red wine tastings, imported beer parties, and those unforgettable performances by our conveniently in-house but inconveniently horrendous chamber music group. This was the Berlioz ensemble, composed of Prateek on ratty high-school bassoon, Ellen on often-in-tune viola, and another friend, the Maestro, on cheap Casio keyboard. The "musicians" seemed to take their inspiration from East African lions—they could scare away any living being within hearing distance of their roar. But I never said anything, not only because I was stunned into silence by their din, but also because it hurts to get hit on the head with a bassoon, even if it is a ratty high school bassoon.

In the living room and around the apartment, we had installed an art gallery--everything framed, everything sophisticated. We had a Jackson Pollack splatter painting, which Ellen and I had done on the fire escape, as well as Modigliani-like oil paintings, an art-deco Che, and an enormous black-and-white photo of an intoxicated but nonetheless inspirational Sinatra. Next to the bottom left corner of our art, we placed typed labels with acquisition numbers, approximate value, and a bit of history. We mentioned if they were photographed or painted in the Turf, or if they had been commissioned to fill a spot on our wall. The painting above the TV, for example, was an abstract nude of a former tenant, Gumi Uquieres. According to its label, Gumi had lived in the Turf in the late seventies. Her roommates had left indications in the hall closet of her history, and she was apparently a quiet girl from Uruguay who frequently entertained both men and women, and sometimes both simultaneously, in her quarters. When she moved back to South America, she ostensibly got a job in "Marketing", but she never revealed the exact details of her work. As a result, there was speculation in the Turf community that she was behind the great revival of South American porn in the early 90s.

Besides the art, the Turf was full of enormous Victorian house plants, never watered, but somehow managing to stay alive on the conversation and the drama of the apartment.

Don't get the idea that because we had all of this junk around, the apartment was unclean. Not at all. It was unclean because we were lazy. Everyone was assigned chores; no one did them. In fact, there were still signs up around the apartment from before we even moved in, when some "Kennan" was being reminded to do the dishes. To be sure, we were all conscious about our slovenly life styles, and every two months we had a coup to overthrow our previously elected cleaning officials. This was a figurative and literal revolution—we rotated the responsibilities, and then everyone went back to doing nothing. Usually the dishes were done only when Ellen took some initiative and recruited me to join the kitchen patrol. Prateek never cleaned anything; his meals were either restaurant leftovers, ordered food, or food from home, so I guess he didn't feel much responsibility for the dirty dishes. Mullins, it turned out, mostly survived that year on pastries: Cheese Danish, jam filled donuts, all sorts of scones, croissants, butter rolls, raisin breads, etc. Oh, and goldfish crackers. He liked them and kept a huge bucket in his room.

*   *   *

If the apartment's décor was unique, its whimsical tenants were no different. Prateek, for example, had an intricate shaving routine which involved, not one, not two, but three razors, including one electric, and a thirteen step process for using said razors, to be followed in exactitude, each time.

"This enterprise," he told me "is a hairy one. To come out alive, you have to have a proper routine, like the one Ellen and I have devised through years of scientific experimentation."

He was part-infomercial and part roommate, and he had a habit of buying absurd gadgets which we would find rusting all over the apartment. When we remarked on their silliness, he would defend them with even sillier sounding theories.

In the previous year Prateek had purchased a $350 hat from Japan which had a tiny video camera situated above the head, recording the wearer's every movement and sound. Anyway, this gadget completely contradicted Prateek's previously expressed theory that hats, except for top hats and bowlers were completely inappropriate for grown men. The other thing is that this ridiculous hat never worked properly, and only recorded loud and embarrassing noises, such as farts or Prateek's mom yelling at him from across the airport. We ridiculed our roommate for it, but to his credit, he wore the hat on at least three separate occasions, until he walked into a low doorway and destroyed the video camera. I could never prove he did it on purpose, but he insisted on his innocence until blue in the face.

Mullins, besides putting his pastry plate in the dishwasher, didn't do much housework. In fact, he never really moved into his room. The entire year he lived out of his suitcases, and what wasn't in the suitcase was either on his floor or lying on the ironing board next to his bed. He never put up any posters, he never put his books on his shelves, and I don't think he ever put a fitted sheet on his bed. He did unpack his computer, which sat on his desk and served as a large coaster for plates and cups of green tea. He would turn it on now and then to "perform his correspondence," as he would say, or perhaps to search for the phone numbers of girls he wanted to ask out to dinner.

Speaking of which, I yelled to Ellen and Prateek. It was time for our meal.

*   *   *

The evening was warm, and I didn't mind waiting at the corner of 18th and Moravian. Prateek and Ellen had invited the Maestro, and three other friends to dinner. When everyone arrived, we started walking down 18th Street and ran right into Mullins.

I asked Mullins if he was joining us. He answered that he had just visited the Blue Fog for a drink and was headed back to meet up for dinner. I gave the signal and the pack continued down the street, preparing to make a right turn on Chestnut.

We strolled, ambled, moseyed, and promenaded down to 11th Street. We walked like we owned the place. And you know what, we did. We were the most carefree sons of bitches around. We yelled, and talked, and laughed nonstop like the city was our backyard. We probably scared some old ladies. Or maybe we helped them remember. Anyway, we were feeling good, and the city felt good too. It seemed to be churning for us, and applauding us for having no obligations but to enjoy, and to live. The air was warm, except on the corner of each block where we felt the breeze of the taxi-cabs passing us at terrific rates. We ignored them, just as we ignored the pollution and the bums we passed on the street. When the city is yours, you see what you want. And for us, everything was glowing as we marched ahead into our future.

We arrived at the Chinatown gate, and just behind it, our beloved Banana Leaf. You wouldn't call The Banana Leaf elegant, but it was stylish in an Asian-metal-modern way. From the two levels of light wood floors, shiny metallic pillars extended to an open, piped warehouse ceiling. Huge fish tanks and modern art lined the walls, lit by enormous tin light fixtures. On the right side of the restaurant, there was a half-open kitchen where you could see bustling chefs yelling in Malaysian. The smells of the kitchen floated through the restaurant, and columns of steam tailed the running waiters with their trays.

It was a weekday, so we got the large round table next to the fish tank. As I sang along with the Greatest Hits of the Eagles playing on the stereo, I waved aside the waitress who brought menus. We didn't need menus; we knew what to eat. Then I remembered that Mullins was a Banana Leaf virgin, and that he might actually want to choose his food from a written list of options. Fair enough. I called the waitress back, and placed an order for nine gin and tonics and one menu. Mullins was sitting next to me, and I advised him carefully on his choices. After a minute or so, we decided he would be a mango chicken man, and I put in the orders for the rest of the table.

Now don't get the idea that we, my friends and I, were habitual sorts of people who just ate the same thing every time. On the contrary, that's why I ordered for everyone else: so they would be surprised. When we went to the Banana Leaf, someone different ordered every time. But our dinners always came quickly, no matter who ordered. Well, except for the time that I tried to order in Malaysian, which practically sent the entire staff to the hospital in fits of hysterical laughter.

As we began to talk, I realized we had big things on our minds. Besides catching up, everyone was thinking about the year ahead, and making those horrible career decisions. First though, everyone wanted to meet our new friend. Next to me, a friend of Ellen's asked Mullins where he was from. Mullins played coy.

"From everywhere, and from nowhere," he replied with a smile.

"But where are you *actually* from?" she said.

"I'm not *actually* from anywhere."

"What do you mean?"

"Well, I've moved around a lot. Here, there and everything."

"Where do you consider home?"

"Right now?"

"Sure."

"Philadelphia."

"Does your family live here?"

"Nope."

"How long have you been here?"

"About 8 hours."

"Have you been here before?"

"Yeah, but that was a few years ago."

"I see." Her food came and she turned her attention to her noodles. The Maestro, who was sitting on the other side of him, continued.

"So where does your family live?"

"In Delaware, but I've never lived there."

"Where did you go to high school?"

"I went to the Indiana Academy for Science, Mathematics, and Humanities in Muncie, Indiana," he said formally.

"So you're from Indiana!"

"No, I just lived there three years."

"You only did three years of high school?"

"That's right, I spent the last year living in Ireland."

"Really?"

"I graduated early and went on an exchange program to stay for a year there."

"What did you study there?"

"Not much. I mostly hung out, and volunteered at a couple of elementary schools. Life's pretty cheap there for an American, and so I didn't have to work or anything. My parents just gave me some money and I had a good time."

Both Mullins' and the Maestro's food arrived, and they stopped talking to start eating. Ellen turned to me as we were being served our food and said:

"Have I mentioned today that we live lives of incredible luxury?"

She hadn't yet. Usually she got to it before dinner time, but I guess we hadn't talked too much that morning or afternoon. Prateek overheard and nodded his approval.

He stood up and dinged his glass with his spoon until everyone was quiet. "Ha ha ha," he said. "And here's a toast to this group of comrades, on the eve of our most glorious year."

Three cheers, we yelled.

"Let us take a moment," he continued, "to remember fallen comrades, who are eating TV dinners or fast food tonight. Let us remember those poor bastards who have to work. And let us remember, how magnificent our lives are. We don't work, and if we do, it's just for a few minutes. Our days are spent expanding our minds, our tastes, and stomachs…" He paused. "It's so good it's sinful. So here's to sin! Ha ha ha!"

"Cheers to that," I said, and we all drank together.

I enjoyed the first sip of my wine, but when I started thinking about the toast, it finished sour. The extremes of good living border the darker continents of egoism and chaos. Prateek and I had discussed it before. We were getting-getting-getting, consuming-consuming-consuming, but not giving or producing at all. We would pay the Banana Leaf bill of course, and even leave a nice tip. But as students living the high life, we didn't contribute too much to anybody worse off than us. We were young, able-bodied, and we never had want for anything. Yet we spent our time stuffing our faces in fine restaurants and toasting that very fact.

Prateek sat down and continued eating. Meanwhile the Maestro got up to get our postprandial cigars from a Chinese joint down the street. He wasn't that hungry, having eaten a late lunch, and he had his food put in a box. On the way out, he swept by Ellen's shoulder and joked:

"Tell me Ellen, how sinful are you really feeling tonight?"

"Where's that symphony you promised me?" she responded.

"I've got the first four bars done. It's gonna be great."

"It better be," she laughed.

The Maestro left.

We ate our meals, chatting about our summers and our plans for the year. As the waiters came around to collect them, the Maestro reappeared at our table. He held up what he claimed were Dominicans 'as good as Cubans.' Then he sat down and gestured to a waiter for the dessert menu.

"One day Castro's gonna die," he told us, and "I'm going to celebrate." The Maestro was a short hairy Pole with beady eyes and oversized forearms. He went to the gym twice a day, and we were never sure if he was most passionate about music, lacrosse, or cigars.

"What did I miss?" he asked.

"Not much," I said.

"Oh yeah?"

"But I'll tell you what you didn't miss," I said. "Some green tea fried ice cream. If that doesn't increase the karma in this world, I don't know what will." Conveniently, one of the friendly Banana Leaf staff came over to take our dessert order.

"So where did you go to college?" the Maestro asked Mullins.

"Yeah," he said, sounding embarrassed, "I went to Franklin."

"What did you do there?" asked Prateek. Prateek refused to ask people what they studied or what their major was, claiming these questions were not only annoying, but demeaning. "Just imagine," he told me once, "if people judged me on my school performance rather than my portfolio of life's activities and enterprises!"

"Um," said Mullins, "according to my transcript I studied Asian languages. Actually that may have been the only thing I learned. Do you go to Franklin?"

The Maestro nodded that he did.

"What do you mean you didn't learn anything about life?" Prateek interrupted abruptly, challenging Mullins. He may have had too much wine. "That was for your Spanish bird to teach you, eh? Wasn't it Mullins?"

"I'd prefer," Mullins responded quietly, "if we didn't talk about that."

"Whatever you say," Prateek agreed, "but it is funny, I mean, don't you guys think?"

"Shut up Prateek," Ellen said politely.

Those who hadn't heard the tale looked confused, so I changed the subject.

"Is everyone free for Tuesday movie nights at the Turf?"

"We are, we are," said the Maestro. "I will bring cigars and brandy."

"Will you bring us some music?" asked Ellen. We were always trying to get the Maestro to compose theme music for the Turf, but we were always in line behind his bar debts. The Maestro was famous at a bar called The Old Wreck for betting his talents on Monday night Quizzo bowls. Unfortunately, more of a Maestro than a trivia nerd, he often ended up having to compose pieces for no-good Quizzo winners.

"I will bring music," he responded. "I am composing a piece called "The Sky Hangs Low," which you are going to love."

"Nice," I commented. "What's it like?"

The Maestro puffed his cigar and looked at me opaquely. He didn't respond. Then he turned to Mullins. "What was Franklin like when you were there?"

"Franklin?" Mullins said. "You know, my opinion on the place changed every year, really every semester. It's hard to separate that from what was permanent. I guess there are some new buildings, but there were always cool people."

"Yeah?" said Prateek.

"Yeah. But you had to look for them. That's because, at least what I remember is that there were a lot of pre-professional people—dorks who saw college as an unpleasant but necessary step between high school and money." Mullins shook his head. "I always wondered why they went to college. I mean, I guess you have to have college to be a doctor or a lawyer, or even a business man. But they just had no interest in the liberal arts classes. They didn't know anything about what was going on in the world, and they didn't connect anything they were memorizing with anything in their life."

"Yeah," said Ellen and Prateek simultaneously. Ellen smiled. Prateek snorted.

"Yeah," Mullins continued. "The social scene was dominated by frat guys drinking themselves sick and screwing sorority girls. People were working really hard, but they didn't know why. That was painful, so on the weekends they got fucked up to escape it. There was too much pressure on these kids, but most of them put it on themselves."

"Maybe they were just ambitious," said the Maestro.

"Maybe," Mullins agreed, "but that's a dangerous thing for someone without some grounding. These kids just went fucking crazy."

"Too bad for them," said Prateek.

"Listen, the way I saw it" Mullins continued, "these were the smartest richest kids around. They had nothing to worry about—they were never going to starve, and if anything happened, somebody was going to take care of them. I guess their biggest problem wasn't that they were lazy or not-interested, but forcing themselves to work hard. It doesn't make sense," he admitted. "I never understood it."

"They had to be at least as rich as their parents. They had to live the same lifestyle. Otherwise they would be unhappy." Prateek explained.

"That's bullshit," I declared, "Even you Franklin jokers are smart enough to know that money don't fill your happy engine." I smiled at the Franklin guys around me so they knew I was half-joking.

Our dessert came, and we started to eat. As we chomped away, our conversation continued.

"It's not money Aaron, it's the things that money brings— the lifestyle—the clothes, the house, the cars, the vacations, the season tickets, all that luxury." Prateek replied "I know I can't be happy if I live a lesser life than my parents."

"What are you talking about?" asked Mullins. "A lesser life? Is that about money?"

"There are widely accepted standards of living in the world. I don't want to go from one stage to a lower one. I would be a failure. I would feel like a failure."

"Are you serious?" asked Mullins. "You think taking a drop in income is taking a drop in success?"

"It's taking a drop in lifestyle. In that sense, you have a lower standard of living, and you have failed to maintain yourself."

"Listen, you're never going to starve. What, you can't get the newest clothes or the latest mocha machine?"

"It makes a difference," said Prateek. "You notice it day to day."

"Prateek, it's only if you choose to notice," I said. "You just have to make other things important."

"But you can't forget your entire childhood! If you grew up taking vacations in Europe, and buying books whenever you felt like it, you can't just start ignoring those needs. You won't be able to."

"Speak for yourself. I'm giving up that bourgeois bullshit for other priorities."

"Yeah," Mullins agreed, "people lived perfectly happily for thousands of years without getting on planes or changing their alligator skin wallets every month."

"Whatever," Prateek muttered. "I'll tell you guys about…"

As he finished telling us about this, that and the other, I could see that Prateek felt attacked, so I backed off and changed the subject.

It was enough. Even if I disagreed, there was no reason to press it. When I was in high school, I learned that keeping quiet is sometimes the best policy. Because, what if you win an argument? What are you really winning? Are you going to change somebody, or even change their opinion? Probably not. I'll tell you what's going to happen 90% of the time when you "win" an argument with friends. First of all, nobody's going to admit you won. You're the only one who's going to think so, and maybe the people who are arguing on your side. Second of all, you're going to feel empty because you were beating on your friend. Third, you might hurt your buddy or your friendship. What's important enough to risk that? Not much. So I decided to finish my ice cream in peace and let Prateek do the same. I smiled at him to show him no hard feelings, and told him when he was rich, he could support my insane CD-collecting habit.

In the meantime the Maestro announced that everyone had to attend a new set of pictures showing at the art museum, and I asked for the check please. We split the damage and got our coats. The Maestro and our other friends headed for the subway, and the rest of us walked to the Turf. It was dark now, but the air was still warm and fresh. I walked next to Mullins, who had impressed me during dinner for speaking his mind to Prateek, who was stubborn like a mosquito at the lake.

"What are your plans for the next week?" I asked him.

"I don't know," he said. "Find a job or two, get settled in Philly. God, it's great to be back."

"It must be."

"Yeah," he said, "until the trouble starts."

"The trouble?" We stopped for a red light.

"Yeah. The trouble happens when things are smoothed out and you start thinking."

"Thinking?" I was confused. If things were smoothed out, where was the trouble? The light changed, and we crossed the street.

"You know—thinking about yourself—your future, friends, women, all that sort of thing." Mullins smiled sadly. "I'm avoiding it this week by being busy."

I didn't know what he was talking about, and I didn't know him well enough to ask better. So I didn't say anything and tried to enjoy the walk back. It wasn't hard; walking through Philadelphia always felt like walking through a movie. We walked past stores, restaurants, and bars. We walked past the taxi-cabs stopped in traffic, past yuppies, and bums, and hippies, past students, parents with their children, and tourists. We walked through the evening lights and under the massive buildings of our city, through the smoke of sidewalk grates and over the cracked streets. We walked without hesitation, and without our end in mind.

We were back at the Turf before we knew it. We had a drink with the Maestro, and then we read for a while in the living room. I was reading "West with the Night," by Beryl Markham, an early aviator in Africa. Prateek was charging through the weekly Economist, and Ellen was reading about "energy healing," or some kind of alternative therapy.

After a few minutes of doing his correspondence, Mullins came out to join us. He didn't have a book, so he went to the shelf and picked one of Prateek's, Madame Bovary. But it was in French.

"Do you speak French?" Prateek asked.

"I learned a little bit in high school, but maybe I'll learn it again now, by getting through this book."

"Good luck!" Prateek pointed to the shelf. "The dictionary's over there."

Mullins took the dictionary and sat down in the recliner. We read for a couple of hours, and one by one we went to bed. In the middle of the night, I woke up and I thought I heard someone cursing. But I figured whoever it was had just tripped in the bathroom hallway, so I went back to sleep.

Chapter Four

In September and October we began the meat of our year. Ellen and Prateek started school at Franklin and were dutifully absent from class almost every day. They believed in "more important" learning experiences, and you could often find them reading in the apartment, or attending meetings in the park on the state of Philadelphia's fresh fish.

Ellen attended foreign films at the Fitz Theatre, hosted meditation classes in our living room, baked fresh molasses bread in the kitchen, and psycho-analyzed her friends at the Blue Fog. To cover her expenses, she worked for a mysterious old millionaire woman, a family friend who would send her research assignments by descending graciously from her limousine and leaving red envelopes at our front door. Sometimes I found the packages and delivered them to Ellen, but she would never show me the contents or tell me what she was researching. Her patron I saw only once, when the limousine was stuck in traffic and the grand dame was about to alight. I was just walking out the front door, and seeing her door open, I offered to deliver the package. She gratefully accepted, handed me the parcel, and drove off.

With his day, Prateek managed small portfolios of stocks and investments, read the entire nine volume diary of Samuel Pepys and spent a respectable number of hours working on his posture. He called this "carriage mechanics."

Both Prateek and Ellen read the New York Times, the Wall Street Journal and the Financial Times daily, the Economist weekly, and an assortment of other publications monthly. In their spare time, they read novels, made notes on their novels, ordered more novels from the internet, and catalogued the novels they had finished reading. These novels had nothing to do with their schoolwork, at least insofar as schoolwork had nothing to do with their education.

I don't know what they were supposed to be studying, and I'm not sure they did either. Prateek refused to talk about his schoolwork "out of principle." What principle he was referring to I'll never know. He claimed that most things he might be learning would not interest me, and if anything did, he would mention it immediately and without "an institutional reference to Franklin." I found his attitude a little patronizing, but he probably didn't mean it that way. If you asked Ellen about school, she would just laugh. School was a great opportunity to learn, she would say. It's too bad people are so closed minded about the location of the classroom.

I think that Ellen and Prateek did go to class, on occasion. They certainly passed their tests. But it wasn't fun or fashionable to talk about it. School was for kids; they weren't kids. School was about surrendering control of your education; they wanted to be in charge. School was about devoting your time to silly group projects, meaningless paper assignments, and an obscene amount of boring reading; they had no time to surrender.

Didn't they? They were students, weren't they? They had signed up for this Ivy League Franklin University, right?

"F.U.!" shouted Prateek when I asked them. "We signed up for access to the libraries and professors when we need them. Do you think we really spent all that tuition money to enslave ourselves?"

"Yeah" Ellen agreed. "I just wanted the college lifestyle, and Franklin sounded like the place where I could educate myself and say FU to the rest."

I might have agreed with them and done the same, had I been at "FU." But my work was completely different, and there was no slacking off. I met with my bass teacher once or twice a week, and I had to achieve results. My teacher was a short man with a goatee and an afro. He wore black turtle-necks, black pants, and black leather shoes, and he always looked sharp. He had played with just about every big name in jazz, and been a soloist with most symphonies in the country.

My teacher was kind-hearted, but his only compliment to students was to kick the floor while they played. Actually he did believe in compliments. He told me in my first lesson that if I played well enough, that would be compliment enough. I would know it, he said, and then I wouldn't even care what he had to say. But that day had not yet arrived, and he still had plenty to tell me. So I spent many morning hours in the woodshed. That's practicing, in jazz speak. Exercises and scales for forty-five minutes, then all sorts of different music for the next three hours. In the afternoons I went to some theory or history classes, and I played in some school groups. Then I practiced for a few more hours and lugged my bass home. Of course, there were always concerts, performances and gigs to practice for, so I didn't have much time to read three newspapers a day. And auditions were coming up in the second half of the year, so I needed a basic mastery of style, technique, and musicality.

I'm not complaining. When I felt the joy of playing right, there was nothing else. Even when I was just practicing and it was going well, I forgot to eat. And there was nothing better than playing a gig at a downtown club, or a party where people really jived with your music. When I was playing right, I felt like I was making waves of electricity surge through the room and into the defenseless hearts of my listeners. I was a maniac, doing something completely pure, and purely beautiful.

Of course that's preposterous. Nothing is completely pure. And I wasn't really a maniac, I was a student with a good imagination. I wanted to feel what it was like to stab random

people in the heart with love. I couldn't do it yet, or only maybe
to myself, and for a few seconds. But I was getting closer, a little
bit each day.

My other homework was *listening*. I had to develop my ear,
so I spent hours *listening* to all kinds of music, not just jazz. Now
there's a difference between listening and *listening*. There is a
difference between listening to Glenn Gould while organizing
your desk, and *listening* to Glenn Gould while closing your eyes
and conducting until you smash the "Champion!" statue you
won at the 4th grade Spelling Bee.

If you're a musician or an artist, it matters how you *listen*.
When you *listen*, things influence you, they enter you. Sometimes
you notice when you hum a tune that randomly occurs to you.
On good days, you can even find your influences in your fingers.
Without trying and without even knowing it, you can play them
on your bass. I was always amazed when I heard my influences.
At the same time, I always wondered about what other things
come out of my fingers and my mouth without me knowing it.

                              *   *   *

Mullins spent his first four weeks in Philadelphia finding
work. I couldn't understand why he was having such a hard time.
As a Franklin grad with all kinds of experience and talents, I
thought he would get jobs thrown at him.

Apparently not. We asked Mullins if we could help, but he
wanted to do it on his own. Surprisingly, he didn't even want to
talk about his job search, so we talked about other things. But one
day he returned home and announced that he had been wildly
successful. We had just finished cooking dinner, and four pillars
of steam were rising from four plates on the kitchen table.

"Ah," he exclaimed, "what a day! I'm finally a working
man."

"So what did you find?" I asked. "Marketing bitch? Pizza
delivery? Indian chief?"

"Close!" he answered. "I did find three jobs."

"Which one are you going to take?" Ellen asked.

"All of them."

"What?" Prateek's face twitched in surprise. "How are you going to work three jobs?"

"Well, I won't have to work them all at once, I hope."

"But what about finding yourself a career? What about joining the real world?" Prateek pressed.

"At this point," said Mullins, "I have to eat."

"Yeah," I agreed. "Probably the same thing will happen to me once I graduate. But I'll be living in a garage."

Ellen finished serving our drinks and sat down. "So what kind of jobs did you get?" she asked. "And why did it take you so long to find them?"

"Why did it take so long?" Mullins replied. "Well, for one thing I refused to work in an office. I hate offices."

"You want to work, but you hate offices?" Prateek looked at him in amazement.

"They're oppressive. And cubicles, God, they're prisons."

"So what are you actually doing?" asked Ellen.

"Let me guess!" Prateek begged. "Gardening! No? Masseuse? No? Journalist? Interior decorator? Carrier Pigeon?"

"Carrier pigeon?" I interrupted. "What the hell kind of job is that?"

"You know," he said, as if everyone did, "the guys who ride the bikes through traffic delivering legal documents."

"They're not called carrier pigeons."

"They are!" he insisted. "It's industry slang."

Was it? Was it indeed? Well, it wasn't slang that I knew. But who cared. Mullins wasn't taking a job as a carrier pigeon, and if Prateek wanted to live in his own world with ridiculous hats, shaving routines and carrier pigeons delivery boys, that was fine with me.

"You haven't guessed it," Mullins said. "You haven't even guessed one of them."

"Well, they clearly aren't normal jobs." Prateek remarked.

"Clearly." Mullins grinned. "Well, I'm working three days a week at school for the blind as an assistant librarian."

"You're what?!"

"Um, I picked up some brail when I was a kid. Two of my first cousins are blind. So I found this private school which is building up a collection of books, and people come in and read during the day, mostly kids, students in the school, and I'm just going to help them out, and you know keep the library clean. I guess I'll have to bring my own reading material though." He stroked his chin.

"That's great!" Ellen congratulated him. What else was he doing, she queried.

"Well, I got part time work for a DJ company doing audio and emceeing at concerts and parties."

"What? Do you know anything about audio equipment?" asked Ellen.

"I will soon!" Mullins pulled a book out his backpack, which he displayed to us proudly. The cover said: "A Guide to Audio Equipment (for Blind readers). Full Brail Text."

We burst out laughing.

"No no," he said, "this is great. I go to all the fancy-shmancy concerts and parties, and take advantage of the catering. All I have to do is set up the microphones and say "Heeere's Johnny. It's cake.""

"Literally," said Prateek, still shaking his head in disbelief. "And your third job?"

"Nocturnal baker!" Mullins announced. "Three to four nights a week I'll be baking the most delicious breads and pastries that you can imagine for a place called the "The Green Hose" down on 2nd street. I'm working with the owner, and if his largesse with himself is any indication, I'm going to be eating pastries all night long."

"Wow!" Ellen loved baking bread. Even more, she loved eating bread. I didn't mind it much myself and told Mullins he could bring a few loaves home with him from work.

"I'll do what I can" he said with a grin, "but you have to understand that baking is a serious business, and I can't be distracted by personal greed. Once I put on that apron, the Mullins you know disappears, and I become Mullins the baking-machine!"

"So you're making the big bucks now?" asked Prateek.

"I won't get paid much," he said, "not even with all three jobs combined. But it will mix things up, and maybe I'll find out I want to pursue a career in a related field. Maybe I'll find I have a passion for working with books, or being on a microphone, or selling hot buns." He chuckled. "But really these jobs will give me some time to think, you know, about what I want to do later, to interview people and things. And also some time to have a social life, you know, at the Turf, or maybe a girlfriend or something."

"Yeah," I said. "You get to explore yourself."

"Well," he replied with a grin, "there's a lot out there to explore."

*   *   *

Over the next two months, Mullins began his three jobs. The weather got colder, but we were so busy we hardly noticed. During the day we would all go away to our various tasks; Prateek to his stocks, Ellen to her God knows what, me to my bass, and Mullins to his three jobs. At night we would all meet up and discuss the day's events—that is, if we were not having a party at the Turf, or going out for a concert, meal, or exhibition. Time, in fact, rarely showed up to join us, and maybe that's why I can't remember most days. But I do remember the kinds of stories we used to hear, and the way Mullins would tell us about his work.

On Mondays, Thursdays, and Fridays, he worked as an assistant librarian. His supervisor, the head librarian, was a skinny bald man who wore grey glass lenses and patched tweed. This bookish boss almost never spoke, which Mullins disliked. But when he did speak, he had horrible breath, and Mullins disliked that even more. Apparently, he spent most of his day pacing up and down the library reading obscure books that Mullins never saw on shelves. If Mullins walked over to him and tried to identify the books, his boss would close his volumes and hold them behind his back.

"I really don't care," insisted Mullins. "As long as he keeps his hands off the kids."

Mullins was half-lying. The truth was, he needed some drama to keep himself amused, and when he couldn't sniff out any with his boss or the other assistant librarian, he created some for himself.

"A couple weeks after I started working," recounted Mullins one evening at the Blue Fog, "my boss began leaving the library for three hours during the day. He said to me that I could take charge of the classes. I was just supposed to show groups of ten kids how to find some brail books, and then give them the rest of the hour to read." Mullins laughed.

"How did it go?" I asked.

"It was no challenge," he said. "Boredom was the issue. Think about this—ten blind kids in school, who probably have better imaginations than seeing-people. I'm their teacher, and they have to stay in the library for an hour. Now that's what I call potential for captivation and education, is it not?!"

"They can't see me, you know," he continued, "so it had to be all about the stories themselves—no facial gesturing or wriggling. Anyway, on the second day I had the kids to myself, I told them they could put the books away if they wanted, and that I would tell them a story. I explained that since I was storytelling during their reading time, my tale would have to be educational and completely true. Also, I told them that they couldn't tell my boss or their other teachers that I was telling them the stories. If they did, I said, there would be no more stories."

"How old are these kids?" I asked.

"Second graders," he said. "You can't trust them. So I started telling them a long story, but leaving it hanging at the end of each day, just like in Arabian Nights. That way, I figured, they would want to hear the rest and they wouldn't tell anybody." He took a swig of beer and smiled to himself. "Of course, it could only last so long, and today I got called into the principle's office."

"What was the story?" Ellen asked.

"Well, I won't tell you what I told the kids," he said. "It might scare you. But…"

"Scare us?" interrupted Prateek. "Please. The only thing that scares me is the Fed lowering interest rates again. If that happens, you had better put bars on my window and call my mother."

"Ok," said Mullins, "I'll give you the PG-13 version. But don't blame me if you have nightmares."

Mullins finished his beer and began his tale:

"This tale started long long ago, before you or I was born, before our parents were born, and before even our grandparents were born. It's the story of the Hizzards, the secret evil monsters. But don't worry about them yet—first you have to know where they come from, so you know who they are. The Hizzards were relatives of the Largots, huge hounds brought over on the Mayflower to help the Pilgrims hunt wild boar.

Soon after the Pilgrims had arrived, the Largots went blood-crazy. The enormous hounds had so much wild game to kill in the American forests that they became obsessed with killing. They killed everything they could find with their enormous teeth and razor-sharp claws: poultry, dogs, even horses. Eventually, a particularly crazy Largot killed a plump Puritan child.

Well, the Pilgrims had a meeting and decided this had to stop. They agreed to round up all the Largots and ship them back to England, where they could at least massacre those Godless Anglicans.

The Pilgrims spent the next year rounding up all the Largots and sending them over to England on the Baskervilles Supply Ships. After thirteen months, they thought they'd captured all their Largots and they stopped their hunting. But they were wrong, dead wrong. A few Largots had escaped from the North East, and had made their way to down the Appalachian trail to Virginia, eating unlucky students along the way. The Largots especially liked young children who read books, did what they were told, and were nice to everyone, because those were exactly the children who knew about the Largots, who looked out for them, and who helped get some of them captured.

But though children helped to capture some of the Largots, they didn't capture all of them, oh no. Several Largots made their way around Jamestown into the dark forests of the Appalachian mountains. None of the Virginians knew what happened to the Largots, and no one heard from them for many years. So eventually they decided the beasts must have died, and they gave up the hunt for the child-eating hounds. But the Largots weren't dead, not even close. Three of them had managed to survive in the mountains by joining forces and eating whatever forest animals they could find. They also drank the blood of wild horses. On this diet, they became more and more ferocious, and eventually, the most powerful animals in the forest.

One day, when the Largots were out on a morning hunt, they decided to make a right turn instead of a left, or a left turn instead of a right, I don't remember. Anyway, after crossing a mountain pass they didn't know, they walked right into the habitat of the "Southern" or what we now call the "Tiny" Blond Gorilla, a tiny yellow-furred monkey about the size of a 2nd grader! At first, the gorillas and the Largots were so shocked at the sight of each other that neither group moved. Then, seeing the bloody jaws and gleaming white teeth of the Largots, the tiny Gorillas decided they might be in danger. So they tried to run away. "AHHHH!" one of them screamed.

There was one problem though: blond gorillas don't move very fast. These cute animals had long blond hair growing from all the parts of their tiny bodies, hair which would get in the way when they ran. So before they moved anywhere, the blond gorillas had to comb and brush their long fur with sticks and other forest implements. Faced with the Largots, the Gorillas used their emergency technique and formed a line as fast as they could, brushing each other's hair and tying it with grass so they could escape.

The Largots were astonished. Here was a strange group of tiny animals, clearly in danger of their lives, and they had formed a line to comb each other's hair. One of the Largots walked slowly to the end of the line, opened his enormous mouth, and grabbed the blond gorilla sitting there, tearing it away from its brethren.

"Oooo!" the blond gorilla squeaked, as the hound thrashed it hither and thither. The other gorillas were almost frightened to death, and began to comb even faster so they could run away at some future date.

Spiiiiiiiiiiiiiiit! The Largot who had bitten the gorilla, Terence, spat out the blond animal, still alive, onto the ground. "Too much hair," he growled, "it gets stuck in your throat."

As the gorillas combed furiously, the Largots sat down to talk. What could they do with these animals, dumb-looking and useless to eat?

"Maybe we can have them as slaves," Terence growled. "They could clean our fur and polish our teeth."

But an even fiercer Largot named Eliot replied: "Grrrr. I don't think so Terence. Will we not kill them by accident, biting them when they shed their hair on our furniture or breaking them in half when they squeak?"

"I know," roared the third, Douglas. "We will use them as servants when we need them, and when we don't we will send them back to their tree houses to comb each other's hair."

"Brilliant," said Terence, and Eliot snarled his approval.

And that, my friends, is what they did. The Largots found all the blond gorillas in the forest, and took them as personal servants to their secret lair. They had about fifty each and rotated when they felt like it. And according to Douglas' plan, the blond gorillas had to do everything the Largots desired, and when they were done, they were sent home to comb each other's hair. Many, many times, the blond gorillas tried to escape. But being so slow, they were always unsuccessful, and always dragged back to their part-time servitude.

In the meantime, the people of Virginia, who had initially hunted the beasts, had totally forgotten about the Largots, and had also decided they had hunted all the Tiny Blond Gorillas to extinction. Little did they know, however, that the Largots and the Tiny Blond Gorillas began living among them, as Hizzards!"

"Wait a minute, wait a minute," I said. "Where did the Hizzards come from? What do they have to do with the Largots and the blond gorillas?"

"Ah," Mullins said, "you see that's the part I had to fudge with the 2nd graders, birds and bees and all that. I told them something like the Hizzards were distant French cousins of the Largots who came over on canoes and intermarried with the blond gorillas. But the real story is that the Tiny Blond Gorillas grew more and more attracted to their fierce muscular masters, and the Largots, having left their womenfolk in Northern England, grew more and more frustrated satisfying themselves into tree stumps. One day when a buxom blond gorilla was on her hands and knees scrubbing the dirt floor of the Largot lair, Terence could stand it no longer.

"What's your name, you tiny blond buster!" he growled.

"Stacy!" she squeaked, terrified and shaking. A Largot had never spoken directly to her before, and she wasn't sure what to do. She stood up straight, and tried to adopt several pleasing postures. But each one was more awkward than the next, and she sadly returned to scrubbing the floor.

"Come with me Stacy," said the Largot, and he led the tiny gorilla behind the barbeque grill, where he proceeded to part her fur and take her tiny gorilla virginity!"

"Mullins!" said Ellen. "That's gross! How could you say that to 2nd Graders?!"

"I told you," he said, "I didn't say that to the 2nd graders—I'm just telling you guys the real story. I told you it was gruesome. I warned you."

"Mullins!"

"Go on, go on!" Prateek urged. Ellen and I looked at the Senator, but he had his full attention on Mullins.

"Stacy," Mullins continued, looking at us carefully, "was not the only blond gorilla to serve the needs of a Largot. Indeed, after Terence bragged to Eliot and Douglas about his exploits, the Largots spent a lot of time behind the barbeque grill with tiny blond gorillas. At first, no one saw any consequences to their actions. The Largots were happy to get their rocks off, and the Blond Gorillas didn't mind the male attention. You see, they all happened to be female, because the male tiny blond gorillas had been too lazy to work and had been killed by the Largots.

"After a few months, the Largots noticed that some of the tiny blond gorillas weren't so tiny anymore. In fact, they were growing in size at an enormous rate. They weren't just getting fatter, they were growing taller, and stronger. Before long the blond gorillas were as big as the Largots, and soon after that they were much bigger. Their hair started to fall out, and they began spending most of their time standing up straight.

"Now, in truth, the blond gorillas were pregnant, but they didn't know it. They thought their new hard work had caused them to grow to new heights and new strengths. The Largots didn't know what to do. Their servants had over-taken them, and soon the hounds would no longer be able to control their balding female helpers.

"They didn't have long to worry. Stacy, who had been pissed off since Terence started spending most of his time with her cousin Kelly, formed a militia and led a revolt against the Largots. The assault was well-planned. The gorillas spent a few weeks slowly preparing their hair and sharpening sticks. Also, the Largots were old and scaly by now, and they couldn't put up much of a fight. So the hounds were killed and then skinned and skewered on the barbeque. Then their remains were spread around the forest for all the animals to see what happened to those who fucked with the tiny blond gorillas (who were not so tiny anymore).

"The blond gorillas took over the Largots lair and began their own rule over the forest animals. But they didn't last long either. All the gorillas were pregnant, which meant they had morning sickness and had to stay in bed. They couldn't really enforce their authority in the forest lying down.

"The gorillas underwent their pregnancies with bravery and stamina. Unfortunately the gestation periods were extremely long. Five years later, Stacy was the first gorilla to go into the extended painful birthing process. When the birthing day came, she lay on her bed, legs wide open, as the other gorillas stood around her to help with the baby. But instead of the screams of joy that Stacy remember from attending births as a young tiny blond gorilla, the gorillas standing around her open legs looked shocked and terrified as her child was born. Slowly, the baby was handed to her, and she saw immediately that it was not a tiny blond gorilla. No, it was something else altogether.

"The baby that Stacy had and the babies that all the other Gorillas had were different than anything the forest had ever seen. The owls called them "Hizzards," because owls could pronounce only three syllables, "Hiss," "Arrrr," and "Zzz," and as most animals trusted the wise birds, the names stuck.

"The Hizzards were trouble from the beginning. The boys bit and kicked each other and ran wild around the fort. The girls poked each other in the back with sharp stones and pulled each other's hair. But even scarier than their behavior, the little boy and girl Hizzards looked a lot like what some of the forest

animals called "the bumans". Like their fathers, the Hizzards'
legs and arms were barely hairy at all, and like their mothers
they stood on two feet. Like their fathers they were lonely and
violent, and like their mothers they were prone to escapism. Like
both their parents, they made full use of the grill and took full
advantage of the other forest animals. Like both their parents,
they had no use for forest schooling, and were only interested in
which plants could be smoked on weekends.

"Eventually, the Hizzards grew into adolescent teenagers,
and they became too much even for their gorilla mothers to
handle. Having enough of their childhood lair, they banded
together and ran away from their fort. They crashed off through
the forest toward Virginia, leaving a path of insensitivity and
destruction in their wake.

"The forest animals were right: the Hizzards *did* look
like "bumans." And when the Hizzards got close enough to
Williamsburg, they joined the real-people towns and cities
without even being noticed. But the Hizzards were still an evil
bunch, and they decided that in order to maintain their lifestyles
of laziness and abuse, they had to spread their ways. They
formed alliances and training groups, and they even recruited
new human beings to be taught the Hizzard values and lifestyle.
This meant learning a lot of new rituals. At night, for example,
the Hizzards practiced the gorilla dances of their mothers and
the brutish hunts of their fathers. They would drink ghoulish
drinks, just as their fathers had drank boar's blood, and they
even shared this drink with unsuspecting human beings who did
not know its terrible affects.

"Sinister and smart, the Hizzards took advantage of lonely
young humans who were overcome by the pressures of work,
ambitions, and family. They held parties, disguised as normal
social events, and invited anyone who wanted to forget their
loneliness and pressure. Young people who came were grouped
together at Hizzardic meetings and led to believe they could
escape their pain by the drinking of a ghoulish beverage,

and the association with other lonely depressed individuals. The older, more experienced Hizzards led the way. They demonstrated advanced Hizzardic techniques for imbibing the holy beverage faster than any normal being could, and for using the ancient Hizzardic knowledge of forest botany to enhance the experience.

"After a few of these parties, the Hizzards chose the young people with the most pain and loneliness, those who were most easily manipulated, and those most talented at manipulating, and initiated them into the Hizzardic order. The others were kicked out the door with the trash. The new recruits fearfully participated in long painful initiation ceremonies, which served to unify the pain of recruits into a single welt of united ugliness, and to destroy what remained of their individuality.

"The new Hizzards could only associate with other Hizzards, and had to judge all others by the Hizzard hierarchy. If the person were not a Hizzard at all, the human could either be recruited or completely ignored. More importantly, Hizzards could only mate with other Hizzards, and were required to help other Hizzards in any worldly goals. It didn't matter who was qualified for what or who was stepping on whom; loyalty to other Hizzards came first. Finally, these initiates were given a three letter code which represented their Hizzardic subgroup and defined how they were to think of themselves and others.

"Scary! But unless you're a Hizzard, you never know who is. You never know who you can trust, or who's watching you! Even in Philadelphia, Hizzards are everywhere. Like their animal parents, they will hunt you or take you as slaves! And if you're not careful, you will become one of them, accepting their hideous lifestyle of pain and escape.

"And you want to know the worst part? I was a Hizzard once. That's right, don't look so surprised! For two years after I was recruited I was a victim of their plots. I was a victim of their rituals. I was a victim of their thoughtlessness and self-abuse. Worst of all I was a victim of their hideous women. That's how

I know so much about them and their evil. After two years, I couldn't take any more and I escaped. But I'm still worried about them, they're still around me, around us, and if they get a chance…they'll get you too! "

Mullins took a swig of his beer, grinned, and nodded at us. "I really freaked out those blind kids. Boy, you should have seen them!"

"Mullins!" Ellen chided.

"Unfortunately, some of them were so scared they would get eaten that they told their teachers, who told the crazy librarian. He wasn't too happy with me, and he sent me to the principle for a reprimand."

"Serves you right!" Prateek remarked. "There's nothing wrong with social organizations. They're just a place for like-minded people to enjoy each other."

"What are you talking about man?" I asked. "Are *you* a Hizzard?"

"If such things really existed," answered Prateek, "I'm sure they would have recruited me by now."

"Could be," said Mullins. "But the whole Hizzard story taught me one thing for sure: a career in the world of books and publishing isn't for me."

"Huh?"

"It's just too damn quiet. I need to be in Hollywood or something!"

"Yeah!" I suggested. "Or a lawyer. They tell good stories."

"Good idea," said Mullins, "write that down somewhere."

*   *   *

If he saw them, Mullins learned from his mistakes. He took his reprimands in stride, and he redirected all of his energy toward new goals. So he didn't tell any more stories in the library. He let the children read, and he struggled through *Careers for the Partial-Sighted*, in Brail. Meanwhile, he spent more time at his second job, audio-engineering and emceeing, because it was more "Hollywood-esque." He found performance exciting, he told us, and he liked being behind it all. That is, until a few weeks later when he gave us another story at the Blue Fog.

"So," Mullins said. "What have you guys been up to?"

"This and that" Ellen responded. "I spent last week making architectural diagrams for a summer community on Cape Cod."

"Who asked you to do that?" Mullins inquired.

"Oh no one, it's a gift for my future self. What's your opinion on two story shower heads by the way?"

"As long as the water is hot," he replied. "And you Aaron?"

"I've been transcribing some violin sonatas for the bass."

"Oh yeah?"

"Yeah. My teacher told me this week that I need to improve my classical skills if I want to have a chance getting a job in an orchestra. Apparently I've been playing too much jazz and I'm sounding pretty horrible on the classics."

"How can you play too much jazz?" he asked.

"That's what I said," I insisted. "But I guess you can be playing jazz when you should be eating. That could be a problem."

"It could be," he agreed.

"How was your audio work this week?" Prateek asked.

"Could have been better," Mullins admitted. "I don't think this Hollywood thing is for me. Too impersonal and high pressure."

"What do you mean? What happened?" I asked him. You were so excited about it just one week ago.

"Well, I worked a backyard party, a convention of Republican bigwigs."

"Ah, politics," I sympathized.

"That's when disaster struck."

"Disaster?" said Ellen. "Republicans? My day just got even better."

"Quiet you!" shouted Prateek. "When you start reporting your income you'll understand!"

"Anyway," Mullins interrupted. "I got all dressed up, coat and tie and such, and took the train out to the 'burbs. There were no cabs out there, so I walked for about half an hour with the equipment until I got to an enormous white mansion. I rang the doorbell, and the butler took me around the back to the deck where I set up my sound system. Actually, I should say I was on the second deck, because there were three decks on three different levels, the highest one with tables set up for eating and the lowest one with a swimming pool. This backyard was money."

"Who owned the place?" I asked.

"Some big donor. I asked what the guy did for a living, but nobody seemed to know."

"Money was what he did for a living," Ellen surmised.

"Well, I'd set up my sound system a million times before," Mullins continued, "so I didn't really bother with the sound check. Instead I went to go get myself some white wine and some of those smoked-salmon and cream cheese hors d'oevres. Man that stuff was tasty. Then I was talking to some of those very nice Republican girls in high healed sandals. Say what you will about Republicans, but they know how to recruit some classy women. I was telling them about my Ivy-League days, and they were smiling. I thought everything was going really well. Then all of a sudden, some dudes arrived in pink polo shirts, slicked hair, and boat shoes, and the girls just floated right away from me. I couldn't believe it. They didn't even say 'tootles.'" Mullins shook his head.

"Whatever," I said. "Rich broads aren't worth the silver spoon their daddy bought to feed 'em with."

"Yeah," said Mullins still seeming disappointed. Then he perked up. "Finally it came time for the speeches. It turns out this was a birthday party for another big-time old donor, and a bunch of people were going to honor him with toasts. So I sit down next to the stage and turn on the mikes. Everything worked fine for about two seconds and then I heard a "ZZZZZZZZ!" sound, like a huge buzzing bee, go through the speakers for a second and stop. 'Few!' I thought, that's gone. Then about twenty seconds later, it happened again. Suddenly, I saw some guy with a starched pink collar running over to the soundboard. 'Shit,' I thought, what am I going to do?"

"What did you do?" I asked.

"Well, you know me," he said. "I don't know anything about microphones or audio. I just took this job for the cream cheese and smoked salmon hors d'oevres. So I pulled myself up to my full height, try to look professional, and said to the guy: 'Listen, uh, we're having some interference from the airplanes flying overhead, and I'm getting an interrupted signal." He looked up at the sky for airplanes. Of course there were none. Then I lowered my sunglasses on my nose, stared over them at him and said in a low voice: 'We call this RF217 interference. You know, it's a little like we had in Gulf War.' He looked up at me squeamishly, nodded, and said in a tiny voice 'What can we do? We have to do something!'

'I'll do my best,' I told him. Everyone was sitting down and I announced him and gave him the microphone. Since the speakers were buzzing on twenty second intervals, I decided to cut the stereo every twenty seconds for just a second, and then turn it back on again."

"Oh boy," I said.

Mullins smiled. "Yeah, it wasn't a great solution. This is what it sounded like: some young kiss-ass dorkus in khaki shorts would get up to the mike teary-eyed and say: (Mullins sat straight up and made a dorky southern accent.)

'Uh, I'd like to say something to the man of the hour. Uh, he's the type of guy, uh, just the type of person, uh, whose actions in life we should never, ever, ever…'

And I cut him off!" said Mullins. "His last word, of course, was 'forget', but you know, it was pretty funny to hear that cut off."

"Rock on!" said Ellen.

"Yeah, I wanted to," said Mullins, "but people started to get upset. They kept yelling 'Turn it up,' from the back, which was making me kind of nervous. So I turned it up, you know. And then some guy came up to the mike who was big-time, you know, someone who I think had run for president in the 70s or something. He stands next to me, takes the mike, and starts to talk. And of course, my cell phone goes off in my pocket. It reverberated through the microphone, and was magnified at top volume through the speaker system. And you know, I couldn't get it out of my pocket. I was struggling, fighting with it. I almost ripped my pants off, but finally I grabbed it and shut it off as fast as I could. You'll be happy to know that all of two-hundred of these glitzy ritzy people were looking straight at me, including the president-loser guy. How about that for a disaster!"

"Haha" I joked. "That's what you get for having a cell phone."

"Listen," said Mullins, "I almost always leave my cell phone in my desk, and when I take it out, it's always on vibrate. The only reason it was on is because I had to reset my answering machine, and it just happened to be there at the bottom of my pocket. Fuck! I'll tell you what though—I didn't enjoy that day very much—I don't think this big-time performance stuff is for me," he sighed.

"Well, at least the call wasn't important, right?" said Ellen, trying to look on the bright side..

"No," said Mullins. It was just my audio boss telling me he had given me the wrong equipment that morning. I got his message too late, long after I had to explain to the entire crowd that we were having RF217 interference, and long after listening to my angry host bitch at me for forty-five minutes about my "unprofessional performance."

"Nice," I said.

"Yeah." He shook his head. "I can't be in entertainment. I can't stand to have people yelling at me. I need my freedom."

"Get used to it" recommended Prateek. "Any job that will support you will involve other people. And as sure as there are other people, you can be sure they'll get pissed."

Mullins nodded but I couldn't tell whether he was paying attention or not.

"Of course, the best job," Prateek rattled on, "is to be the CEO of the enterprise. But even as a CEO, you're going to have the board bitching at you, and your big investors, and your vice presidents…"

"And you family too, since if you're a CEO you're probably spending too much time at the office," Ellen interjected.

Prateek looked at her. "Say what you will, but work is the source of achievement."

"What kind of achievement?" Ellen taunted.

"Whatever. Efficiency. Return on investment. Whatever goal I set myself. When I do that, I can work any and all hours to get it done. Then I feel fulfilled."

"Fair enough," said Mullins. "But then why is it that my goal last night was to bake twenty-five croissants, fifteen loaves of brown bread, fifteen loaves of white bread, ten plain scones, ten fruited scones, two carrot cakes, three raisin breads, and ten chocolate pastries, and when I was finished baking all of that, I just felt tired?"

"You're a night-baker, what do you expect?" said Prateek.

"True," Mullins admitted. "It fucks with my clock. But according to what you just said, time shouldn't matter if it's my goal."

"It has to be your fixation, Mullins. Once you're fixated you can think of nothing else. But look at you, you don't even bake every day. And you know what, you still have human requirements. Your body will do more for you than it normally would if you implore it. But eventually you'll get tired."

"Well, I guess baking isn't my great career path either. And man, some nights there with Clive…it's crazy. I wonder if I should even be there." We often heard about Clive's craziness.

He wasn't your average boss. Of course, Mullins wasn't your average employee. What was the problem?

"You see," Mullins had explained, "Clive Bar Cokeba, who sports of a walrus-mustache, if you haven't seen him, used to be a track star, a professional marathon winner in Northern Ireland. Now he's a super-energetic baker and I'm his victim."

"His victim?" I asked.

"Oh yes, I think anyone spending nights with Clive is definitely a victim. He throws things at me, gets drunk, and forces me to participate in baking competitions where if I lose, I have to eat what I made."

"Where does this guy come from?"

"Well actually, the New Yorker did an extended piece on him which is on the wall at the bakery. Apparently he was famous in the 70s for finishing his races by jigging the last mile, far ahead of the closest follower. His methods for winning were ruthless. All the way through the race he would sing Irish ditties into the ears of his competitors, intimidating them with tales of "Bray Malarkey" and "Finnegan's Nose Hair.""

"Jeez," said Prateek, shaking his head.

"Yeah," Mullins agreed. "And when he arrived at the finish line, he would grab a six pack of Guinness from his wife and chug every can before the 2nd place runner even arrived."

"Skills," I said. "Skills."

Mullins nodded and continued: "So apparently he became a national hero, and everyone thought he would be the unifying symbol for the Catholics of Northern Ireland to oust those pesky English, once and for all."

"What happened?"

"Well, one day, after his usual morning pint of whisky, Clive walked out the front door for his morning training and tripped on a garden hose. He fell down his stone stairs, permanently shattering his left knee. His face was only saved from serious damage by a pastry, strangely left on his garden path near the hose."

"Wow, so then he saw the light and moved to Philadelphia to start an international baking empire?" Prateek suggested, fingers clasped and eyes lit-up.

"Not exactly," Mullins responded. "As he could no longer run, Clive was asked by various political groups to become their spokesman. But when he refused to enter politics, he was too rude about it. Part of the problem was that he would go to TV interviews drunk, and once he even mentioned that the people pestering him to work were a bunch of "prattle-fouks, who ought to stuff their du-has in their shizzle-tobeys."

"Really!" Ellen exclaimed, amazed that you could say such things on TV.

"Now that's a big insult in Ireland," Mullins explained. "Clive's only chance to avoid angry Irish militants was to leave the country. So he took his wife, and left for Philadelphia, where his distant cousin had come for college. He used his marathon profits to start The Green Hose in a tiny hole-in-the-wall kitchen in Old City, and here we are."

"Wait, that isn't the end of the story," said Prateek. "I've heard Clive's name before—doesn't he own some other places?"

"Oh yeah," said Mullins. "Clive recently bought our favorite convenience store on 10th street."

This store in question, the Boobery, had no boobs. But, as a consolation prize, it did import the most delicious beers from all over the world. According to Mullins' discussion with Clive, the name came from Southern German monks, who used massive quantities of delicious ale to help them imagine the boobs they missed so desperately. When Clive found out that Mullins liked his imported brews, he made our roommate a member of his family. "So last week," Mullins continued, "Clive invited me to one his "Irish Seders".

"That's a contradiction," Prateek pointed out.

"What's an Irish seder?" I asked.

"Oh," said Mullins, "it's one of these feasts that Clive has at his apartment on South Street." He laughed. "Nay, it's more than a feast. It's an extravaganza. Last week Clive served leg of lamb with green mint jelly, asparagus, green beans, green Jell-O pudding, and green beer."

"Wow," Ellen added. "The guy loves Ireland."

"I think," Mullins said "it's less about Ireland than about home. After we ate Clive got super drunk and decided to help us remember his Irish roots by singing the bawdiest bar songs he remembered."

"Like what?"

"All the greats. There was "Mary the Hairy," "Patty McPherson: My Guinness ain't your buid-ness," and the Bar Cokeba classic: "The English are wankers.""

"Sounds like a rocking good time," Ellen observed.

"Yeah," Mullins agreed. "At the end of the evening, I was the only one left standing, so I told the drunkards a made-up story of adventure in Ireland. There were conniving leprechauns, pots of gold, and various leafy plants. Total BS, but they ate it up. Especially after Clive had his "Irish Stoagie"."

"Is Clive sober enough to keep conversation at the bakery?" Ellen asked.

"I don't think I would call it conversation," said Mullins. He made a grizzly Irish voice, shifted in his chair and spat out:

"Ay in thar forest aye one upon eirn filo darnin go bar mathia killigan quittle mcjamie society tone solomon der HAHAHAH rusheen in thar…" Mullins trailed off, staring doubtfully at the ceiling.

"Sounds profound," I said

"Clive thinks so," he said. "After his proclamation last night, he started staring at me and grunting, and when I didn't say anything, he picked up all the buns on the table next to him and threw them at me."

"He what?"

"Well, he's a bun-thrower. He sang me a limerick once that said something about 'you can tell how good a bun will taste; by the way it explodes on somebody's face.' I don't remember the whole thing."

"What did you do?"

"Well, I retaliated of course. You can't just let a drunk Irishman abuse you like that. But I was smart about it. I knew that any pastries I destroyed I'd have to bake again, so I launched a bag a flour. Direct hit."

"Did that stop him?"

"No, but the next forty pound bag of sugar did."

"Sweets."

"Exactly."

We laughed, finished our drinks, and headed back to the Turf. We laughed, finished our drinks, and headed back to the Turf. We laughed, finished our drinks, and headed back to the Turf.

What's that? Did I make a mistake? No I didn't. That's how it was, over and over again during the year. The stories, the laughs, the drinks, and the heading back. The stories, the laughs, the drinks, and the heading back. It wasn't a routine though, it didn't feel like routine. The stories were always worth drinking over, and the conclusions usually eliminated one more career idea and created at least one or two new nicknames.

"I have your title: you're an I-baker!" Prateek told Mullins excitedly that evening.

"What the hell is that?" asked Mullins.

"Like an I-banker, investment banker. You work crazy hours—through the night, and hate what you're doing! You're only doing it in the short term until you get a high-paid consulting job or something!"

"Thanks Prateek. Now I feel important."

"Well, Mr. I-baker, what will you be doing with all that dough tonight?" asked Ellen.

"Not funny." I said. Ellen thought she was the queen of puns. In actuality she was the queen of string-cheese puns.

"No, I like baking," said Mullins. "It's a catharsis for me. And don't you know it's the reason why so many middle-aged housewives don't commit suicide? You shouldn't make fun of something so important."

"What are you talking about?" Ellen exclaimed.

"Kneading bread," he said, and then demonstrated. "It removes their stress and malaise. It's zen."

*   *   *

Some two weeks later, Mullins showed me why he had objected to the term I-baker, and convinced me conclusively that neither he nor I, nor anyone else in their right mind, would want to be associated with I-bankers. We had just finished dinner at the Turf. One of the light bulbs in the kitchen had burned out and we were sitting in semi-darkness, finishing off some surprisingly good wine from Indiana.

"You see, there *are* good things about Indiana," Mullins informed us.

Ellen was in her pajamas. She always changed into her pajamas when she was in the apartment. She and Mullins were listening to Prateek and I debate the merits of teaching English abroad. I was telling to Prateek about the benefits of teaching for the French government where you got a week's wages for twelve hours' work. In response, Prateek denied the financial feasibility of the program, despite the fact it had been running without problems for twenty years. Only solid careers like banking could support the economy. Prateek finished his food and left to check "his indexes."

"I don't know about Prateek," Mullins said.

"Don't worry about him," Ellen said. "He's a training to be a corporate crusader. They're tough."

"Oh, I'm not worried about him now," said Mullins, looking up. "I'll be worried about him when he's forty and grey-haired, a slave to his desk who drives all the people around him to hell. Then, if he realizes where he is, he'll regret his greed."

I asked Mullins if that was fair. Banking probably wasn't the most exciting career, but it was a service that peopled needed, and it was something, some kind of job. Besides, we all knew that Prateek had an intellectual interest in business.

"Clearly," Mullins said, smiling at me, "you do not study at an Ivy League University. For those who do," he explained, "the crusade of the corporate warrior is well known." And then Mullins began his tale:

"Generally, the solider dons his uniform as early as possible. For the lucky ones, the summer after freshman year is the first mission. The armor is standard: there's the gray, blue, and black suits, the starched white shirts with cuffs, the conservative ties and shoes, and of course, the commands to 'cut my hair as if I was everyone else in my office, or failing that, my boss.' If the crusader is lucky," Mullins said, "he can head straight for his Jerusalem; sometimes though, he has to start in LA, Chicago, San Francisco, or the low of the low, Philadelphia. But even through those lesser sacred places, the voyage is gruesome before the crusader can make his pilgrimage to the holy Wall."

He raised his eyebrows seriously and continued.

"The solider has to prove his holiness during extreme rounds of interviews. Since he is indeed going to war, his recruiters test him for battle. They intimidate him with outrageous questions, and they poke at him to test his mettle. Sometimes they tie him to a chair and then bend over in a far corner of the room—just to see how quickly the student can escape to kiss their asses."

Ellen laughed, and Mullins went on

"Not everybody can stand it; lots of soldier-wannabes don't make the cut. Maybe they hadn't displayed iron will and outrageous confidence; maybe they flinched when asked if they would work more than one hundred hour weeks; maybe they presented their resumes upside down, or had coffee stains on their leather binders. Worst of all, they may have accidentally, totally unintentionally, in a moment of extreme weakness, revealed *a personality.*"

Mullins stopped and made the sign of the cross. Then he continued:

"For this reason, most crusaders train long hours to get rid of such rubbish. But not everyone is so skilled. Some exit their interviews crying, some cursing, and others drooling the sloppy saliva of failure.

"For those who do succeed, who receive offer letters with unimaginable bonuses (life-insurance payments in advance), the summer is set. They travel to a great financial kingdom and prepare to fight longer and harder than their opponents. Their barracks are menacing glass menageries, and if they are lucky, they are granted a semi-private sixteen cubic foot box, in which they can wage holy war. They are not expected to leave. No, they are expected not to leave."

Mullins took a breath and raised his arms like a priest.

"And so the armies of crusaders in their camps toil day and night, week and weekend to achieve certain digits on certain screens, representing a victorious battle for the kingdom of God. No one knows how many battles are necessary to win the war, and it seems sometimes like the life-draining crusading might go on forever.

"Will God, they wonder, ever arrive to say 'Nice work: Now go to the beach and don't come back!'? No, no, they have to remind themselves, that's just a silly fantasy inside the minds of homesick soldiers. You had to expect that kind of thing. In war."

"Hardcore," I noted. "What happens?"

"Hardcore," Mullins agreed. "What happens? If the solider can contain such fantasies inside him, if he can survive the mine-laden battle fields of twenty hour a day seven day a week war, if he can survive the lack of sleep, the trench food, the smell of death and vile conquest around him, and if he can survive the loss of his humanity and individuality that war causes—and that is a big if—then he might be offered a permanent position after his college graduation."

"Shit," I said. Mullins continued.

"That is the lifestyle that I am worried about for Prateek. Should he really spend his life fighting in the trenches year after year? Will he eventually lose all interest in his life, or regret spending all his youthful waking hours (and those he should have been sleeping) battling to win an un-winnable war?"

"So why do they do it?" I asked. "These are intelligent self-respecting college kids. Why do they join this, this holy crusade?"

Mullins laughed. "Clearly," he replied, "they're a spiritual bunch. Selfless! They know a higher good. They're saints, sacrificing themselves and their lives for the holy war. Where do you think Prateek gets such righteousness?"

"I don't know, I…"

"You're right, Aaron," Mullins responded calmly. "Are they really saints? Or are they just innocent and naive, innocent of war's blood, war's torment, war's insanity? They don't read poetry or history, so it's possible. It's possible that they are drawn in by the promises of unbelievable spoils. They know that when a battle is won, the armies receive such loot as can hardly be compared to any peacetime or civilian remuneration. This loot, this booty, the key to God's green kingdom, has got to be very, very tempting."

Mullins voice began to grow in volume and intensity. "The students know that if, one day, they can escape the war, a possibility that dwindles with wives, children, mortgages, apartments, cars, timeshares, college costs, yachts, retirement plans, etc, they can enjoy a golden vacation with no more financial worry. Money lets you become the God that never arrived!"

Mullins took a deep breath. "The problem is, once you go to war, you're never the same. Even as you sit on a deserted beach in the Florida Keys that you own, you are still twitching, waiting for your army radio to the sound the battle cry: "SELL SELL

SELL!!" (retreat) or "BUY BUY BUY!!" (advance). You sit on the beach, in your three hundred dollars sunglasses, and you don't know what to do with yourself. Then it all falls apart."

Mullins stopped, and after a minute of silence, I remarked that at least Prateek would never be alone in the trenches.

"Oh no," agreed Ellen cheerfully. She had been listening with amusement. "He'll be joining the fifteen dollar martini crowd."

"Huh?"

"What do you think soldiers do when they get a respite from duty?" asked Mullins. "Haven't you seen any World War II movies? They drink. And if they're lucky, they womanize. Usually there are women who know where the soldiers work, and they know the bars where the soldiers go for a good time. Sometimes the women are from the other side, you know, the people the soldiers are looting. In that case, sometimes they try to wile themselves a solider husband... "

But I still couldn't understand the motivation. "Why do these people go to war for nothing? How can they stand the horrors if they can rarely enjoy the loot? And how do you know all this?"

"I was a victim one summer. Oh yes, I fell prey. I don't know what I was thinking—it seems so ridiculous now, but I guess I'm just blind sometimes, completely blind to what I'm actually doing."

"It always seemed like a trap to me," Ellen remarked. "But, you know," she continued sarcastically, "the market's smarter than anybody, especially the government, so I guess it makes pretty good traps. Also, maybe some people are made to be soldiers. Why should we try to stop them?"

"Well, if they're your friends, maybe they just need some perspective..." I suggested.

"I agree," Mullins agreed, "They do. Or else their blind perseverance will drive them to hell."

Chapter Five

Mullinstein, Aaronburg, Isaac Singer, and Karen ushered in the Sabbath with reverence and prayer. They stood four in a row at the back of the shul, silently participating in the Friday night services of the Franklin Hillel. When the congregation sat, they sat. When the congregation stood, they stood. When the congregation chanted "oi yoi yoi," they chanted "oi yoi yoi." When the congregation listened to the sermon, they listened to the sermon. And when the congregation retired to the dining room to eat from a grand, sumptuous, and free buffet, they were first in line.

"What's not to like!" Mullinstein exclaimed loudly. The others nodded vigorously in agreement, their mouths stuffed with hallah bread and herring. The four were sitting at a large round table with four other Shabbat Jews.

"Delish!" added Isaac Singer. "Just like bubby makes it!"

"Oi!" said Aaronburg, "such chulent I've never eaten!"

"What kreftig nosh! I could...nosh...all night" Karen agreed.

"Excuse me," said the Shabbat Jew sitting next to Mullinstein, who introduced himself as Daniel, "but are you guys Jewish?"

"Of course my little mensch, I'm Mullinstein, and it's an honor," said Mullinstein, extending his hand.

The other three introduced themselves to Daniel, and then to Chaim, Chaim's younger brother Ari, and Joshua. These four regarded Mullinstein and Aaronburg, as well as Isaac Singer and Karen with some suspicion, but maintained polite conversation.

"Oh, sorry about that," said Ari. "We just haven't seen you here before. Where do you guys hail from?"

"New York of course," Isaac Singer answered quickly. "The Lower East Side."

"All four of you?" asked Joshua.

"Oh yes," Mullinstein nodded, whilst kicking Isaac Singer under the table.

Daniel and Joshua turned out to be from Oregon and Alabama, and the brothers were from Arkansas.

"So, what did you guys think of the D'var Torah?" Joshua asked the newcomers. The four began to ponder and Aaronburg finally said "I don't know, what did you think Mullinstein?"

"It was...good..." Mullinstein replied, slowly, kicking Aaronburg under the table.

"Yeah, but I thought he really strayed from the Parshah, didn't you?" Chaim asked.

"Well, ... I'm not sure if that's a matter for the dinner table," Mullinstein declared with a serious face.

In the meantime, Ari had become quite taken with "Karen," who may have been displaying slightly more cleavage than was appropriate for a Sabbath dinner.

"Your name's Karen?" he said. She nodded, her mouth full of smoked salmon. "You have to excuse me Karen, but I've never seen a Jewish woman of your...well, who looked so...what I want to say is, you're extremely...do you know what I mean?"

"Oh no Ari, what DO you mean?" she chirped sweetly. As she grabbed another loaf of hallah, she batted her eyelashes and continued to eat with the other hand.

"Your, well, your skin, and hair and eyes...I just..." His voice trailed off, but his mouth stayed open and his eyes stayed glued.

"Oh Ari, that's just bubkes," she flirted. "I'm just the like everyone else in the shul mischpacha."

"So, Aaronburg," Isaac Singer said loudly, drawing the attention of Daniel and Joshua, "did you hear Reuben kvetching about that shmendrick wife of his? Oi, I was just shvitzing when I heard it!"

"What?" said Aaronburg, not understanding half of what he heard.

"You know Aaronburg," said Isaac Singer in a strained voice, his face reddening slightly, "I was smoozing with Reuben, and boy oh boy what tzoress! Apparently his Miriam brought home some trafe food on Pesach by accident, and didn't even have the chutzpah to tell him! A regular goyishke kup she's got! What a noodle!"

Aaronburg looked at Isaac Singer blankly.

"Who are you guys talking about?" said Daniel, "and what's up with that Yiddish?"

"Oi gevalt!" said Mullinstein interrupted, "what shtick! Isaac Singer, do we always have to listen to the whole megillah!"

"Hey, who *are* you guys?" demanded Chaim. "Ari, stop drooling on that girl!"

"Chaim, I can practically see her pupick!" said Ari.

"Who are we?" intoned Isaac Singer offended and motioning to the others to eat faster, "listen, mashugine, we've been shlepping around all day, and here we are trying to have Shabbat kodesh, and you give ask us this? Watch your goyim pisk!"

"Us?! Goyim?!" Chaim exclaimed. "You're the goyim. She's Asian for God sakes! You're Indian! And you're...Ari, close your mouth!"

Karen smiled at Chaim, but he had seen through her guise, and he grabbed his younger brother.

"Aaronburg, Isaac Singer, Karen," said Mullinstein, "there is no reason for us to listen to this facacta nebbish! Let's go."

And so, the four Sabbath Jews rose, and wished their new friends mazel tov. They then left the shul, their pockets stuffed full of nosh.

*   *   *

"Hey," yelled Ellen from her room, "where are we having the Rumpus meeting tonight?"

"How about in the Buntsman Building?" Prateek yelled back. The Buntsman building was the new business school building at Franklin. It resembled a brick barn with an enormous silo next to it, and the silo was topped with a glittering golden dome. As the newest building on campus, the Buntsman building was packed with extremely high tech equipment and run by a huge central computer. Some called it the Death Star; others, Scrooge's money bin, or the Golden phallus. Prateek, however, loved the Buntsman building. According to him, it was "obviously superior on all academic and professional levels to any other learning environment."

"No way!" Mullins yelled from his room, "I have vowed never to step in that building."

"All right everybody," I announced, "we'll do the Blue Fog." I emailed the Rumpus members and told them to meet up at the Blue Fog for our discussion on "Being a Tourist."

Rumpus was an unofficial discussion club run by the Turf. At each session a member would provide some readings and lead a talk on a subject of his or her choice, at least until the discussion drifted elsewhere. We addressed such modest topics as: "What are the implications of photography for painting?," "Are progressive tax codes actually progressive?," "What are the best ways to give and receive gifts?," and "New Models for Alternative Education." In addition, we had a website that Prateek made, and we even had a constitution, which the Turf members had written together over the previous summer. Most importantly, we had a slick name: "Rumpus." I have to boast—

the name was my idea. It was mostly a joke, since I only half-respected the intellectual project of the group and thought that we made a lot of silly noise. But I convinced the other members to accept the name by arguing that should we ever need to attract new members or hold an event, our name would be irresistible to undersexed college kids who heard "Rumpus" and thought "Rump."

In addition to the Turf members, we could usually depend on three or four regulars and a couple of newbies to attend our weekly meetings. This week Ellen was leading the discussion on being a tourist. In her summers, Ellen had voyaged across Asia, Europe, and South America, and she alerted the members attending the discussion that we would be talking about the best methods of being a tourist in a new place.

After dinner we headed over to the Blue Fog and took over the enclosed back porch. The Maestro showed up, as well a few other regulars. As we were arranging the chairs, I saw Drew sit down at the main bar smoking a cigarette and drinking out of a flask. I went over and asked if he wanted to join us.

"Why da fuck not?" he said. "It can't be any worse."

"Ok," I said, and after he ordered a double scotch, we joined the group.

"So," Ellen started, "I wanted to talk about being a tourist. I want to know the best of way of being a tourist, to develop a theory to best capture your experience in a foreign country. What do you need to do? What do you need to avoid? What rules can you always follow?"

Ellen liked this method of discussion; she liked to feel like we made progress and that from analyzing our knowledge, we could figure out useful rules for ourselves.

So, we talked about being a tourist. Some people wanted to see everything, other people wanted take their time and chill. Some said you have to learn the language; others said don't bother, everyone speaks English. Some said you had to go exotic places and eschew the tourist attractions; others said you might as well hit the popular attractions; they wouldn't be touristy if they weren't cool. The highlight of the evening were Mullins' stories about getting arrested in rural China (he met a woman at a bar who went wild and trashed the place), and the time he was stuck in Prague for two weeks with a maniac woman who wanted to kill him. Ellen liked the stories but was disappointed with the lack of theoretical conclusions. Apparently, it seemed, you couldn't discover an ideal way to be a tourist, even with the combined experience of the Rumpus members.

I felt a little bad that I didn't have much to say. That usually happened—one of us just wouldn't feel like participating. Either we thought the topic was stupid or the readings were boring or the discussion was uninspiring or we just wanted to be with our own thoughts. Drew didn't say anything either. So after everyone had summarized their positions, I asked his opinion.

"Uh, I don't really do this sort of thing," he replied.

"What sort of thing?" Ellen inquired.

"Um, well, touristing, for one. I've never been out of the country. I'm fucking terrified of airport security."

"That's ok," she said. "Have you been to any new places in the US? What did you think about them?"

"Well, I have, but I don't philosophize about the experience. That's sophistry."

"Sophistry?"

"I mean, it's ok for you I guess, but it's not my thing."

"What is?"

"Sitting around figuring out the way to live. I don't do that anymore." Drew spoke slowly with intense conviction.

"I don't really understand," Ellen admitted.

Drew took some more scotch and continued. Everyone leaned in to hear him.

"I decided a couple years ago that doing shit was a lot more important than talking about it. Maybe if I had been traveling I could talk about it. But I never have. Sometimes I had to go away from Philly. But it was never about finding some other place."

He paused to smoke. "You can't escape yourself. It's like that platitude says---wherever you go there you are. I couldn't really ever leave Philly, even if I got on a plane and went to Europe."

Mullins cleared his throat and asked, "What did you find when you traveled?"

Drew took another drag on his cigarette and blew the smoke upwards. "I listened to people," he said. "I heard their stories, and told 'em mine. I tried to get some perspective. That's why I say I wasn't a tourist. I didn't go anywhere to see anything. I didn't go anywhere to be anything."

We were silent. Drew took another drag of his cigarette and finished his drink. He got up.

"Uh, thanks guys," he muttered, and walked out the door to the bar. I could see him sit down on a stool and order another drink.

"Well, on that note," said Ellen, "we will adjourn this meeting of Rumpus. Next week we're talking about psychological traumas caused by the internet. Aaron will email you guys with the readings and the meeting time."

Everyone got up to go.

"Mullins," I said, putting on my jacket, "what are you up to tonight? You want to hit a jazz club?"

"Actually I think I'm going to stick around and have a drink with that Drew guy. He seems interesting."

"Yeah, he's something," I agreed. "Rare around here."

I decided to walk back with Ellen and Prateek to the Turf. We were all pretty tired, and we went to bed soon after we returned. But I couldn't sleep. So I got up and read some short stories from a book my parents gave me. I read a story about mowing the lawn, and how it makes you feel. I read a story about a guy who ate M&Ms until he started blinking like a traffic light. I also read a story about finding God inside your body, right next to your spleen. God was a little brown guy who explained that the reason he wasn't around very much was because you never called him up to hang out, and he had gotten a little tired of waiting for you.

Mullins came home while I was reading, and he must have seen my light on because he knocked on my door.

"Drew's quite a character," he said.

"I know. That guy could be in a movie or something."

"I like him though; he's honest."

"He is honest," I agreed.

"Well," said Mullins, "I've had about enough of this day. I'm out of here."

*   *   *

Although Ellen and Prateek were anti-classroom, they were not anti-professor. It's true—some teachers they despised, and some they ignored. But others they liked, and a few they even respected. Ellen had invited several professors to present at Rumpus meetings, and one had led a very fine discussion. This week, the week before Thanksgiving, we had invited two professors out to dinner, with the naïve but well-meaning hope of discovering whether academia was a decent profession or a complete waste of time.

The two professors were Sam Gounder, an English professor, and Gary Mafter, a music professor. Ellen and Prateek had both taken their intro classes and enjoyed their lectures. But was their research—where they spent most of their time, as interesting and useful as their teaching?

We took them to L'Arbre, a nice French restaurant in Old City famous for the deciduous tree in the center of its authentic cobblestone floor. Mullins and I headed over early to get the table, while our roommates met our guests at the door. When they arrived, we all introduced ourselves and ordered our meals.

Handing his menu to the waiter, Prateek said "Well, Professors, my roommates Aaron and Mullins are thinking about a career in academia, and they wanted your opinion." This wasn't entirely untrue, although we were drawn more to the lifestyle than the work itself. No 9-5, no losing your job if you have tenure, nice campus and work environment, year-long sabbatical vacations every so many years, and almost complete freedom over how you spent your time. I explained this to the professors and they laughed.

"Don't forget that you actually have to *get* tenure first," said Mafter, a white-haired gentle-looking man in his sixties. His round face was wrinkled, but his blue eyes shined with youth. "That takes years of toil and it's very competitive."

"And you can't just work on anything," said Gounder through his impressively thick black beard. He was a younger man who taught contemporary poetry. "Academia is trendy like everything else, and department politics can be harsher than you might imagine."

"But it's the life of the mind, right?" said Mullins, "I mean, you're really trying to expand the horizons of human thought and knowledge, wouldn't you say?"

"Ideally," said Mafter, with a smile. "But day to day you are just trying to get published. If you're lucky it's something you like, or something important; if you're not, then it's just like any other hard work."

"Well, what do you guys work on?" asked Ellen. "In your classes we didn't really talk about your research. I mean, how do you really spend your time?"

The professors glanced at each other to be polite, and Mafter answered first.

"I'm a musicologist, and I work on comparative music theory."

"But what is that? What do you really do all day? What's the title of your research project?"

"Well, if you really want to know, I'm deriving a mathematical model to predict the inconsistencies in monastic chant of the middle ages before the development of modern notation. I work with a lot of manuscripts, historical texts, and statistical models to express the probabilities of the inter- and intra-monastery variation in chant, both as compared with other branches and other linguistically corroborative brotherhoods."

Before he could say more, our salads arrived.

"So," Mullins asked bravely, "what is your methodology?"

"Ah," replied Mafter, swallowing some salad, "by using a relatively simple model of tonal structures and chant variation in the socio-historical context, we can extrapolate mathematical probabilities for human psycho-linguistics and aural expressivity. Ergo, we can create predictive strategies for understanding creative harmonic culture within the modes of vocalizing and the Cziksentmihalyian paradigm.

Ellen leaned over to me and whispered "Ergo."

"And do you like it very much?" Mullins followed.

"I'll tell you," said Mafter, leaning in as if to share a secret, "it's what I think about when I go to the bathroom in the middle of the night. You young people don't understand that yet, but you will, you will."

"Bladder control," agreed Prateek, "now there's a subject for research." I kicked him under the table.

"Plus I like teaching," Mafter continued. "Seeing my students learn. It won't make me a millionaire, but every day when I get home from work at 3 pm, I can take a stroll around with my wife, go see a movie, or read a book. I don't have to worry about a bottom line; I just worry about my students, who are real human beings to me."

"That sounds good, Professor," Ellen said. "So you think it's a worthwhile career?"

Before he could answer, a waiter swept by to remove our salad plates and set the table for the main courses. Mafter whispered something to Gounder, and I adjusted the napkin on my lap. After two more waiters stopped by to fill our water glasses and drop off our main courses, Mafter continued.

"You have to love it," he said to Ellen, "or it's as meaningless as anything else. You see this steak," he said, picking up a piece of meat from his plate. "I'm really enjoying this, but some butcher had to kill this cow, which I would not find enjoyable, and someone had to cook this meat, which I have no skills to do." He ate the meat off his fork, chewed, swallowed, and concluded: "The academy, and I mean the humanities, is about appreciating and analyzing man's and nature's creations, to the highest and most profound extent."

"That sounds good Professor," said Mullins. "But what do you think about the common criticism that academics are closet artists without the courage to write or make art themselves?"

"It's just like I said," Mafter responded, "different people have different talents. Some musicians may be able to create a beautiful melody on the piano. I have the talent to explain what that melody is in notation and language, and to explain what about that melody makes it attractive or absurd or why it evokes certain emotions. Besides, oftentimes artistic temperaments do not make for good teachers. Our society needs people who can appreciate art deeply, and teach it without a vested interest."

Mullins nodded and thought for a moment. "That's interesting. And what about you," he said turning to Professor Gounder, "what do you make of it? What kind of research do you do?"

Gounder had been listening intently to the conversation. "Well," he said slowly, "I just finished a book on new Holocaust poetry. But I guess you could say I'm not a traditional Humanities academic like Gary."

"Why's that?"

"Well, I run the Poetry and Prose center for the University, so I spend a lot of time doing community organizing—more than most professors. I work on getting poetry readings on the radio and poetry in the newspaper. I try to bring published poets to Franklin and to help the young poets at Franklin learn how to write. I also work with West Philadelphia schools to create some kind of poetic interchange between the kids in my classes and the undergrads. So I don't really spend as much time as I should on research."

"That sounds pretty good though," said Ellen, "like you're trying to spread poetry in the community."

"It's really a great way for people to learn how to talk to each other," he replied. "Plus, some of the young students I have are great writers—so fresh and exciting, even in a conservative institution like Franklin."

"Do you get pressure from your department to publish more?" asked Mafter.

Gounder laughed. "Not since I got the last US Humanities grant. As far as the university's concerned, it's as good as five books."

"What division did you apply for?" Mafter inquired.

"The teaching division—using electronic resources in the classroom." I remembered Ellen telling me how the internet was part of her poetry class.

"Not so easy to do in music," said Mafter.

"I suppose not," said Gounder, smiling kindly.

"And in your opinion," I asked, "is academia worthwhile?"

"If you know what you like, and you're willing to sacrifice a lot of time for it," he said. "In English, for example, you could spend six to seven years living the impoverished life as a student, and then not be able to find a job at a decent university, or at all. It's very political who gets hired and where. So I think if you can love what you're doing enough to withstand the poverty, long hours, and some of the dense people you run into, it's worth a try."

"That's not a glowing recommendation." Prateek folded his arms.

"Listen," said Gounder, "all careers have their ups and downs. This one has big benefits if you make it, but don't think that making it in academia, or at least in the humanities, is any more a reflection of pure genius and honest scholarship than in the business world."

"But where's the bottom line in the academy?"

"There isn't one. It's your resume—what you've published and where, and who you've worked with…but even that isn't enough. Something like seventeen tenure-track spots open up in US university English departments every year for eight thousand candidates. That means it's a challenge to get in."

"And aside from the barriers of entry?" Prateek followed.

"You have to be able to work alone, to motivate yourself to keep going, and frankly, you have to be sharp. And like I said, it's a political game, even at our level." He gestured at Mafter, who nodded.

"But this isn't to discourage you," Mafter said. "If your life is about the life of the mind, you should go with what you've been given. There's a lot of glory when you make a discovery, even if you don't get a pay-raise."

"Totally," said Gounder. "Now tell us about what you guys are interested in. What are you all majoring in?"

We spent the rest of dinner and dessert telling the professors about ourselves. They listened enthusiastically and said they thought we'd all make fine professors if we gave it our best. When the meal was over, we picked up the tab for their food and thanked them for their time.

"Our pleasure," said Mafter, "it's so rare to find students who want to engage their professors."

"And vice versa," said Ellen. "Goodnight!"

We said goodbye to the professors and, stuffed to the gizzard, walked slowly up Chestnut Street to the Turf.

"Those are great guys, and that was a great discussion," said Mullins enthusiastically. He thought for a moment. "But I'm still confused about academia—do I want to be a scholar, or just one of those guys we met? Well, I'm not feeling the passion for study right now. Back to the drawing board I guess." We walked quietly for a few blocks and then he spoke up again: "I know!" he exclaimed, "I liked what we did tonight. How about a career for all of us interviewing people? We could be like team Charlie Rose!"

"Ha ha," said Ellen, "Charlie Rose works because he's by himself and because of the intimacy with his guests. You think the four of us could do the same?"

"I would rather be Robin Leech," I said. "He must be getting old. Who's going to look after the rich and famous when he's gone?"

"No no no," said Prateek. "Your goal should be to be interviewed by Robin Leech, not to be Robin Leech."

"I don't know, Robin Leech gets to meet a lot of cool people."

"Well, speak for yourself," said Prateek. "Being rich and famous is part of my master plan."

"Right after 'Buy the Green Bay Packers?'" I retorted.

"Right *before* 'Buy the Green Bay Packers?'" he answered.

"I don't know about the Packers," said Ellen, "but there are definitely mandatory luxuries necessary for happiness. Remember that Rumpus meeting?"

"Like?" I asked.

"Like a wine cellar, a sauna, a fully-stocked kitchen, a nice set of leather luggage…"

"On wheels?" Mullins interjected.

"On wheels," she continued, "lots of vacation time, a great stereo, et cetera, et cetera."

"Not bad," I said. "And don't forget about your threads."

Ellen dressed in high fashion. However, she never discussed shopping, and as far as we could tell, she never actually went shopping. Prateek asserted she had a personal shopper, and my theory was that she ordered all her clothes online. She would confirm neither.

"Ugh," said Mullins. He tripped on a stone, but recovered before he fell. We were walking over the Chestnut Bridge, which was lit beautifully. The Skukyll River gleamed black and flowed smoothly past the garbage on its banks. We were silent for a while, admiring the Center City skyline.

"What about architecture?" I suggested to Mullins, as we hit 22nd street. "You could be an architect and design impressive buildings!"

"Too much drudgery and too many long hours." He picked up a stone and tossed it over the bridge. "Plus do you know how many years of school I'd need to do that!? I didn't take a single math or science class in college. We'll keep working on it."

*   *   *

The next night Prateek and I went to a movie at the Fitz with a friend of his visiting from Portsmouth College. Grace was her name, and she was in Philadelphia for a job interview. Ironically, she was almost nothing like Prateek. She was effervescent, sensitive, and suspicious of tradition. Maybe that's why they got along so well. Grace was Hawaiian, but for some reason she was studying art-history on the East Coast. As she was also a senior, she had applied for a highly-esteemed curatorial job at the Philadelphia Art Museum. Only five others had been selected for the interview, and all of them had more experience than she did.

We got home from the movie and put on some Cannonball Adderley. Then we helped Grace practice some interview questions, until she had a terrible realization. She had left her dress in New Hampshire!

Grace was beside herself with dread. There was no way she could interview in the clothes she brought, they were much too informal. All the stores were closed, and none would open before her 9 am interview. I suggested she try some of Ellen's clothes, but she looked at me and frowned. Ellen, I supposed, was a different shape.

No matter! The Turf rallied to her cause. We quickly developed a list of all the girls we knew, and then put them in order of who looked most like Grace. Then we started the mass phone calls, all four of us at the same time.

We couldn't find anyone her size. We must have called thirty people, and visited at least ten. But each time a young lady opened the door, either she or Grace would smile, and we would politely say 'no thank you' and leave. It's funny: as discerning as Prateek and I claimed to be with women's figures, we had no real conception of comparative body size.

Finally Prateek remembered that the Maestro had a roommate whose clothes might fit Grace. It was the same girl who had tried to seduce me our freshman year. I had rejected her advances on the official grounds that I had a girlfriend at the time and was unavailable, which was untrue. In reality I found her repulsive. No offense, but I don't date pasty-skinned girls who have a Zorro moustache, a neck hairier than my legs, and the teeth of a cable-movie cave monster. Otherwise, she was a good-hearted girl, and we stayed distant friends.

Prateek made the phone call, and learned that the Maestro's roommate wasn't home. So he convinced our buddy to let us raid her closet, and assured him that we would do whatever necessary to make it up to her. Not wanting to worry our guest, we told Grace that it was the Maestro's sister, who surely wouldn't mind the intrusion.

The three of us ran over to the Maestro's apartment on Walnut Street and he buzzed us in. We thanked him profusely for the service and then made a beeline for his "sister's" room. He told us we only had a few minutes before she returned so we had to be fast. We rushed Grace into her room, and I tore open her closet doors, saying: "Go!"

She began trying dresses on over her clothes. The first few didn't fit, she said breathlessly, but it looked like some of the others had potential.

"How can this one not fit!" Prateek shouted, as she took off one of the black dresses. It's stretchy, look it even fits on me!"

Before we could say anything, he yanked the black dress from the chair, pulled off his shirt, and wrenched the dress over himself. It was far too tight, and exposed the price of tasty home-made Indian food.

Suddenly, we heard footsteps in the hall, and a female voice call: "Maestro, I went shopping!"

We all looked at the door. She was coming!

"Shit!" whispered Prateek, and he slammed her door closed. "Hide!" he yelled.

There was nowhere to hide. Her tiny room had a single futon on the floor, an undersized desk, and a beanbag chair. The bottom of the closet was packed with shoes and suitcases.

Prateek ran behind the beanbag chair and tried to hide himself. You could see about half of him.

"Come on guys!" he yelled.

I laughed. We had no chance. The Maestro's roommate burst into her room to find the Maestro and me standing next to Grace, who was wearing one of her dresses. The rest of her dresses were on chairs or on the floor. "What's going on!?" she screamed. Oh I got forget to mention, for a good-hearted girl, she had an explosive side.

"Don't worry, I can explain everything," said Prateek getting up from behind the bean-bag chair and extending his arm like a Roman emperor. He said this as suavely as he could, forgetting that he was wearing a tiny black dress.

"I hope so, Prateek," she said, almost in tears, "and you can start by telling me when you became a drag queen!"

"Oh! Shit!" he said, remembering the dress. He pulled it off and replaced his shirt. She was not amused.

"Baby, baby, come with me for a minute," said the Maestro, saving Prateek.

"But…" she protested.

"That dorkus isn't going anywhere," he said. "Grace here is a friend who had a dress emergency." He whispered in her ear for a moment, and her eyes widened.

"Really?" she said. She looked at me, and I shrugged innocently. Then the Maestro whispered more.

"Ok ok," she said pushing him away with a grin, "you guys finish up in here, and I'll be back in a few minutes. By the way" she said to Grace, "the blue one hanging in the closet would look nice on you." She left the room.

"What did you tell her?" Grace asked.

"You don't want to know Aaron," he replied, grinning at me.

"Why Aaron, why Aaron!" I said, suddenly very nervous. What had Maestro done to me?

"Go ahead and try on that other dress," he told Grace. Then he went over to help Prateek hang up the clothing.

"Aaron," he said when they'd finished, "why don't you just hang around for a little while after Grace and Prateek leave."

"What?!" I said. "What did you get me into?! What did you say! Damn you Maestro, what's going on?!"

"Don't be angry." He put his hand soothingly on my shoulder.

"I'm not angry, I said, "I'm only frightened, like a tiny blond gorilla."

"A what? Listen, we'll have a chat, Aaron," he said. Grace giggled and she left with Prateek for the Turf.

I'm not going to subject you to what I endured that evening. Suffice it to say that the Maestro had appeased his roommate by telling her I had organized the whole charade as an excuse to visit her. She was so touched that she decided to attack me with her most feminine weapons. But I withstood! I did not cave in! That's it, I say no more.

All right, listen I know you're curious, and I should probably come clean. I may have inadvertently come into contact with this young lady's chest. But I assure you, I had nothing but the purest intentions. In fact, I was a perfect gentleman. It's just that when a large heaving bosom moves in your direction after you've consumed the majority of a six-pack of beer, *and* you receive a simultaneous attack to the lap, you cannot easily avoid the assault. You have to make a decision: what will you sacrifice?

But I did not lead her on, I tell you, I was just doing my duty. And if she emailed me constantly for a month afterwards, I swear she just wanted to go to meals, concerts, ice cream, tea, coffee, and movies with me *as a friend.*

I lumbered home around midnight. Mullins was drinking green tea and reading Madame Bovary in the living room. He had a blanket on his knees, and he was calm. The only light on was a lamp next to him, and I sat down on the couch in the shadows.

"Where have you been?" he asked. I assumed Prateek had informed him of my predicament, so I said:

"Oh you know, a little this and that."

"What?" he asked, surprised. "I thought you were hanging out with the Maestro."

"That would have been safer," I joked, "It's important not to play with heavy machinery when you're drunk."

"What are you talking about?" He didn't know about the Maestro's roommate.

"Oh," I responded, "the Maestro's roommate used to like me a lot, and I had a couple of drinks with her, and then…you know."

"Wait, is this your new girlfriend?"

"No way! I mean, she liked me freshman year, but I wasn't interested in her. Tonight I wasn't all that interested either, but I was in a predicament, you understand? I sacrificed for Grace!"

"A predicament!" he said, sounding shocked. "How do you fall into that kind of predicament?!"

"You don't," I told him. "It falls onto you."

"That's crazy! How come it never happens to me?" He smashed his arm down on the table next to him and knocked the lamp onto the floor, smashing its base. But the noise didn't seem to have woken Ellen or Prateek, and being intoxicated myself, I continued talking as if nothing had happened.

"I don't know. I never look for it though. You can only see it peripherally. Like this." I motioned to the sides of my head, to explain 'peripherally.'

Mullins bent over in his chair and stared at the floor. I could barely see him in the moonlight. "I don't know, man. I don't know why it isn't working for me. How come I'm here reading about a crazy woman having affairs, and you're out having them?"

"Listen, you just moved here, and you don't know that many people." He looked pretty down, and I wanted him to feel better. "And listen," I added, "she really isn't special to me at all. She isn't even that attractive…" I shuddered to show him. Maybe I deserved to, what with my callous behavior and brute insensitivity. Like I said though, we didn't go that far. Besides, to some extent I was giving this girl what she wanted, what she had wanted for a long time. Wasn't there some merit to that?

"I meet girls," he moaned, "but something just doesn't seem to work. I don't know what."

"You could easily find a hook-up at a campus bar or a frat party," I instructed.

"I know," he replied, "and sometimes I really feel like doing it. But it's not me, you know. I'm not that guy. And I don't think it's really what I want. Plus, I'm just not good with girls; I just keep fucking up for one reason or another. You've heard the stories."

"Mullins," I said, suddenly thinking clearly, "do you ever wonder if you get locked in your own stories?"

"What do you mean?" He sat back and sipped his tea.

"Do you think what happens to you happens to you because you're living your story?"

"I don't know what you mean," he replied. "Of course I'm living my story."

"But what I'm saying is, you're not letting your story unfold on its own …."

"Listen Aaron, I tell a lot of stories. My life is definitely one of them, or at least the material for a lot of what I say. What's wrong with that?"

"I don't know exactly, Mullins," I said, "but I feel like something might be."

"Like?"

"Well...well, I don't know."

"I don't think so," he said. "All the stories I tell about myself are funny. I mean, people always laugh. When people laugh I feel good, so no biggie."

"No biggie," I repeated, mostly to myself. I didn't know what to say. Frankly, I didn't really know my own thoughts. I felt like I was on the verge of seeing something. But, I couldn't yet. And I couldn't worry too much about it either. My God, not while the Maestro's roommate was out to get me.

"Well Mullins, I think I'm going to hit the sack."

"Ok man, I'm going to read for a while. Could you turn the other lamp on for me?"

"Sure," I said. "Watch out for sharp pieces when you get up."

He nodded, and I turned on the other lamp, and left him there, reading with his blanket on his lap.

*   *   *

The next day Ellen and Prateek asked me about the broken lamp. I told them Mullins would explain, but they said that he'd walked to the Art Museum with Grace and was going to spend the morning there.

"Well," I admitted, "Mullins smashed the lamp by accident." Then I explained our conversation of the previous night.

"You got it on with the Maestro's roommate!" said Prateek in disbelief. "Jesus Christ! I would have smashed the lamp too!"

"It was nothing," I said, defending myself. "Can't it just be nothing? We barely did anything." I looked at Ellen for support, but I didn't get any.

"You better be careful Aaron." She was serious. "You don't want to hurt her."

"No more," I said, "I promise. Anyway, I'm sure Mullins will get another lamp."

"I think," said Prateek, "that we need to help our man with his woman situation. I'll call up you-know-who." He was referring to the dark-haired nymphet who lived below us. She came from a very traditional family, and was also in heat more hours than the sun. We never knew exactly how far she went with her men, but we often saw her male guests entering or leaving the building.

"I don't think he wants you-know-who," I said. "I don't think that's going to help him."

"Should we try to hook him up with somebody else? Maybe we can go through your black book," he joked.

"Not funny."

"I think we shouldn't do anything," said Ellen. "What can we do? We don't know what's going on in his mind. It's too dangerous to fool around with his life. Besides, like you said, what would we do? Have an intervention?"

Prateek disagreed. "No, no, no. I'm for doing something. We should support our buddy with all our resources. He's still new to Philly. And he's working in a bakery for God's sake."

"It's not our business," she insisted. "People have to figure out these kinds of problems on their own."

"What do you mean? You don't even want to talk about it?"

"Oh well, I don't have any problems talking with him about it. I'm just not sure we should sit him down for a here's-what's-good-for-you lecture. He's a big boy. Let him deal with his own problems."

"Ellen, you know it's not easy for gentlemen to talk about his feelings." Prateek adjusted his posture. "He won't bring it up on his own, I assure you."

"Too bad then. It's his deal."

"But we're not making deals," Prateek argued, "We're trying to help Mullins. Let's do something."

"I want to help Mullins," she said, sounding frustrated. "But, I don't know, what can *we* really do? He just hasn't figured himself out. That's what it is."

"Is it?" I wondered. It didn't really make sense to me either. If Ellen was right that Mullins didn't understand himself, what could we do? "Well, we ought to at least..." I began to suggest.

"What is his problem exactly?" Ellen interjected. "You said he doesn't just want to get laid? What does he want, the love of his life? That's a lot to ask for."

"I don't know, I don't know."

"Well, I think we should call you-know-who," Prateek said. "Maybe our boy just needs some feminine attention."

*   *   *

Four days later, we left south for Thanksgiving vacation. Ellen had invited the three of us to her home in South Carolina, and we agreed immediately that it was an ideal trip. Her parents and brothers were on a cruise, and we would have her place to ourselves.

But even after making the executive decision, it took us at least two days to figure out a departure time, method of transportation, and route that was acceptable to all. Finally we decided that we were to rent a car, and "take to the great American roadways." We would drive down together on Wednesday night and drive back on Sunday morning, except for Mullins who had to fly out Saturday. We protested his decision to leave early, but he said he had an interview which might be setting him up "for the big time." He would not divulge its nature.

The day before we left, I had suggested that we take a train. But Prateek disapproved of trains.

"They're cattle transport!" he yelled. "Overpriced, unreliable, bovine box-cars!"

"Ok then," said Ellen, "what about renting a car?"

"Superb!" said Mullins, suddenly standing up at the kitchen table. He turned his head left, and looked up at something I didn't see. "The great American roadways!" he exclaimed. "How I have waited for this day! Each will take his turn at the wheel, driving his country with the justice of democracy and equality! Let us depart with reckless abandon, and make for our destinies together!" He stopped and looked at us.

Prateek snorted, and the three of us tried not to laugh.

"What the hell was that, Mullins?" Prateek spat between breaths. "You think you're Emerson or Winston Churchill or something?"

Mullins glanced at him quickly and then looked at the floor. "No," he said in a quiet voice, "I was just practicing. Drew said I should practice with…"

"Drew?"

"Oh, never mind. Listen, I'll go rent the car." He left and went into his room.

"What was that about?" Ellen wondered.

"Strange," Prateek added.

"No idea," I said, "maybe we'll find out on our trip."

*   *   *

The next evening we met at our designated time to pick up the rental car. But, not having much experience (any experience), renting cars, we were highly unprepared. Mullins' Driver's License had expired while he was out of the country. Ellen announced that she couldn't drive at night. Prateek had sprained his right knee having tripped on the stairs in the Buntsman building and was unable to use the accelerator, clutch, and the break. I didn't have a credit card. Eventually, we had to put two under-25 drivers on Prateek's credit card. And if you do the math, you'll see that I had to drive the whole damn way.

Not that I'm upset about it. No, there's nothing more pleasant than driving 11 hours straight overnight after a stressful day of auditions. Especially if you happen to hit a freak snowstorm when you are surrounded by 18-wheeler tractor-trailers driving eighty-five miles an hour. Prateek, of course, was nonplussed.

"Drive faster," he instructed me evenly from the middle of

the back seat. This was after I had been driving for eight hours with one short break in a Wendy's bathroom. We had dropped off the Maestro in Washington and were continuing south. According to the radio, snow only fell in North Carolina once every ten years. This was the mightiest storm since 1963.

The others were asleep, so I whispered back. "Prateek, I'm going sixty-five and the limit's fifty-five. I can't see 10 feet in front of me, and I can't see the sides of the road at all. There are huge trucks around here that could squash this car, and you know what, I can't even see where they are."

"Ridiculous," he scoffed. "You're driving like a granny."

"What are you talking about?!" I said, straining my voice. "You're insane."

"You clearly don't know how to drive in snow," he said, still at normal volume.

"What, faster's better, is that your rule?"

"In these conditions, granny driving is even worse."

"Aw man," I muttered, and continued at my snail's pace of sixty-five.

Prateek continued to make comments about my "Sunday driving" over the next two hours, but I was too tired to listen. "Thank God he sprained his knee," I repeated to myself.

Ellen woke up for the last hour and directed us to her house in Greenville.

"I don't understand it," said Mullins, as we unloaded the car. "First of all, it's only Thanksgiving. And second of all, we're in fucking South Carolina. We went *south* for vacation, just to avoid this kind of weather."

Prateek scowled. He informed me that because of my driving, we had missed two of his alternate bed times.

"What are you talking about?" I snapped. I had just driven him 11 hours across too many states, and I wasn't in the mood for complaining.

"I can only fall asleep at certain times," he whined. "We missed three of them this evening."

I took a deep breath. I didn't have the energy to fight. We filed into Ellen's house and crashed on various couches and beds. I haven't slept that well in a long time.

We spent the weekend relaxing and wandering around Greenville. There wasn't a whole lot to do by our standards, especially since things were closed for Thanksgiving. So, we ended up watching a lot of movies, taking a lot of walks, and sampling all the rare and expensive liquors that Ellen's parents had hidden poorly under the kitchen sink. Of course, we replaced the volume of what we drank in cans of Sam Adams. That's a respectable beer, you know, for what it is.

Saturday morning I got up early to drive Mullins to the airport. He was dressed in a suit, and he had a notebook with him. In the car, I put on a CD of Charles Mingus and Mullins asked me, "What do you do when a guy tells you his wife left him for a fat loser, and that pigeons love to shit on him during his lunch break? How do you respond to that?"

"I don't know," I said. "This guy sounds like a real character. You can't cheer him up?"

"I don't think he even wants to feel better. Have you ever met someone like that?"

"Jesus, I don't think so."

"At first I had pity for all his problems," he said, "and then I started to find him really crazy. Now it's just funny. It's like he enjoys telling people how unhappy he is, you know, with these bizarre stories."

I was quiet as I merged onto the highway. I didn't really know what to say. "Sounds like you have it figured out," I finally told him.

"I don't know," he murmured. "But anyway, this guy is helping me a lot, working his ass off for me, so I can't complain."

"All right," I said. We listened to Mingus until we arrived at the airport. "Good luck," I told him. "On whatever the hell you're doing."

"Thanks man," he said. "I'll see you in a few." He shut the door and was off.

When I got back to Ellen's place, she and Prateek were having brunch with one of her high school friends. The guy had apparently started a computer company when he first got to college, but it went broke, and he continued making cash by pirating software and customizing skateboards. He said when he graduated he wanted to work "probably in HR, but only if it's cool," and that he "wouldn't mind sales either, as long as there are major perks."

Ellen wasn't so close to this guy, I knew, but she liked to visit him when she was home. I sat down to the join the three of them and ate a few too many Danishes. When my arteries started to protest, I moved over to the piano in the corner to bang out some melodies. It's hard for me to be away from music for long.

"So," I heard Prateek ask him, "tell us about Ellen in high school. Tell us all her dirty secrets, ha ha ha."

I turned around and saw him smiling his evil smile. Ellen shook her head and started clearing dishes to the kitchen.

"Well, I don't know dude," said the high school buddy. "She was generally pretty clean."

"But," Prateek insisted, "there must have been something. Nobody is spot-clean. Ha ha ha."

"Oh Prateek," Ellen laughed, carrying some dishes out, "we're not really in high school any more, are we?" She stayed in the kitchen to wash up.

"What," Prateek pressed on, raising one eyebrow "about guys?"

Ellen hadn't told us much about her high school dating. I tapped out 'In a Sentimental Mood' on the piano.

"Well." Ellen's friend coughed, sounding embarrassed, "I don't know."

"Nothing?" said Prateek, sounding really disappointed, "I thought you were her friend?!"

"I am," the friend insisted. "I mean, I guess there was this guy she was in love with. But I really can't talk about him!"

"Whatever, it's been five years, I'm sure she's over it," said Prateek quickly. "What's the story?"

And so Ellen's friend presented to Prateek the tragic romance of her 11th grade year, a story of unrequited love which destroyed a friendship and caused a year of emptiness and desolation.

I had never heard the whole tale before, although Ellen had told me some of the pieces. But that was a long time ago. I let the piano get louder and played for about forty-five minutes while Prateek and Ellen's high school buddy talked. Eventually I heard their conversation die down, and I stopped playing to go get some water in the kitchen.

When I was filling up a glass from the sink, I realized Ellen wasn't there. I went into the living room where Prateek was instructing his new friend in the statistical method for winning fantasy football.

"Guys," I interrupted, "have you seen Ellen?"

"Nope," they said and went back to their discussion. I checked upstairs and Ellen's door was locked. I knocked but she didn't answer.

"I'm going for a walk," I announced to anyone in particular. She didn't respond.

"OK," Prateek responded from downstairs.

I left, and when I got back from my walk around three-thirty, Ellen was sitting on the living room couch with swollen eyes. Prateek was checking his email upstairs and the other guy had left.

"Where have you been?" I asked innocently. I put some water on to make tea and got John Coltrane playing on the stereo. Ellen sat without speaking and smiled at me sadly.

"What happened..." I asked her.

"No," she interrupted, smiling tightly.

"Are you upset?"

"I don't want to be," she whimpered.

"Laugh it off," I almost said, and then reconsidered. "Go ahead and scream at me," I said. "I deserve it."

"But you didn't do anything," she said, staring at the floor.

"OK. But it's just as bad."

"I don't know. I don't know, Aaron"

"Oh Ellen," I said. I gave her a hug and we drank our tea in silence.

*   *   *

Ellen didn't talk much to Prateek the rest of the day, but I don't think he noticed. Nor did she talk to him in the car on the way home; she slept the whole way. Even after we got back she was unusually quiet, but Prateek remained oblivious. I, on the other hand, felt the tension and was uneasy with her silence. I told her about it— I told her that she had to say something. But it took two days for her to speak with Prateek. I remember now that when I was eating lunch the following Wednesday, he came out of her room and stared at me without saying anything. I stared back, not realizing what they'd talked about. Then Prateek went into his room and shut the door.

A few days later Prateek and I were going food shopping, and he told me about his conversation with Ellen. "She said," he related, "never to tell anyone what she told me or to ever talk about that guy."

"You don't seem to be following orders," I pointed out.

"Ha ha ha. Silliness," he responded. "She's being ridiculous. Everybody has stories from high school, and everybody should be able to laugh at themselves."

"Yeah, well if she's pretty sensitive about it, we should probably drop it, don't you think?"

"That's absurd! Anyway, she shouldn't be repressing her memories. Think of how upset she could be if she ever meets this character again. I've alerted her other friends to be on the lookout for him."

"You've what?"

"What? Oh, I told all the members of the Turf extended-family to be on the lookout in case he shows up. You never know, he might have changed his mind or something. Everybody should know in case he does."

"They should?"

"Oh yes, that's very important. And as for you, if you hear or see this character around Philadelphia, I want you to alert me immediately."

"You do?!"

"Yes, that's critical. Then I'll put my plan into action."

"Your plan?"

"Yes, my plan. I can't tell you about it of course, but it's perfect."

"Why can't you tell me?"

"Well, as you know, I keep a policy of never revealing information about myself unless absolutely necessary. I like to keep people on a need-to-know basis."

"Oh. Right. Glad to know you're on top of things."

"Ha ha ha."

I made a note to myself to keep Prateek on a need-to-know basis.

Chapter Six

About a week into December, it got cold. No, wait a minute, it got cold in November. In December it got *really* cold. We're talking about the kind of cold where you stock your cellars for the next ice age. The kind of cold where if you're old, you stay in and risk starvation rather than take your hips out on the frozen sidewalk. The kind of cold where you cover *every* part of your body or chance losing a frozen limb without even knowing it. And the kind of cold where you thought the liquid in your eyes was going to freeze solid, if the air in your lungs didn't condense and suffocate you first.

On these cold days, no one opened the window to check the temperature. Ellen claimed to be able to estimate the degrees Fahrenheit by looking out the window and carefully observing the expressions of pain on people's faces. But to me, figuring out the temperature didn't matter; the expressions of pain told you enough. Those were the expressions that made you all the more glad that your hips were young and strong, that you spent most of your day inside, and that you lived in Philadelphia and not Alaska!

That's right, it wasn't *that* cold, not like Alaska or anything. The truth is that I find complaining about the cold pretty boring unless I exaggerate it into a story of frozen hell. But I wasn't exaggerating everything. It was still cold enough to prevent us from going to parties, to restaurants, and to class. It wasn't cold enough, though, to prevent us from going to the Blue Fog for hot toddies. And, it sure wasn't cold enough to stop Mullins from inviting new female friends to come along too.

Mullins had decided that he needed to maintain the Japanese skills he had learned in college, so he had advertised in the Franklin paper to meet Japanese language partners. Only girls were accepted.

"Isn't that a little transparent?" Ellen asked.

Mullins feigned innocence. "Have you ever tried making small talk with a Japanese male? Fah-get about it. My first language partner in college sat across the table from me without uttering a single word in four meetings."

"Didn't you ask him about himself?" said Ellen. "What did he say?"

"As far as I could tell, he had no interests or hobbies. He just sat there like a lump of clay. He didn't do anything, and he when I asked him about himself, he just grunted."

"What was he doing at Franklin?" Prateek wondered.

"You'll be happy to know, Prateek," Mullins smirked, "that he will be one of your future colleagues. He was in the United States to improve his English in order to speed up his career in banking."

"Maybe he was just shy."

"No. He showed no emotion, not even shyness." Mullins said. "He didn't even blink. He didn't ask any questions, and he didn't answer any either. Just like a solider," he said to me.

"Why did he sign up to be a language partner?" I asked.

"Beats the fuck out of me," said Mullins. "I said to myself: either he expected a chick and was severely disappointed or he has absolutely no character. I mean, how was he going to improve his English if he didn't talk at all? Well, maybe he was never planning to use English anyway; maybe it was only important on the resume."

"There's nothing necessarily wrong that," said Prateek.

"Sure," said Mullins with a tone meaning 'there absolutely is.' "Now I'm not saying that all Japanese men are like this," he continued. "I've met a lot of Japanese guys who were communicative, inquisitive and emotional. But you know, that's pretty much guaranteed with girls. That's why I asked for a girl."

"Chauvinist!" accused Ellen, half-jokingly. She wanted Mullins to admit he was on the hunt.

"Listen," he retorted, "I'm not a misogynist. You know I love women!" Prateek and I laughed, and Ellen made a sour face.

"Ellen, I just can't overcome these institutions by myself—if girls talk more, I look for a female language partner to improve my Japanese. End of story."

That, of course, was not the end of the story. But who cared, anyway? If Mullins wanted to date a Japanese girl, and he found one who wanted to date him, so what? So what? Well, what if he found one who didn't want to date him? What if he found someone who just wanted some language practice?

*   *   *

Mullins entered the Blue Fog with a young Japanese lady just as Ellen and I were starting our second round of hot toddies. Prateek had stayed home "to trade." Ellen waved to Mullins, inviting him to sit with us. I saw Mullins acknowledge her and then look around quickly for other tables. As there were none, he came over with his friend to join us. "Look," he said to her after introducing everyone, "we might as well get to know each other in English, since my roommates don't speak Japanese." She agreed.

His language partner was short, stylish, and carefully preened. Mullins told us later that she got up an extra hour early in the morning for her beauty routine. She was wearing knee-high leather boots and a short leather skirt, and under her coat, a very tight shirt.

She was training at Franklin to become an international fashion lawyer. She was very smart, but I learned that afterwards. At the time, I thought she was cute and opinion-less. She laughed at everything I said (not all that much, and not all that funny), and didn't really have much of her own to say. But Ellen knew something about this Japanese laughing. Apparently, there is a different laugh for every kind of response, and if you can interpret them, you can know if someone is laughing in joy, anger, or disgust.

Mullins, however, was not able to understand his language partner much better than me. He quickly became frustrated with his inability to figure out what she was thinking about him. He made jokes and then, after she laughed, apologized that they were stupid. She laughed at that too. As time went on, he got more and more animated and dramatic, trying to feel out what she was thinking. He told stories about his travels and about some of the previous girls he had wanted to date, and how he found out later that they were insane. The stories were good, but they didn't provoke his language partner to voice her feelings in a way he could understand.

I'm not sure if this young lady was only able to express herself by laughing, or if she was just un-provokable. But the result was the same, and Mullins couldn't get much out of her. So after an hour and a half of performance, he signaled to us that he was ready to leave. We paid the bill, and Ellen got up to say hello to another friend. I decided to hit the can before we left, and as I got up, I heard Mullins ask his language partner if she'd like to go to dinner in two days' time. She laughed and said she would check.

"Check what?" I heard him ask as I walked away.

When I got back to the table she was gone, and Mullins was talking with Ellen.

"You know there's really two ways to see this girl," he said. "One is that she's reached some kind of enlightenment, and being so peaceful and calm she avoids creating conflict and argument.

On the other hand, what the hell does she think?! She's really smart—I know it, and I know she's a top student at Franklin. But how can we talk so much without saying anything?! She's not giving me any idea what she thinks about me!"

It seemed that Mullins was not satisfied with his Japanese lessons.

"Mullins," I admonished, "you just met her. What's the big deal?"

"I don't know," he conceded. "I guess that she didn't go for my stories at all. I mean, she laughed a lot, but I didn't get the picture she really was letting them affect her."

"Affect her? How exactly did you want to affect her?" Ellen demanded

"It's not that I should be able to control her emotions," he said slowly. "It's just that I get no emotional response from what I'm doing. Part of it is that she's a relaxed person. But there's got to be more, right?"

Mullins sighed. There were too many people, he said, that he couldn't predict. And why were so many of them attractive girls? He could tell a damn good story. He *knew* it. But the ladies didn't seem to follow the plot.

"Ah," said Ellen, looking at me. Her eyes lit up, and I knew it was theory time.

She ordered another round of drinks and then said "Mullins, how would you like to hear my theory on this situation?"

"Um…" he mumbled.

"Two theories may apply here," Ellen continued, ignoring him. "One is that beautiful people are always screwed up…"

"They are?" he interrupted. "What?"

"Haven't you noticed?" she remarked.

"I'm not sure, what are you saying exactly?" he asked skeptically.

"Don't you see?" she replied. "Beautiful people are screwed up because other people have been lying to them their whole lives. Regular people, most people, will say anything to be around beautiful people, to make the beautiful people like them. Imagine the extreme. Imagine that you're the most attractive girl in your high school. Guys are saying everything to you. The confidant ones are messing with you and laughing at you when they don't succeed. The diffident ones are either creating calculated stories to win your company or else they're too nervous to talk to you at all. Are you getting this?"

"Interesting," said Mullins, "But I don't see why she's necessarily screwed up."

"She's not screwed up necessarily. But she may be sick of people trying to screw her!" Ellen spoke with intensity, leaning over the table. "Come on Mullins, you admitted yourself that you're trying to manipulate her, and now you're upset that you failed. My God! People, men, have been trying to manipulate her for her whole life. Don't you think that's a little annoying? Don't you think Asian girls in America are a little sick of having guys invite them over to learn Asian languages only to find that they are the objects of yellow-fever sick-fantasy fetishes?!" Standing over the table, she looked as if she was pushing it into the ground with her forearms.

"Whoa, whoa" I said. This sounded personal. Ellen didn't hear me and continued glaring at Mullins. "Ellen!" I said loudly. I grabbed her forearm. She looked at me now, but didn't see me. "Calm." I told her, squeezing. "Deep breath." She took a deep breath and sat back down. She shook her head and smiled. I stared at Mullins, trying to let him know to be careful with how he responded.

"I think that's a little extreme," Mullins suggested. "It's not all about sex, you know."

"Which brings me to your second problem, and my second theory." Ellen's muscles had loosened, but she was still speaking more quickly than normal. "If you were interested in her as a person, you shouldn't have been trying to stimulate her, or to get her worked up by your crazy stories. When will you guys learn?" She shook her head.

"I learned," I announced. "I learned! The real question is, when are womenfolk going to learn to respect my emotional needs!"

"Aaron," she said, not looking at me, "you don't know your ass from your elbow." She didn't laugh and continued staring at Mullins. "If you are trying to stimulate her, to work her up, or to get her excited about you," she told him, "it's already too late. You've already lost." She gazed at him darkly.

"Now that's a happy thought" declared Mullins, staring back, clearly annoyed at her reprimand. "She's very helpful isn't she," he said to me. Then he turned back to Ellen. "Can you cheer me up with more theory?"

"Even if you are just trying!" She ignored his comment. "You've already lost. You have forgotten the cardinal rule."

"And what, pray tell, is that?"

"That, pray tell, is that you're not going to convince anybody of anything. You're not there to impress her by trying to. Trying is failing," she snapped. "You should be being, not trying."

"Your theory is useless," he informed her angrily. "It's 'do nothing and you'll succeed! Wait around and expect something to happen!' Well, I'm tired of waiting! It's been 24 fucking years, and I'm tired."

"Mullins, you're just making it difficult on yourself. Why didn't you just treat her like a friend?"

"She's not a friend. We couldn't even have a decent conversation."

"My God!" she yelled, standing up. "So why are you trying to date her! You're treating her like an object! Don't say you didn't want sex—that's exactly what you wanted!"

Mullins kicked his chair back, stood up, and yelled: "NO! I did not! I'm a good guy!" Everybody at the Blue Fog was now staring at my roommate, but he didn't care. "I'm talented, I'm smart, and I'm a good guy! I deserve something! I deserve better!"

"Shhhhh," I tried to tell them, but they didn't listen. Then I turned around and waved to the other customers to tell them that everything was ok.

"You don't deserve shit!" she spat back at him, "except yourself and what you get. And you certainly don't deserve to have an Asian woman as an object to fuck, one you can't even talk to!"

"I didn't want to fuck her," he snarled back through his teeth.

"You did!"

"How the hell do you know what I want?"

"Because you're acting like stupid cock."

"Fuck you!"

"No, fuck you Mullins, fuck you!"

Before Mullins could respond, Ellen was overcome with an extremely loud fit of sneezing.

"Bless you," I said, as she sneezed over and over again.

Mullins looked at her strangely and was silent, but after the fourth or fifth sneeze began to say "bless you" as well. Soon the entire café was blessing Ellen for her sneezing, and the Blue Fog had become a chapel. In total, Ellen sneezed at least fifteen times, and when she was finished, we were all well-blessed. Exhausted, she sat down in her chair, and Mullins, still looking surprised, sat down too. I continued waving to the crowd and finally convinced the other customers to return to their business.

"Damn it Ellen," he whispered to her. He wasn't angry any more, but detached now. "Why are you so upset?"

Ellen sneezed once, and then shook her head. "I know," she agreed. "God, I'm surprised at myself. I'm sorry!"

Mullins shook his head. "What?"

"I didn't know I…" Her voice trailed off.

"What?"

"I didn't realize that I had such a problem with…"

"Yeah," he said softly. "Well, it's ok if you have a problem, I mean, we can talk about it more in a calm way, but let's not take it out on me."

"No," she agreed. "No, I should solve this problem on my own. Don't worry about it."

We got up to leave, and Ellen walked over to give Mullins a hug.

"I really didn't mean it," she said. "I know you're not a chauvinist."

"I'm not?" he said.

"No, you aren't. But sometimes you provoke the wrong people."

*   *   *

That Saturday night was India Night at the Turf. We had India Night once a semester, when we invited all the Indians we knew to come over for vodka-lassie drinks, good Indian conversation, and athletic Banghra dancing. Prateek, being somewhat Indian, was connected with every ethnically Indian student on campus, whether they were from India or Indiana. I don't know how this network functioned, but it guaranteed a large number of guests for appropriately advertised social events.

To me, the Indian kids at Franklin all seemed sharp. They were sharply dressed. They were sharp thinkers and had sharp tongues. They had sharpened their ambitions, and they always seemed to have scoped out the fastest paths to success. I was a little disappointed that so many of the Indian students at Franklin were focused on business or engineering, but you know, these things are cultural and you can't feel bad about them. Besides, some of them had good reasons to want financial success.

In the past, Ellen and I had been the only non-Indians to attend India night. We were accepted just like the other FOBs (fresh off the boat) because when the tunes came on, we Banghra danced like Parsees from Ghatkopar. Prateek, on the other hand, did not dance. Ever. He refused, said it was beneath him, beneath his dignity, et cetera. We had tried many times to convince him, and we had always failed. But this time we had a new secret plan, one that was sure to work. It was called: Plan Absinthe.

The ingredients of Plan Absinthe were sent to us illegally from Prague by the Maestro, who had spent his Thanksgiving in the Czech Republic visiting his brother. His package had contained: 1 woolen cap, 1 leather-bound menu of exotic teas, 1 restaurant business card, 1 plastic model of the Charles Bridge, and 1 bottle of absinthe. What is absinthe, pray tell? Absinthe is the reason why we have art and music from the 19th century. It is a liquid hallucinogen that looks and tastes like mouthwash. And it was the most widely used stimulant in Europe until it was banned. Why was it banned? Well, it's poisonous—it's made of wormwood. It makes you delusional. And if you drink enough, it makes you dead.

In addition to supplying our absinthe, the Maestro was also our source for cigars. Prateek liked these especially and we planned to use them in addition to the absinthe to get our friend dancing. Was our plan foolish? Was it unfair? Manipulative? Perhaps. But believe me, Prateek has done much worse. Which doesn't justify anything, I know. But I'm not trying to justify that night; I have a hard enough time remembering it.

At the party, the stereo was provided by the Bop, Godfather of the Indian students at Franklin. The Bop was a prince from a small state in India, but upon his arrival in the US, he took up a more American role: Mafia Boss of the Indian community. There were good reasons for the switch. At home he had twelve personal servants, but he only brought two with him to Franklin University. Thus he incurred the services of several other Indian students, who became his minions and henchmen. The Bop always wore black leather and silver jewelry, including a $15,000 watch. He exuded power, and you never got close to him without getting through his entourage first. We heard that several Franklin students were $50,000 in his debt, and that he had recently "confiscated" the car of an Indian student who had crossed his path. Some said he was involved in big illegal activities, that he masterminded fraud and gambling schemes to finance his lifestyle of extreme luxury. Others said his power was overblown, that the Indian students could have mutinied at any time. I don't know. All I can tell you is that when you met the Bop, he had already decided your fate. You just had to hope you would like it. By the way, he was a Communications Major with a Theatre Arts minor.

How did we know the Bop? Well, Ellen lived across the hall from him freshman year. Although he never stopped to talk to her, she noticed one day that his servants had forgotten his folded laundry in the basement laundry room. When she presented the clothes to her neighbor, he took off his glove and slapped his servant across the face. Then he yelled something in a guttural voice that she couldn't understand. The servant, trembling, spoke:

"The Bop doesn't forget your service." The servant nodded to her and she left. Since then, the Bop had always responded to her requests, or rather, had one of his servants respond. He never had time to accept any of her meal invitations, but occasionally he would show up to her parties for a few minutes. That was, when he hadn't rented out entire clubs in downtown Philadelphia for his friends and all the Indian women around.

The Bop had heard about our Indian party and had immediately sent a messenger who told us that He, the Bop, would be providing the stereo and music. Mind you, he didn't *ask* us. He told us. But, you know, one less thing to worry about. So early the day of our fête, some of the Bop's freshman minions had brought in his $20,000 BOSE stereo and a stack of fifty CDs. One of them told me nervously that he was to be the DJ for the night, and that the Bop had personally selected the music we were to enjoy.

We spent the afternoon mixing lassies, and moving the furniture and appliances out of the living room and kitchen, our dance floor and party area. We hung Christmas lights from the ceiling and sent apology-in-advance letters to our neighbors. We also sent out reminder emails to our seven-hundred best Indian friends and a few other close accomplices, and worked out a few of the night's best Banghra dancing moves.

When our preparations were complete, we adjourned to the Tandoor Palace for a hearty meal of lamb vindaloo, steamed rice, and keema naan. Then we went back to the Turf and commenced our final preparation stage: intoxication. We drank a few G&Ts to finish off the tonic water, and then moved over to Brooklyn Brown Ale, one of the excellent brews of the tri-state area.

Our guests began to arrive around 10:30, except for the DJ, who arrived promptly at 10 and began playing music at top volume "as he was instructed." There was no one in the living room to hear it.

When the guests arrived, Ellen took coats while Prateek dolled out the vodka-lassies. I introduced Mullins to the Indians that I remembered and introduced myself to the Indians that I didn't. Then Mullins and I wandered through the dancing students. We observed that our guests dressed up—the men in shiny patent leather shoes with a matching belt, black slacks, and reflective silk shirts in all the primary colors. They all seemed to have gel in their hair. None wore a beard or mustache. Most of the girls sported expensive-looking dresses and open-toed high heels. They were all well-coiffed, and made up, and their smiles gleamed more brilliantly even than their jewelry.

As I meandered, I heard rapid-fire stock-tips yelled above Banghra backbeats, some discussion about class, and a lot of Hindi and Tamil that I didn't understand. But at that point, I wasn't too interesting in conversation, I was more interested in who was busting what moves. In fact, the dancing varied in quality tremendously—some were smooth and flowed with the music; others looked as though they were missing certain joints or had their feet nailed to the floor. I was tempted to join in myself, but I decided to wait until Ellen was with me.

Eventually, Mullins and I made our way back to find her, and she suggested that we go into Prateek's room to have some absinthe before we started. We signaled to Prateek and he agreed. And so, the music blasting, the lassies flowing, and the brown bodies shaking in our living room and kitchen, we left our party and closed ourselves off in the bedroom to take our poison.

I sat down on Prateek's chair and put on some Jamiroquai, just loud enough to drown out the DJ. Prateek turned off his light and opened his curtain, so the room was illuminated only by the orange reflection of the alleyway streetlamp. Then, from under her dress, Ellen revealed a small glass bottle of absinthe.

"Straight from Prague!" she said. "Nothing like it."

Prateek was surprised, but refused no challenge to his manliness. "I'll drink it now!" he ordered.

"No, no," said Ellen. "You can't just drink absinthe straight. I mean, you can, but it just *isn't done*, you see. Instead, you dip a spoon-full of sugar in your glass and then light the spoon. You then dump the lit sugar into the glass which sets your absinthe on fire. The fire doesn't burn long, and when it stops, you drink."

We followed her instructions drank. We lit our cigars. We toasted each other, the world, India's contributions to culture, and drank. Then we drank some more. After that, Ellen refused to continue, and she gave her glass to Prateek. Mullins had previously had some bad experiences with absinthe, so he didn't want to drink much either, and gave his glass to me. They switched to chilled rosé.

We heard a knock on the door. It was the Maestro, who had brought along his roommate. I avoided making eye-contact, but luckily she didn't seem interested in me.

Instead, Prateek and I finished the absinth bottle. We didn't have to, but it was a small bottle, and I didn't mind. You see, I didn't drink as much as Prateek. He went crazy. Taking the bottle from his desk, he chugged, puffing on two cigars at the same time. Then he lost it.

"Frosty!" he yelled at the Maestro.

"What?" said the Maestro.

"Frosty, l'homme de neige! You are Frosty, l'homme de neige."

"Thanks Prateek," said the Maestro.

"Frosty!" he yelled again. His eyes glazed over. Then he threw some pens from his desk at Frosty.

The Maestro and his roommate left to get some lassies and when they returned, they tried to get us to come out and dance. But we were still chatting in a cigar-smoke haze, and no one felt like moving. Except Prateek.

"Ug!" said Prateek and threw his shoes at the Maestro's roommate.

"Ow, shit!" she said when they hit her on the knee. Prateek was unapologetic. He didn't seem to realize what he had done.

"Hey, watch it Prateek," said the Maestro.

"Ha ha ha ha ha!" he replied slowly. Then he messed up his hair and kneeled on the floor. He began to hit his head on the bed.

"Wow!" Ellen laughed. "We gotta get this on tape!" She left the room and Mullins left with her. Two minutes later, she came back with her video camera and some beers. "Hey Prateek!" she said, "drink this!"

"Hey!" he growled, barely able to stay on his knees. She tossed him a beer which he could not catch. It hit him lightly on the chest and then fell on the floor. As Ellen raised the camera to her face, he moved his head slowly in the direction of the floor and noticed the beer.

"Ug" he grunted. Then he picked up the beer and pegged it full force at Ellen's head.

Direct hit. The full can of beer hit Ellen's camera and then ricocheted off her forehead, giving her a mighty gash. She screamed "Eeeeeeeeeeegk!" and put her hand to her head, where blood began to ooze.

"Ug," he replied. He had put his little finger in his belly-button and wasn't much interested in what anyone else had to say.

Ellen ran out of the room to get some paper towels for her head. I stumbled out of my chair and smacked Prateek on the forehead, in return for which he tried to bite my leg. Quickly, I escaped out of his room, and collapsed in a chair next to the door. Next to me, I remember Mullins talking to a pretty Indian girl in a fake British accent.

"Quite right!" he said, "I'm British, but how *could* you tell!"

"Well, I've been there before. God it's so wonderful to hear a British accent again!"

"Indeed!" he said, "indeed!"

"Where are you from in England?" she asked.

"Oh, London of course."

"Where in London!" She was suddenly excited. "I studied there last year!"

"Quite so!" he said, stumbling a little bit. "You know, of course, North London I suppose."

"North London? I LOVE North London!"

"Me too," he told her, "Of course I do, that's where I'm from. North London." She smiled at him and opened her mouth to continue. But before she could ask another question, he interjected:

"And what do you come from Miss?"

"Oh, I'm from Bombay, but I plan to live in New York after I graduate. You know that British accent is just so good to hear again."

"Why thank you. Some say I do like to hear myself talk. Maybe there's a good reason!" Mullins laughed, and she laughed a second later, not really understanding.

"Wow," she said. "So, what, like, are you doing here in America? I'm just here, like, because of New York you know, but otherwise I would definitely be in London."

"Well, you know, the pound is very strong right now, so I figured it was a great time to pop over the pond and have a little holiday stateside! Do you like it here?"

"Oh well, you know, New York is, like, fabulous. There are so many, like, places to go."

"Indeed. And where do you stay in Philadelphia?"

"Chi Omega," she declared proudly. "You look older," she continued, "do you work?"

"Do I work!" he said. "Of course I do. Why, you could probably even guess what I do!"

"A banker!" She clapped her hands, like a child in front of her birthday cake.

"Noooo," he said nicely, and encouraged her to try again.

"A trader!" she said, and clapped again.

"Noooo. I don't work in financial services."

"Equity!" she squealed, and clapped again.

"No, no, no, I don't do anything in New York, and I don't work in the finance industry. Can't you guess anything else?"

"You aren't…" she said shyly…"a middle market man, are you? I dated one of those, and it wasn't as good as Goldman, but still…" She smiled hopefully.

"You don't seem to understand," said Mullins losing some of his British accent in his frustration. "I don't do anything with money! Nothing!"

"Hmmm," she said, either disappointed or completely stumped. Then she looked at him. "Are you…a consultant?"

"No." He sighed and tried to change the subject. "So, how do you like your sorority, Chi Omega?"

"Oh, it's just fabulous. The girls are so sweet. Most of them are dating…bankers." She looked up at him and pouted. Mullins stretched his neck to the left and noticed me sitting near him. Then he yelled:

"Hey Aaron, what about that Banghra dancing you've been promising us?! Let's see some."

I smiled at Mullins and told him I was taking a rest. Meanwhile, I heard his new friend bragging to her accomplice:

"Just met…British guy…finance…but he won't tell which department he works…"

Then Mullins spoke to me again, clearly needing an escape. So I did it. And to this day I do not know how. I managed to get off that chair and do some serious Banghra dancing. It was so good that the whole crowd circled around me cheering me on. Until I fell flat on the floor and passed out.

Isn't that something, what we do for our friends!

*   *   *

A week afterwards we left for winter break. I don't remember much from that week, except recovery and cleaning in silence. By the end of India night, everyone had drank too much, and we spent the next few days suffering through unpleasant hangovers.

Prateek especially had to appeal to his fruit-shakes, which he called "Health in a Bottle." He claimed these would cure him instantly.

"This is like adding hearts to my character in a video game. I can feel myself getting better with every drop," he told us as he drank. "Can't you see me getting better?" he demanded. "Can't you see the improvement?" Two minutes later he threw up (again).

After signing a pact that 1. we would never drink again, and 2. unlike the last seventeen pacts of this nature, we would observe this pact, we took the next few days easy. Then we all went to our respective home states for Winter break and wrote emails to each other.

*   *   *

To: Aaron, Ellen, Mullins
From: Prateek

Fellow prisoners,

The rents have begun a new reign of terror. I have been barred from my computer and cannot trade options. I estimate I am losing approximately $87 a day due to this ludicrous parentage, which I will of course be charging back on their credit card.

Otherwise, I sleep, read, eat, and shit. Sleep, read, eat, and shit. Eat some yummy. That's it.

Prateek

P.S. About your head, Ellen: I have always thought that scars were extremely flattering, as a mark of war or conquest.

To: Aaron, Mullins, Prateek
From: Ellen

hey guys!

smiles to everyone on feeling better! are you all having fab times at home? what have i been doing? not much i'm terribly sorry to say. i went to visit some friends briefly, and i've been loitering in bookstores and getting kicked out of cafes. What's wrong with reading for three hours in one place?! i swear you'd think they have other customers.

i discovered recently that salmon can be baked with honey to delicious golden results. also, i finally figured out a way to hypnotize my brothers to get them to shut up.

i've been working for my mom's friend's husband to make a little extra cash. i sit in a cubicle for eight hours and pretend to do work. don't tell them, but i'm really reading newspapers and books on the internet. haha. what they give me takes about twenty-minutes, but they are under

the impression that it's eight hours of
work. why should i tell them otherwise?
    what are you guys doing?

    hugs,
    Ellen

    P.S. Screw you Prateek. A scar on a
woman's face is not flattering, so you're
damn lucky I didn't get one.

    To: Ellen, Prateek, Mullins
    From: Aaron

    Hey roommates,

    You'd think what with me being an
extremely highly trained bass-player and
musician generally that my parents and
neighbors would appreciate me entertaining
them at "all hours of the night." What do
you know, they don't. Instead, they prefer
to waste their nights snoozing and spend
their days entertaining me in real-world-
speak. Apparently my parents are concerned
with my potential to get health care next
year. They have also instructed me to look
into Roth IRAs, which is something about
retirement. I responded by buying a small
plastic pig and telling them I prefer the
more doing things the old-fashioned way.
    What else? I take walks. I watched the
24 hour James Bond marathon. Yesterday I
also started applying for music teaching
jobs, in case I can't play for a living.
    When I got home I tried to do some cooking,
but my kindly mother vetoed the use of all
dairy products, fat, non-vegetarian, and
sugar items---basically, all good taste has
been banned from our kitchen. Yesterday I

snuck out to get a couple packs of Oreos
from my high school vending machine.

See you,

A-

To: Aaron, Ellen, Prateek
From: Mullins

AKK

   I have finally escaped my mother, who
has been after me all week about cleaning
my room and getting a "real" job. She also
wants to know all the details from Philly,
and I just don't feel like telling her. So
I told her I was going to look up porn on
the internet now and that she could join me
if she wanted to. She scurried off.
   So I emailed this Franklin senior at
the beginning of vacation, but she hasn't
written back. She's the one I met at the
Fitz. Do some people not check their email
at home?
   I have to go back right after New Year's
to start work. I'll bake some pastries for
the Turf before you guys get back.

Time for green tea,

Mullins

                    *   *   *

   Everyone was glad to get back to the Turf, even though no
one looked forward to more school. Don't get me wrong, we
all loved our parents. It's just, once you live by yourself and
can do whatever you want all day, there's no fun in having
somebody asking after you all the time. Even if they love you, it's

annoying. We weren't trying to be ungracious—we just liked our independence.

Independence, of course, has to be gotten. For us, it had to be gotten intellectually and financially. We were struggling to separate what we were told from what we actually observed, and to understand why we could live the lifestyles of absurd luxury that we did, and then why we would be in the gutter the very next year.

"College is a four year luxury hotel," Ellen remarked at brunch, "even if you have to work through it." A good meal at the Turf always brought out her philosophic side. "Where else do people pamper you, take care of your every need, provide you with almost every resource you could possibly want, and ask you almost nothing in return?"

"You do work," Mullins disagreed. "I did work."

"But you have to admit," she said, "it's nothing like *work*. I mean, people ask for two-week-long extensions to turn in 3 page papers—could you do that at the bakery?"

"No, but I'm not talking about schoolwork. I'm talking about everything else I did at Franklin."

"Oh yes! We typed your name into the internet and found out you were quite the busy boy."

"You did?" he asked, surprised. "What did you find out?"

"Oh, just about your failure in the porn industry and such things." Prateek told him.

"Very funny Prateek. No, what did you actually find out?"

"Well, Mr. Franklin *valedictorian*," Ellen said, licking her lips, "your college resume was online. We saw that you did just about everything."

"Listen, I didn't do that much," Mullins protested.

"Oh, but you did," I said. "You did a lot. That's a lot of talent. That's a lot of drive."

"Well, I didn't say I did them well."

"You did them well," said Ellen. "That's in the school newspaper article about you."

"Oh," said Mullins. "But listen, I don't think I'm that special or anything. I hope you guys don't think I feel that way. I mean, I really believe that what I did, anyone can do."

"Is that right?"

"Listen," Mullins told us, "most people can do most things. They just don't bother."

"Then how come I can barely finish practicing each week," I said.

"Because you're throwing dinner parties, painting paintings with Ellen, going to concerts and movies, cooking meals, playing squash, reading all those books, listening to music, and drinking beers with your friends," he said to me. "Don't tell me you're not doing anything."

"It's not the same," I responded. "Yours were official things, in groups. Mine are just things I do on my own."

"So what?" he retorted. "You think that means less?"

"Ah," Ellen observed, "but none of us are valedictorians at the same time."

"So I test well," said Mullins, "that's all. And I hope you see from my current situation in life that testing well is not everything."

"Of course not," Prateek pointed out, as if he had informed Mullins himself.

"Right now I would trade being a valedictorian for…a couple of things. You know, it's really worthless. You can't even talk about it without sounding arrogant. You can't even tell people! What good is that?"

"It's good on your resume," Prateek suggested.

"But I don't care about my resume!"

"Even so, it makes a difference," Ellen said. "Mullins, you should be more proud of yourself."

"Should I? I didn't think pride was a great virtue."

"It's not," she said. "But everybody's allowed to have some pride, you know, to keep you going."

"Umm," he mulled and poured himself some more grapefruit juice.

We finished our brunch and went to have some beers at the Blue Fog. It was nice to be back, even if I had to start practicing like a maniac. This was the last semester, and none of us had any idea where we were going next.

*   *   *

"Those who are not givers are takers," Mullins said, "just as those who do not tell the truth must be liars." He looked at us in the eye and then spoke again: "But are they? Really? Is it so simple? Is the world black and white?"

"That's a nice start," said Ellen. We had enlisted Mullins and his rhetorical skills to justify our latest activity of questionable moral rectitude: copying CDs from the library.

As Mullins argued, copying from the library is not really stealing at all. When you steal, the property has to belong to someone else. But the library's property belongs to everyone. So you're just making use of what's yours, right? Plus, the library's there for *you*, isn't it? It's there for *you* to take what *you* need. In terms of how long you take it for, two weeks, one month, forever— that's just a small matter of policy. We simply had a different interpretation of the rules.

Were we advocating the destruction of "good for all," that each man and woman should plunder the earth solely for his own good, ignoring their fellow human beings and the generations to come?

Of course not. We were saying that with the right words and the right smile, you can justify anything, even to yourself.

"Now, we're not actually 'stealing' from the library," Mullins continued. "In fact," he intoned, "by copying CDs, we're actually expanding the library's collection, pushing back the frontiers of ignorance, repelling the darkness, and adding to the sum total of human understanding.

"But the cost, naysayers yell, the cost! The cost? But what is the cost? Does Mozart or Beethoven care where is their joy is kept? You can't cage their art; it exists beyond the meager walls of the library! Anyway, Mozart and Beethoven don't get any royalties. Neither do 98% of the jazz and classical musicians whose work we are liberating from this dirty capitalist Bastille!"

On the contrary, Mullins argued, we were giving life when it might be dead, lending ears when there might have been none, and best of all, spreading the word so that our friends and classmates and the world over could rise up as a tide of swelling aesthetes to do the same. From our example, everyone would learn to patronize their libraries and bookstores, and most importantly, to support their local artists.

(This assumed, we noted, that our friends, classmates and the wide world did not take the same tactics as we did. But that was simply a matter of policy.)

We at the Turf became more and more obsessive collectors until each day we would arrive at the fourth floor and take the scenic route to the CD collection. Navigating asthma-inducing stacks under unforgiving florescent light, Ellen, Mullins and I burst into the library's music section every day and checked out six-ten CDs each. Then we copied them (and those the others had checked out).

Soon we owned the entire productions of artists and musicians, then composers, then record labels. Similarly we photocopied entire books and bound them. The results were less aesthetically exciting but exciting none the less. Now what's so bad about that? We weren't selling them—only enjoying them. Every one should have such a library.

One day mid January, Mullins and I made our way to the CD room to find a cute work-study student with long red ponytail and freckles guarding the collection. She was perched on a stool, and sat with her back straight and her proud chest forward. She was wearing a Franklin Crew jacket, jeans, and the look of a librarian about to be victimized.

"Ah, you're new here," said Mullins, leaning over the counter on his elbows with a smile.

"How did you know?" she answered.

"Oh," said Mullins, nodding to me. "We spend more time here than most of the employees." I smiled and thought of our justificatory scheme. It was brilliant, unanswerable, and total bullshit.

"What's your name?" he asked.

"Caaaroline" she answered. "Or Caaarrie, that's fine too."

"Where are you from?"

"Paraaamus." She had nice posture and a lovely nape, but her seductive powers were mitigated by these 'aaa's and by 'Paraaamus'. Paraaamus was not my paradise city.

"Ah, the Garbage State," Mullins said, smiling. "Did you know there are more garbage dumps in New Jersey than anywhere in the world? And I'm not just talking about the towns." Mullins, as I have noted, was a provocateur. And he especially like to provoke people with good posture, which according to him, was maintained by an intricate but fundamentally weak stick system centered between the buttocks.

Caaarie did not respond to his provocation well. "Veeery nice. You know, most people here are from New Jersey." She did not smile.

"Indeed, indeed." he said, brushing off her displeasure. "Sometimes I just can't help myself. Well, what blissful music should we have today? Any suggestions, Caaarrie? What do you think?" He smiled like a jackass.

She stared at him for a moment, still annoyed. "You know, I think you should get some real music. The stuff in here is dead, and for old people." Unfortunately, this heinous admission had no effect on Mullins, who, when thinking properly, would have scoffed at such boorishness. Instead, he tried to change her mind.

"Caaarie, have you ever experienced the majesty of Johann Sebastian Bach, or the passionate yearnings of Brahms?" he asked, leaning closer. I don't think she had, and I don't think she cared. But Mullins wanted to dance a little. "Have you taken the time to experience a Mahler symphony? Have you…" And on and on he went, pointing out how her "popular" music really descended from this music, bla bla bla, which grasped the subtleties of profound human emotions, bla bla bla, and was humankind's greatest legacy, bla bla bla. He told her how Ravel had changed his life, bla bla bla, inspired his art, bla bla bla, and how he had never experienced joy and sorrow as when he listened to Puccini, bla bla bla. She wasn't looking at him. I think she had a book in her lap. Anyway, he wasn't speaking her language—she didn't talk art bla bla bla; he wasn't in her world.

Still, there was her posture. And her nape. Most importantly, she was attractive, and Mullins was still single. But we left without her number or email address, hoping in fact, not to see her again.

*   *   *

That same conversation, and so many like it, were repeated in the Turf as Mullins' stories. He felt, he said, like some kind of blind senior-citizen.

Ellen was silent as Mullins finished, but Prateek was enthusiastic, and advised Mullins to call whoever it was up, and let her have it.

"Some people's ignorance is astounding," he said. "Why, senior citizens are some of our greatest resources for wisdom and experience. I myself take advantage of the resources of several senior citizens, whom I value tremendously as people."

"Prateek, they're your grandparents! And you invest their money," Ellen scolded.

"All the same," he countered, "they had the wisdom to give it to me."

Chapter Seven

"What's that spider doing?" asked Mullins. "It looks like it's caught in its own web." He was standing on the coffee table in our living room, staring at the ceiling.

"Ignore it," Prateek instructed, not looking up from his Wall Street Journal. "It's not hurting you, is it?" He underlined a sentence he had just read and harrumphed.

"Ok," said Mullins and sat down on the coffee table. "By the way, did I ever tell you guys the story of the time I got attacked by spiders in Cape Tribulation?"

"You didn't." Ellen was sitting next to me on the couch. We were reading sections of the Sunday New York Times and drinking Mullins' green tea. "Where's Cape Tribulation?"

"Australia," he replied. "East Coast, on the Great Barrier Reef."

"What were you doing Down Under?" I asked.

"Hanging loose. My Dad had a two-week conference in Sydney, and I went along for the ride." Having our attention, Mullins proceeded to tell us the story of how, staying alone in a ramshackle hut on a remote beach cove, he was attacked by crocodiles, snakes, and spiders in one night. The story was as riveting as it was unlikely.

"So what do you think of that!" Mullins concluded excitedly. He stood up on top of the coffee table and began to move his arms around as if he were doing a modern dance.

"What are you doing?" Prateek inquired without looking up from his paper.

"Tai Chi," Mullins replied.

"And *why* are you doing it on the coffee table?" Ellen asked.

"And why...not?"

"You might have more space to move around if you were on the floor," I suggested.

"Space is not important. It's my inner space—my composure and cool frame of mind. That is the secret to concentration and confidence, both keys to attractiveness."

"Huh?"

"Ahghgh!" he replied. In waving his arms, he had hit the spider web on the ceiling and knocked it down on his head. He rubbed his hair feverishly with his arms, trying to get it off. I stood up to help him, but before I could do anything he ran to the bathroom and stuck his head in the shower.

Prateek shook his head and grunted. "I always say to clean that ceiling. Keep it spider free. It's a good insurance policy."

Mullins came back with wet hair, looking sheepish.

"Another tribulation, I guess," Ellen joked.

"That's my story," he admitted and sat down in the recliner to read Madame Bovary.

*   *   *

There was rarely an awkward silence in a room with Mullins. In fact, there was rarely a silence at all. I don't know if Mullins liked hearing himself talk, or if he had a fear of silence, but he always had something to say. Once, after a dinner party where he had interrupted all the moments of quiet, Prateek had told him that if he wanted to help himself, he ought to shut up more. Mullins was offended, and told Prateek to kiss his ass. But Prateek was not upset by Mullins' response, and he replied that our roommate was scared of himself.

"Don't worry," he explained sympathetically to Mullins, "you're not alone. I've observed many kids at Franklin who do everything they can to hide from themselves. They drink, they yap, they have to be with people all the time. No torture is worse than leaving them in a room with nothing to do. Not because of boredom—because they're afraid of being alone."

"Uh, ok," said Mullins, not really listening.

"And it's not totally your fault," Prateek concluded happily. "You can always blame your Rents."

That was how Prateek called his parents, the people who not only had raised him from birth, but paid for his education, and sent most of his food fresh from Wisconsin in re-used butter spread containers.

"Wouldn't it be more appropriate to call them 'The Cafeteria Staff?'" I asked.

"Anyway," he continued, "even if your greatest goal is to reject your Rents, you can't. That's because they've got you from the inside out. No matter what you do, you're eventually going to see a picture of yourself where you look like them, or hear yourself on tape where you sound like them, or worst of all, find yourself making an argument for 'responsible investing' like your Rents might make. Even if you moved across the country or across the world to escape them—they're always with you, inside your brain and your body. So don't worry or blame yourself for all these things Mullins—it's mostly in your genes."

*   *   *

One afternoon in early February, I wandered in from my bass lesson and made my usual survey of the Fredrick the Fridge to avoid my music theory homework. Everyone had their doors closed except Mullins, who was seated on the windowsill in the living room. He had moved aside the Green Perrier bottles which normally enjoyed the view and was staring down at 18th Street.

"At any time" he said without turning around, "my future could arrive." He swiveled slightly and looked at me with one eye. "I could inherit billions from an unknown relative. Or maybe a beautiful woman will see me from the street and make it her life's quest to find me and love me. Frankly, I don't even care which one."

"If she saw you from the street," I said, "it wouldn't be very hard for her to find you."

"How does she know I'm living here?" he responded. "Perhaps I'm just enjoying the view."

"That's possible, I guess, but then why wouldn't she just knock on the door?"

"Oh," he said, not really listening. He sighed. "Couldn't anything happen on 18th Street?"

I shrugged my shoulders and he turned back to the window. Looking down he said, "At this very moment the future is arriving in a AGH! NOO!"

I asked what it was, and if he was all right. He yelled again: "AGH!"

Ellen and Prateek hurried out of their rooms and asked what the matter was. Ellen had been in one of her hippy-bliss-out-self-hypnosis-trances; her hair was all over her face and she had not yet returned to reality. Prateek had been reading Business Week in his favorite suspenders, and he left his room with the magazine rolled in his hand, ready to swat a fugitive in the apartment.

Before anyone could talk, the buzzer sounded. Had Mullins' wishes come true? I looked at him and he gawked back at me as if he was terrified. But what was so scary about his beautiful new lover, or the lawyer of his new estates?

The problem was that our visitor was neither. In fact, it wasn't his future at all. The future does not arrive when you ask for it. When you ask for it, when you beg for it, the future does not arrive at all. Instead, the past arrives with a funky hat and some shiny boots.

In this case, the hat was 10 gallon and the boots were black as coal.

"Brad J Mullins" we heard as our door slammed open a moment later. (mind you, no one had buzzed him in or opened the door). The voice was big. But what followed was bigger. Brad J. Mullins stepped into our apartment, one hand on his belt buckle. Then he extended his other massive arm.

"Matthew's Dad," he told us. "Delighted." We introduced ourselves briefly. "Now," he said, looking around, "where's my son?" We looked around too. Mullins was not in the kitchen. He was sitting in an arm chair in the living room, seemingly immersed in a book of essays by Gore Vidal. His father swept past us, and we followed him into the living room.

"Son, we're in town and we're taking you out to dinner. You fellows wanna come?" he asked us.

We began to nod when Mullins sighed loudly. Then he spoke, with a southern twang we'd never heard before:

"Why'd you have to show up like that, no warning or anything? What the hell, Pop?"

"Son, don't curse in front of a woman!" He scowled. Then he continued: "Now I heard there's a good restaurant in town. The Peach and Oranges or something?"

"Le Péché d'Or," Prateek volunteered, in his best French-for-businessmen accent.

"The Peach and Oranges it is!" Brad J. bellowed. "Ya'll coming?" he asked, still staring at Mullins.

"Sure," we told him.

"Five minutes please?" Ellen asked, in her most feminine voice, only used for especially big men and especially nice restaurants.

"Sure." Brad J. hollered, and smiled charmingly at us before he lurched out the door.

*   *   *

We all got dressed and followed Mullins down the stairs. He hadn't said a word to us or looked at anyone directly since his "Pop" arrived. Ellen, Prateek, and I exchanged smiles. The Rents were always more fun for the roommates.

We opened the front door of our building and found ourselves standing before an enormous white Mercedes. The car was so large that Brad J. sat comfortably in the driver's seat with his hat on. It was certainly larger than my room, and much cleaner too. I couldn't see if there was a passenger in the other front seat, but Mullins opened the door to the back seat and we all piled in behind him with room to spare.

Little had we gotten settled and begun the seatbelt hunt when an orange melon appeared before us between the two front seats. Actually, it wasn't an orange melon, it was an orange face shaped like a melon. After a moment, the melon spoke:

"O! Moyyyyyyy. Gawwwwwwd, Matthew, ya roommates are soo cute!!"

I knew that accent after the first two syllables, and I knew it was not southern. No, this was another animal altogether. This accent came from the land where neurosis had been invented, the land where black stretch pants had become appropriate attire for all occasions. This was a land where the rich lived rich, but where pronunciation of the English language had been so far sullied that it had become as sharp as chalk razorblades scraping on a chalkboard. This island off mainland America, though a catalogued part of literary history, was for us an elongated stretch of rotten eggs. I dare not invoke its name, but to those of you who have seen the uniform and heard the drawl of its denizens, I say: I'm sorry. I could only hope that Mullins' mother was not a model citizen.

"Yes Mom, thank you."

I also felt a little bad, both for Mullins (having a melon for a mother), and for her tanning bed (which must have given itself cancer by now).

Is that a little harsh? I should say something nice: Mullins'
Mom was the only one who used his first name: how sweet is
motherly affection!

"Mom, can't you call me Mullins like everyone else?" he
implored.

She ignored him and turned back around in her seat. "All
right Bradley, you can go," she screeched. She was petit, but
Bradley could not have missed the signaling flags, which, on
second glance, were long plastic red nails extending from bright
orange hands.

Anyway, Bradley didn't go. In fact, he didn't appear to have
heard his wife at all. Instead, he put down the map he was
scrutinizing and turned around.

"Where's this joint, son?" he asked.

"A couple of blocks down Walnut."

I asked where Mullins' parents where had come from, but
before anyone could answer a car swerved close to the Mercedes
and Brad J opened the window to converse with the other
driver.

"Now fuck you, you piece of shit! Do you want me to ream
you a new asshole?" The driver did not. In fact, he didn't even
want to continue the conversation, and he quickly pulled away.

Slightly embarrassed, we didn't talk until we arrived at the
restaurant. Mr. Mullins gave the car keys to the valet.

"If you scratch her..." he told the young man, "it's your
hide!"

The valet answered with a Philadelphia "Yo!" and leapt into
the car to drive off.

"Now, who's hungry for some oranges and peaches?" Brad J.
snorted. "I hope they fry 'em," he joked.

No one from the Turf was particularly interested in fried
peaches, but, still being interested the most exclusive and
well-renowned restaurant in the city, not to mention the most
expensive, we followed our Texan host into the Péché d'Or.

The restaurant was a bourgeois fantasy of 19th century lavishness. After proceeding through the lobby where our coats were taken, we entered a long rectangular space luxuriously decorated in red velvet trim. The walls were lined with gilded gold-framed mirrors like the palace Versailles; each table was flanked by two waiters in starched black-tie; elegant silverware shimmered next to sophisticated place settings; fresh flower centerpieces sat surrounded by golden goblets and every other implement of opulent eating imaginable. The guests dazzled too, especially the trophy wives.

And the food—oh, I don't dare. How can I capture the experience of oysters with champagne followed by a rabbit thigh slowly cooked in a white wine sauce of its own juices—a sauce that had seven or eight different tastes in it—a sauce that could have been its own meal, or even seven or eight of its own meals, and this sauce served with a fennel puree on which sat a cylindrical tower of apple and smoked salmon, each brick the size of a rice grain? No, no! Nor could I do justice to the desserts, all fifty of them, each an architectural masterwork in its own right, which arrived on a handsome cart and which were literally limitless—you could have as much or as many of any gourmet pastry or cake until you died, after which, I heard, you could be buried with the éclair of your choice. But I wasn't worried about making that choice; after all, why die when you've already gone to heaven?

*   *   *

We sat at a round table. I sat next to Brad J Mullins who sat next to Mullins, Prateek, Ellen, Mrs. Mullins, me, etc. Brad J grabbed a menu from a passing waiter, looked at it quickly and then commanded "Some weeters and bubbly, and the full menu for everyone."

As we waited for our hors d'oevres, Ellen and I gave each other toothy grins, soaking up the restaurant, the clientele, and our hosts. We knew we had to enjoy the sights, smells, and tastes because the conversation probably wouldn't be terrific. It wouldn't be the Rents fault. That's just the way it was. As youths, we didn't want to offend our generous hosts so we didn't say anything too interesting or provocative. And as parents, they didn't really know how to relate to us.

Over the hors d'oevres, we talked about the weather, the city, our apartment, and the economy. The economy conversation continued as the waiters cleared the sea-food plates and cutlery, and by the time the main meal arrived, our discussion had reached the inevitable economic meat of any parent-college-student dinner: the return on investments, or "what are you going to do with your life?"

This is the most asked and yet most unfair question that all college students must bear. Why is it unfair? Because no one knows the answer, even if they think they do. Nobody knows where they'll be in ten years. If you guess right, you should have been buying lottery tickets instead of yapping. But the question still gets asked—parents are investing a lot of money in college, and they want their kids, like their brokers, to assure them it's worthwhile. They don't remember how most youth spend their early twenties floating about like water lilies with outboard motors, searching for meaning and direction, finding what they didn't expect where they didn't expect it. Friends, relationships, jobs, careers – nobody has written the book on it, and even if somebody did, it would only be something to laugh with, not to expect or to believe in.

Still, since most college kids are on the parental pay role, you had to keep up appearances. Prateek answered first, gingerly revealing that he was going to be an investor. He would, he joked, give money from the rich to the very rich, an enterprise which the market demanded, and which someone might as well profit from. Brad J. and the Melon nodded their approval, and turned to Ellen.

She explained slowly that she wanted to work in education reform and build a group of private schools where people learned what was really important. Brad J. and the Melon again whispered something like "very impressive!"

Finishing off my fourth glass of champagne, I told them I was in music school, but that if I couldn't find a job in an orchestra or a fulltime jazz band, that I planned to move to Hawaii and become a private detective in the service of a rich but conspicuously absent British patron.

"Higgins!" Ellen interrupted excitedly, pointing at Prateek. We had named Prateek "Higgins" because of a thought he had mistakenly voiced the previous week while reading his *"GQ"* magazine:

"Balderdash! The only cravat I will ever wear is a silk one!"

Prateek didn't read *Men's Health* which he called "a plebian guide to machismo," and only read *GQ* begrudgingly because Ellen had banned him from renewing his Playboy subscription to the apartment.

"Higgins!" I repeated, and toasted him with my champagne flute.

"I never!" said Prateek crossly, although he was probably kidding.

Brad J. and the Melon laughed and congratulated me on my plans. Then Brad J spoke to Mullins:

"Now son, why don't you do something interesting like your friends here. Just look at them, so full of great career ideas—they're definitely going to be successful."

His wife nodded her approval. "You know, your father and I would still be happy to support you going to law school. Or if you don't want to do that, why don't you have a talk with your roommates about your future—maybe they can give you some good suggestions?!"

Mullins was silent, his arms folded and his attention elsewhere. He looked completely lost, as if he was sitting at the wrong table or listening to a conversation in a foreign language he did not understand. After a moment, he wiped his mouth with a napkin. Then he began to talk rapidly. "Parents, I have a story for you about a friend of mine from Franklin.

"This guy, whose name I can't tell you, was a great success from childhood through adolescence because he always did what his parents told him and accepted all their wisdom. He was smart and conscientious, and polite and respectful. He was friendly with everyone at school and he didn't threaten anyone— he wasn't competitive except with himself. You see his parents had told him not to worry about the other kids-- *he* was his own greatest opponent to success. So he followed their lead happily."

"A likely story," interjected Prateek, who'd also been drinking champagne. "He was probably whipping himself in the closet."

Mullins ignored him and continued: "My friend never partied in high school. In his family, "staying out late" or "spending hours idly" just wasn't done. So he didn't drink or go to parties. And it wasn't too tough because no one invited him. When he felt lonely, he consoled himself by remembering that even if they had, he wouldn't have gone. Besides, he couldn't relate to kids his age—they were crazy. They did drugs, had sex— it was another world. In his world, bedtime was consistently 11:30, and "going out" meant going out for school supplies. He didn't trust people who drove fast, did their math homework in permanent ink, or smoked cigarettes. Outside of school, he took piano lessons and practiced, but he was never *that* good. He volunteered at the local library and he was an "ambassador" at his school for new students. He…"

"What's the point here?" Brad J. interrupted. "And what does this have to do with your career?"

"All right, I'm getting there. So my friend got into Franklin easily, but it wasn't easy for him to be there. He rejected most of the kids who spent their time destroying their brains with TV or beer. That wasn't how he had learned to be. Instead he called his parents every night, and they helped him get through it. They were solid—there for him, helping him get through all that bullshit and continue on to law school. He did well in college too. He made the dean's list every semester. He was in the honors program and he was one of the top students."

"Sounds like a good boy to me," said the Melon.

"Listen to this: at the beginning of senior year, when all of us were preparing for our futures, this guy was getting ready to apply to law school. Everybody knew he could get in, but before he could even apply, a terrible thing happened to him. You're not going to believe this when I tell you, but he started to disappear. I'm not kidding you, I was there. First it happened to the back of his legs. You would look at the backs of his legs and not see anything. They were transparent, you know, and you could see whatever was behind them. Then it was the back of his arms, and then parts of his back, and his shoulders, and then his waist. If you touched him, he was still there, but his body was just no longer reflecting light—he was becoming invisible to the human eye."

"Jesus, what happened then?" I asked.

"Well, I stopped seeing him after that," said Mullins. "And not just literally. He went home to Denver and spent all his time seeing doctors. He emailed me about it. Apparently his parents made him wear sunglasses, long sleeve shirts, and gloves, and one of those masks that burglars wear so they could see his facial expressions. It was horrible; he was always burning up."

"What was happening to the poor boy? What did the doctors say?" the Melon asked.

"Nobody knew," said Mullins, "nobody could figure out what was going on, although when they analyzed his cells, they could tell that it had been going on for a long time."

"Did he die?" asked Prateek, "And who got the TV-movie rights?"

"He didn't die," replied Mullins with a smile, "he moved up to the Yukon territory, where he had an excuse to cover his body with clothes all day. His parents got him a job as a farmhand in a tiny town where no one would bother him."

"Wow," I said.

"And then did he die?" Prateek followed.

"Nope. But he suffered, oh God did he suffer. All through the frozen winter, he was completely alone. He couldn't tell anyone about his condition, and he had to live in almost complete isolation except when his parents could visit him."

"Did you visit him?" Ellen asked.

"I wanted to," Mullins replied, "but at the time he didn't want any one else to see him in his state. I tried to go anyway, but even his parents wouldn't tell me where he was and I couldn't track him down."

"What happened?" I asked.

"Well, while he was out in the Yukon, he developed a love of flowers. Flowers were his main source of beauty, he told me. They didn't judge him or tell him what to do. So he decided to write a book about flowers."

"A book about flowers?" Prateek noted suspiciously.

"What was he doing with flowers?" Ellen asked.

"Writing about them," said Mullins. "And the craziest thing happened. As he was out doing research for his book, just out walking around the different flowers, he started to re-appear. He didn't know if it was something in one of the flowers that cured him—like pollen or some crazy chemical. In fact, he didn't even notice that he started reappearing because it was the back of him which reappeared first. I can tell you though, how excited he was the day his right arm reappeared. He wrote me the most gushing letter."

"Wow," said Ellen. "So he went back to normal."

"Well, eventually. Basically he kept working on his book, and by the time it was finished he had completely re-appeared."

"Shit!" said Prateek, and then looked around sheepishly to see if anyone had noticed his choice of words. No one reacted, so he continued: "Did he come back to Franklin, to sell his book, or the movie rights, or what happened?"

"Nope. He gave away a few copies of his book, and he never came back to Franklin. Instead he moved to Seattle and got a job working for some newspaper out there. I haven't gotten a chance to write him to since I went abroad."

"That's amazing," I said. "What's his name?"

"Sorry." Mullins smiled. "He asked me not to tell anyone. He started his new life and he doesn't want to be hassled with the past."

"But think of the cash-potential of his story!" exclaimed Prateek. "The books, the movies, the t-shirts, the cults, oh man, it's a silver mine!"

Mullins laughed. "You get it?" he said to his parents.

They shook their heads in the negative. But Mullins didn't seem to care, and he didn't tell them more. If the story had no effect on his parents, it had reminded him of whatever lesson he was trying to share, and he finished his dinner in peace.

Mr. Mullins leaned over to me and smiled, his teeth full of pureed fennel. "You ought to help my son find a career," he said to me. "His mother and I have tried to help him, but it's no use. Kids don't listen to their parents anymore." He took another bite of food and continued. "I think the boy would make a really good lawyer. He's a good talker and has a wiz of a memory. Plus it's a surefire way to get a job. You know, I'm in business, which is precarious and sometimes worse. We've had to move all over because of it. But we have a neighbor at home now who's a lawyer, and so far as I can tell, all he does is show up to board meetings and answer silly questions about firing people. Don't you think Mullins would be a good lawyer?"

I agreed that my friend definitely had the necessary skills.

"Well," he said, "if you can give him a little jump start, his mother and I would surely be grateful, and I think in the long run, he would too."

"Sure," I said.

Then Mr. Mullins asked me about classical music, which he liked, and the Melon joined the conversation to comment on the sad state of orchestras on the East Coast.

"There are so few places worth playing anymore," she said. "What do you plan to do?"

"At this point," I told them honestly, "I'll be lucky to play at all."

We finished the last bites of our entrees and our plates were whisked away by the staff. I wiped my face with my napkin and thought about dessert. Looking to my left I could make out the dessert cart at the other end of the dining hall, pushed by two muscular servers in tuxedos. After stopping at two other tables, these culinary oxen began pushing the massive trolley of deliciousness in our direction.

Finally, after what seemed like a slow-motion odyssey across the ancient world, the cart arrived and the oxen began doling out the sweetness. I waited anxiously for my turn, jealous of those who came before me. But my drooling was interrupted by Mr. Mullins, who bellowed:

"What are you kids doing tonight?"

"Goofing off," said Ellen.

"Drugs," said Prateek (meaning studying the markets).

"The nocturnal animal safari," I added.

"The what?" Brad J. asked.

"We like to walk past the crazy frat parties," Ellen explained. "But we don't go to them."

"But why?" asked the Melon, totally befuddled.

"To remind ourselves who we're not. It's not elitism; it's anthropology," she said, as if it were our motto.

"You mean you don't actually go to parties-- you just gawk at kids from the outside? How is that fun?" the Melon responded.

"It is," said Ellen, solemnly.

"You do this too, son?" Brad J. asked.

"I do," he responded, "but I don't tonight. Tonight I'm going to the opera with a young lady."

Cue group stupidity. The ladies cooed. Prateek and I mouthed "shwing" and Mr. Mullins hit his son on the back so hard that the boy spit out his chewed piece of triple chocolate raspberry double-decker éclair.

What a travesty! Why do people do such embarrassing things? (For the record, I just like the sound of the word 'Shwing'.) Especially when desserts are on the line! Still there was always more dessert at Le Péché d'Or. And we were excited for Mullins.

"Who's your bird?" asked Prateek.

*   *   *

We didn't hear about the opera until the following supper. Mullins had run off from dinner right after dessert to meet his girl downtown. Brad J took the rest of us home in the Mercedes, which Prateek managed to scratch heavily with his fleur-de-lys cufflinks.

"Don't worry," Brad J said, after pulling over and getting out to look. "That's just a $10,000 paint job."

"Sorry, uh, sorry! I'll pay for it, I promise. I have options!" We scooted back, all of us, near the door, and Prateek pushed Ellen in front of him. Paying wasn't the issue; he was afraid that Brad J. would smack him silly.

Brad J. stared at Prateek and then said, "Aw shucks." He chuckled, "I was just fixin to change her dress anyway." Relieved, we ran up to our apartment before we could do any more damage.

Ellen and I spent the rest of the evening watching old Eric Rohmer movies, while Prateek tended to his stocks. Mullins didn't return before we went to bed.

"What a mess! What a fool I am!" he told us the next night. "So, after I finished my dessert, I warned my parents that I would kill them if they ever visited again without asking, and then I walked down to Broad and Locust Streets to meet my date."

He told us her name, but we didn't know her. Describe her, we demanded.

"Well, she's a junior at Franklin. She comes into the bakery a lot to shop for her family, who live on 20th Street. I knew she loved music because she always hums to herself in the store. One day I talked to her and found out that she wants to be a musicologist—she studies medieval music, and she even won awards for some of her papers."

"What does she look like?" asked Prateek.

"Hmm," said Mullins. "She has fair skin, freckles, and blue eyes. She's six or seven inches shorter than me, and I wouldn't call her "tanned and toned" but she isn't carrying around too much junk in her trunk either. But her most striking feature is her…"

"Would you say her curvilinear structure would correspond more to the Alps or the small knolls of Northern Georgia?" interrupted Prateek. Ellen gave him a death stare and gestured for Mullins to continue.

"Her most beautiful feature is her long straight black hair. It's thick, thick but loose. You can't see through it but you can still see individual strands of hair, long and straight."

He sipped some green tea and continued. "She was dressed really nicely, a fancy skirt and top, and a pea coat, and I felt like I was living a dream walking to the Academy of Music with her. Like I had achieved some sort of movie fantasy, you know. That, combined with the effects of the Le Péché d'Or's shiraz selections and sugary desserts was the beginning of the end."

"Uh oh," I said.

"The dinner—the date--the whole damn feeling of it— loosened my tongue and I talked. A lot." Mullins looked sullen. He scooted back from the table and looked down at his feet. "And I told her about my passion for music, and how she could come with me any time to the opera which I attended frequently and I told her about my family and their visit and my roommates and my work at the Green Hose and…" He trailed off, looking miserable.

"That doesn't sound too bad!" said Ellen, "for an evening's conversation. Very nice in fact."

"You don't understand!" Mullins cried. "That was while we were waiting in line to get our tickets ripped!"

"Classic!" said Prateek.

"The ticket guy ripped our tickets and pointed right to a staircase which we followed. But, the stairs were endless. I had asked for the cheapest seats, bakers and bankers being spelled differently, but I had no idea how bad it would be. At the symphony all the seats are ok. Anyways, we climbed up red carpeted stairs, then the metal stairs, then finally the wooden stairs, until we arrived at the highest balcony."

"Good exercise!" said Ellen. "Always fun on a date!"

"But it was a staggering distance from the stage," Mullins continued, "how embarrassing!"

"Well…" I said, ready to assuage him.

"Hold on Aaron," he interrupted, "It gets worse--I had bought one blocked seat, for myself, since it was cheaper. I figured the roof would be low and I wouldn't be able to see the subtitles or something. I wish. What it meant was: between my legs was an enormous column. It was like a huge phallus, right there, and I couldn't see a thing. I was totally embarrassed, so I started laughing…

"But, but, she had no idea what was so funny, so I had to explain it to her—but she still didn't think it was funny—what a mess. So there I was –on a date with a pole between my legs and a woman who didn't appreciate it. After all, she studies dissonance."

"What?" I asked

"The girl is an ivory-tower academic. She studies music, but she doesn't listen to it. She prefers to read books about music— she claims she can 'get lost in a text,' like in nothing else."

"Strange," said Prateek.

"Yeah," Mullins agreed, "it was a little strange. She spent her winter vacation at a conference called "The Implications of Durkheim, Bourdieu, and Hegel for medieval musicology. She really loved it."

"Too bad," said Prateek. "I'm guessing you didn't get to show her your Hegel."

"No," Mullins muttered.

"Jeez Prateek! Wait a minute Mullins," Ellen said, "I thought you said she was humming in the bakery?"

"I asked her that!" he moaned. "It turned out she was humming variations on a twelve tone row!"

"Wow," I said, "did she have any interests outside of musicology?"

"She plays the zither," he said.

"What is that?" I asked.

"I have no idea," Mullins admitted. "But at the time I didn't even think about it. I hadn't finished my shift as Mr. Klutz."

"Well, what did you say when she was telling you all of these things?"

"I didn't say anything. I tried to talk my way out of that conversation by telling her the plot of the opera. I didn't want to hear any more about John Cage, so I wouldn't let her interrupt me. Because it was a great story, you know." He sighed. "But it turned out after I finished that she already knew the story. Then, to make up for that, I asked how her parents were doing and if they were enjoying the pastries. It turned out her mother had left her family two weeks ago with an old boyfriend who'd been released from jail!"

"You couldn't have known!" we protested.

"But I did!" Mullins said. "I had just forgotten, with everything that had happened. In fact, when I invited her to the opera, it was to get her mind off her family troubles!" He stopped and shook his head.

"Now," he continued, "you are saying to yourself: the nice thing is, it can't get any worse. I wish. I was so embarrassed by my pre-opera conversation that I couldn't concentrate on the opera at all. So I decided to point out all the clever lines to her. You know, smart girl, I thought she'd appreciate that kind of thing. Not at all. She pretended like I didn't exist, so I thought, you know, she just wants to get into the music. I decided I would get into the opera no matter what and I closed my eyes and swayed to the beat. This was probably equally annoying and even more embarrassing for her."

"Wow," I said.

"Then, during intermission I asked her if she wanted something and she said a diet coke. But after waiting in line, I realized I had left the cash in my other pants when I changed to go out with my parents. I tried to bum five bucks but nobody had pity so I had to come back empty handed."

"An uninspiring performance," said Prateek.

"Yeah," Mullins agreed. "During the second act, everything was great except when I dropped my program over the balcony and when my cell phone started vibrating in my pants during the critical last scene."

"You and your cell phone," I joked.

"Yeah," he moaned. "I almost jumped out of my chair. It was, of course, my parents, so I hung up on them. Oh man."

"What a story!" said Ellen.

"No joke," he replied. "After the show, I didn't even bother to ask her out for coffee. I could see she was tired, and I didn't blame her. But walking her home, I told her that I had had a great time with her and was wondering if she was free for dinner on Tuesday. She said she would have to check."

We looked at him in surprise. "I thought you said she was a crazy nerd?" I asked. "Plus that date was horrible, why did you ask her again right away?"

"I was really into her, you know, she made me feel nice to have her by my side."

"Is this the first time you went out with her?"

"Sort of," said Mullins, "Actually she invited me over for dinner at the beginning of the year, and I tried to seduce her. But that didn't go too well."

"What?!" Prateek said. "You never told us that!"

"Well, I was never successful," said Mullins. He laughed. "No, I didn't seduce her at all. She just invited me to dinner at her dorm one night. For pasta."

"And?"

"And I showed up in a tight black turtle neck with a bottle of red wine."

"Huh?" I said.

"Bad idea."

"A little too much, but not ridiculous for a date," I insisted.

"This was a communal kitchen though—there were twelve people cooking dinner in there and everyone, including her, was wearing jeans and a baggy sweatshirt. We ate at a table with everyone else."

"Ooo," said Ellen.

"Ooo is right," said Mullins. "Then I asked her to go to her room for a chat."

"In front of everyone?" Ellen said.

"Well, while people were doing dishes," he said.

"Bad move," Ellen told him.

"Yeah, I know," Mullins said. "She wouldn't return my emails or phone calls after that."

"Well, how'd you ask her out again?"

"I hung out at the bakery during the morning. I knew she was bound to come back."

"Mullins" I declared. "This is not your greatest triumph."

"Don't worry," he said, "I press on."

*   *   *

The Maestro's Rent, his father, also visited him that month, and he also took us out to dinner. But it was a different gig this time. His dad was divorced and living on his own in upstate New York. Believe it or not, he made his living as a woodcarver, so we took him out to The Banana Leaf.

I had known that the Maestro's dad had been carving for a long time, but it was Mullins who discovered that there was more to the man than chips and chisels. I listened to their conversation while the Maestro talked to Ellen.

"Where did you learn?" Mullins asked him between slurps of noodles. "I mean, carving?"

"Taught myself," he said. He was tall and thin, with a shock of white in his otherwise curly brown hair. His handlebar moustache was bushy and seemed to dwarf his thin frame. But it didn't dwarf his arms, which were thick like posts and bulging with blue veins. He must have been in his sixties, but he moved around with the ease of a teenager.

"How did you teach yourself woodcarving?" said Mullins.

"Well, I took a long tour around Africa and Europe as a young man, making sketches of the masters and buying a few here and there. When I met guys who did it, I asked them for a lesson, but that was pretty rare. I was there for a couple years. Then I went back and got some tools and some wood and went at it. I had some advice, sometimes, from a guy down in Iowa who I sent stuff to, but it was mostly pretty general tips."

"So you never went to school?"

"Not for carving. No I got degrees, but nothing to do with that."

"What did you study? It had nothing to do with carving?"

"No, I did undergrad and a PhD in English lit," he said. "But you wouldn't know it from looking at me." He flexed his worn hands.

"In New York?"

"No, no" he chuckled. "I was in Cambridge, Mass for the first one and Cambridge, England for the second."

"Wow!" said Mullins and nudged me.

I was thinking the same thing. I couldn't believe this guy gave up an intellectual career to pursue woodcarving. He could have been big time with those schools on his resume.

"That must be quite a jump," said Mullins, almost laughing. "I mean, from the height of academia to woodcarving."

"It's the lifestyle," he said. "It's what I like to do, and if I can say so, I do it pretty well."

"But you didn't know it in school?"

"I didn't know anything in school." His eyes shined. "And I didn't learn anything until I was traveling around Africa with my girlfriend from grad school. We had almost no money and no ambitions either."

"No ambitions?"

"No, you know Mullins, it was the sixties, and the world was going to hell around us."

"But?"

"But we had to survive, and that was where we started. We ran around Africa for about a year, and developed a new perspective on what was important to us, you know, and how to live."

"That must have been amazing."

"It was tough, is what it was. But I learned something too."

"About woodcarving?"

"About myself, and about how not to waste things."

"I see," said Mullins.

"After that I knew I wanted to work with my hands and create something, you know, something that I could see and hold. I had enough of paper. I was going back to the source of paper to really do something of my own."

"Haha," said Mullins, "that reminds me of a quote I heard when I was in Spain. 'To be original means to go back to origins'."

"Yeah!" said the Maestro's father. "That's it. Of course, you know, it doesn't always work out for me. Sometimes I have to work part-time doing other things to pay the bills. But when I'm carving, there's nothing else."

"You don't wish you had gone into consulting or editing or publishing or something?" said Mullins. "No regrets?"

"Well, I wish I could give my son more," he said, "but that's the only time I've really cared. Oh, I think it would be nice to own my own place, at my age. You know I'm sixty-three years old, and I've never owned my own house. But I never really cared about that either. I guess what I'm saying is that you need to find out what you can stand. I could never stand working for someone else, or working in an office, or working 9-5 Monday through Friday. But then again, I didn't care about missing movies or not being able to drink good wine or take women out to nice restaurants. I can eat beans in a can most nights a week and be happy." He gave us a wide smile. "But I'll tell you something, I'll never stop ordering pizza!"

Our woodcarver was his own man. But was he a model for us?

"I don't know," said Mullins, later that night. "I guess in following what he loved. But I didn't really understand how he came to love wood-carving. I mean, of anything? Why didn't he at become a shepherd or something?"

"Yeah," I said, "He's got a good story to tell."

"Or write a book about Africa then…"

"But if it was woodcarving, it was woodcarving." I remarked.

"Truedat," Mullins agreed. "Well, you know what Aaron, we can always start our own company, you know, if nothing else works out."

"Oh?" I said. "What will this company do?"

"An alcohol education center!"

"What to teach people about the effects of alcohol? You can find all that stuff on the internet."

"No, no, we're going to teach people how to be good drinkers. How to tell a Trappist Ortvale beer from a German Doppelbach;

how to know a sensible Bordeaux from a cheap Australian Shiraz; how to pour your Guinness so it's *absolutely perfect*."

"Sounds good to me," I said. "But who's going to front the cash for this operation? Prateek?"

"We'll tell him it's an investment. We're a start-up, and we need funding. Surely he'd like nothing more than to play the financier, eh?"

"Maybe. More likely he'd ask to see our resumes, references, and a detailed business plan."

"Oh well. Maybe we can get some of the fine beer and wine companies to front us. We're creating new clientele after all."

"You can handle that end," I told him. "I'll be the official tester. Somebody has to make sure our beer is fresh."

Who knew? Thirty years down the line, maybe we would end up in a crazy business together. Or not. Snow was falling outside our window and it made me sleepy. Mullins and I finished our green tea and decided to call it an evening.

Chapter Eight

"There's no such thing as a good reason," Drew muttered. "Unless you get real lucky. I know that for Goddamn sure."

I was sitting with Mullins and Drew at the Blue Fog. It was Drew's round so we were drinking rioja.

"Usually," Drew continued, "you just get fucked." He took a swig of the red. "But sometimes you don't. Anyway, whether you do or you don't, reasons aren't worth a dime. You can't eat reasons or frame 'em, or trade 'em into the bank for a million bucks. All you can do is whine 'em to yourself and the people who'll listen. But usually that doesn't help too much either. That's my experience, anyway."

Mullins was sitting between us at the bar and feeling sour. Drew had helped him to apply to a couple of scholarships, and he'd gotten rejection letters that morning.

"I hate interviews," said Mullins. "How can you find out if someone is worthwhile in thirty minutes? It's bullshit!"

"You can't," I agreed. "That's why I told you to wear those *short* shorts!"

Drew cracked a smile.

"Don't worry Mullins," he said. "*Something* will happen. Really it's not worth worrying until you find out you're really screwed. And when you're on the street, there's always a place for you on my couch. Unless you sully my rug. Never sully my rug—it pulls the whole room together."

"Thanks a lot Drew. But I don't want to work the night shift in a bakery for my whole life."

"Listen, kid. You're not going to die, so stop whining. And, fuck, even if you do die, fuck it, that's not worth worrying about either. Dead people don't care at all!"

*   *   *

From the balustrade of March, we could see the end. It was still small and out of focus, but it was there all right. No question about it. In March we started to feel pressed. None of us had jobs, or contingency plans in case the jobs we didn't have didn't work out. Nor did we have a lot of time to find them. Everyone was busy with his or her life and didn't want to sacrifice the remaining time for an uncertain future. I, however, had no choice, and had started flying all over the country with my bass to audition for orchestras and teaching positions. I hate auditioning. It's hell for me. Can you imagine sitting in a waiting room with your bass and with six or seven other guys from Julliard and the Manhattan School and Eastman, and Oberlin, and thinking "I'm better than them?" It's a bad feeling, and it's one you don't want to associate with your music. Of course, I might have thought, 'there's no need to be like that, so competitive.' But at that time, I felt like I needed competitive energy to give me an edge.

My attitude had its price. Many nights I lay in bed trying to sleep, consumed with my future: "Why is music so competitive, why is it stressing me out? This is crazy, I just want to relax. Why are there so few jobs? I practically have to kill people to get them. And I can't even focus on Philadelphia and the Turf because I'm just trying to stay afloat with my schoolwork and practicing and auditioning and gigs. Jesus."

Before I fell asleep I would usually calm down. I would remember my last year in high school, which was also a great social year, and which also had its stressful rounds of auditions. God, I hated those auditions too; each one put my nerves and my self-confidence to the limit. My best audition, my audition in Philadelphia, happened after I had given up all hope of getting into conservatory. The Bok Institute was my last chance, and I thought I didn't think there was any way I would get in. So I didn't make a big deal of it. I ate a lot of cheese-steaks and drank a lot beer the night before the audition. Yeah, in retrospect, cheese-steaks are the key to good classical music. That explains a lot.

*   *   *

I wasn't the only one worrying. And I wasn't the only one who couldn't sleep. I often heard Mullins get up in the middle of the night to read Madame Bovary in the living room. Sometimes Prateek or Ellen would join him, and I would see them reading furiously if I got up groggily to pee. Funny enough, we never talked about it the next morning. Nobody wanted to remember why they couldn't sleep.

The best times were when we forgot about the future altogether. We would go to a hilarious movie at the Fitz or see one of the ridiculous performing arts groups at Franklin, and just laugh until we couldn't even remember what had been troubling us. That was when we hatched crazy plans. For example, we once decided to create a fake company which would hire a bunch of interns from the Franklin business school to attract clients and build web-pages for them. We would hire these interns without paying them, by promising impressive titles for their resumes. This would be a multinational company whose only headquarters would be on the internet, but who would keep Swiss bank-accounts.

Naturally, this scheme was never hatched, although Prateek did launch a presentation webpage. On the other hand, the scheming itself was incredibly valuable, distracting us from our quest for insecure jobs and our inability to feel secure without

them. Plus, not all of our schemes were imaginary. Our dinner
parties, for example, were real, and really good. If we couldn't
find opportunities to be professionals, we told ourselves, we would
at least eat professionally, until we were too full to do anything
else but sleep.

*   *   *

How high-class can you make a menu? How subtly can
you choose your guests? How sophisticated can you make a
dinner party? Actually, these are rhetorical questions. I know the
answers. I lived the answers.

In most college apartments, the biggest party questions are
"whose books are going under the keg?" or "Who forgot to buy
the frozen hotdogs?" I'm not kidding. I've talked to people who
live this way. Real people.

We didn't live this way. At the Turf, the questions were "Who
will bake the bread?" "Who will make the entrees (and therefore
pick the wines)?" "Who will make the appetizers?", "Who will
lightly sugar the desserts?", "Who will set up the candles, music
and ambiance?", "Who will choose the dinner guests (carefully,
to spark interesting conversation…and sexual tension)?" and so
on. Each time we had a dinner party we probably spent over
an hour screening our various fifty cookbooks and calling our
foodie relatives for recipes and presentation ideas. Then we
would choose the company, divide the various tasks, and print up
a menu (invariably in French) and post it on our door. Of course,
that was two days in advance of the meal. The day of the meal
we would skip class. We would shop in the morning and cook in
the afternoon.

Now Ellen and I cooked our meals most days. On any given
afternoon you could find us making fresh hazelnut pesto, sherry
cream sauces, or Moroccan poached chicken. But a dinner party,
by contrast, was a whole day's affair, one that was as social as it
was culinary, and one that culminated in a meal of such luxury

that none of our guests even dared to reciprocate. We didn't blame them.

Does this sound extreme? Pretentious and absurd? Maybe it was, for a multi-ethnic bunch of students in Philadelphia. But, like so many other silly rituals, it was fun. And unlike so many other rituals, it was ours.

The atmosphere was candlelight and Miles Davis. We usually dressed up, and invited our guests to do the same. Graduate students knew to bring a bottle of wine or some fine beer, but undergraduates were reminded that an invitation to "The Lush Life at The Turf" meant a culinary or alcoholic contribution. Boxed goods (except from The Green Hose) were not accepted. If someone did bring a box good, we would put it aside with a smile, thinking to ourselves: "the dogs will feast tonight!"

We tried to hold the dinner parties as often as possible. In March we held one a week. We rotated being head chef, and everyone had their own specialties. Although he mostly ate his Indian-food care packages, Prateek used the year to become an expert in spicy mushrooms and nouveau Italian food, which he cooked over and over again. He also came to master various North African chicken cuts and fish seasonings. Ellen's repertoire was classically French, from sensuous desserts to fish and potatoes. I was the only one who cooked red meat, so when I could, I made lamb, veal, and steak. I also liked making cream soups and precariously balanced appetizers.

Mullins was our dependable baker, but was also quite able with sauces, spreads, and desserts. He never used recipes, but he could make over twenty-five distinguishable brownies, all delicious enough to make you eat past your fill, experience a terrific sugar high, hear your stomach gurgle, wish you were dead, empty your stomach, wish you were dead, and eat more brownies if any were left.

After our desserts, we liked to end with a spectacle. Spectacle? Oh yes. That was our coffee and cappuccino maker, the Takahashi-3000, which we had ordered from Japan for a price that even my boastful ego will not let me disclose. Suffice it to say that in making our postprandial drinks, this machine provided an enormous display of flames which always impressed our guests (if they didn't run flaming out of the room). And between the flames, the coffee, chocolates, and port, everyone left so full of caffeine, sugar, and alcohol that they floated home across the hazy dew covered streets of the early Philadelphia morning.

*   *   *

Delectable dishes and sophisticated ambiance are key ingredients for any dinner party. But they alone don't make an evening. It's the people that keep things interesting. That's why we always chose guests who would stimulate us. We liked, for example, to invite several people we didn't know at all. They more than paid for their meal as fodder for post-dinner psychological analysis. For the same reason, we invited people who didn't know each other. Finally, we always had to have a bizarre string of characters, both for entertainment and distraction.

Such were the grad students Géorg and Frita (pronounced fri-, like the twi- in twitter), from Albania. Having traveled widely in Eurasia, they had many strange perspectives and oddities of taste. They always wore spats, capes, and big fur hats, underneath which were furry heads of unwashed hair, green checked suits, and socks so holy they had already ascended to heaven. When questioned, Géorg and Frita insisted that they wore only the latest fashions from Saville Row. They told stories about Gypsies and sometimes taught us Roma gambling. For dessert, they accepted only fine marmalade on crumpets and usually brought their own. But in spite of their idiosyncrasies, they never ran out of interesting observations on what everyone else considered quintessentially banal.

Géorg and Frita were just some of the many standard Turf guests. There was also Brian Book, a perennially silent hippy-type who, unsolicited, re-painted the sides of Philadelphia buildings he found unappealing. Brian's response to most things was to giggle, as if whatever you were saying was ridiculous. We alternated in believing he was zonked on drugs or had reached nirvana.

Then there were Clark, Khatari, and Egg—an inseparable threesome of fashion diviners. Always looking sharp, they were inseparable even during our parties, and often formed their own parties in corner or rooms of our apartment, completely oblivious to anyone else. I don't think they were misanthropes, just highly visual people.

There was Mona—who spoke so enthusiastically with so much energy about any subject, that everyone else's hair seemed to stand up, as if blown by a violent tornado.

There was Mort, an obsessive basketball nut who ran for every student government office available and used every means (*every* means) to get elected. Mort was also an amateur folk-singer, and sometimes entertained us with songs of woe.

There was Barry the decathlon athlete who, as a sophomore, had solved Philadelphia's financial crisis by re-writing its tax scheme. In fact, Barry was very smart on every subject, and would argue with anything you said, no matter how obvious it seemed to you.

Then there was Mattie, who never really said anything interesting, but who looked so good that you never could get anything out either. Conversations with Mattie consisted of her smiling, you smiling, her smiling bigger, then you falling on the floor. At that point, Mattie moved to her next victim.

There was Mr. Pore, a Shakespearean actor, Socratic philosopher, brain-surgeon in training, and all-in-one crisis resolution center. Often Mr. Pore brought his girlfriend, a tall slim Freudian with an un-returnable squash serve.

I also remember Molly and Grady, the hard-core Catholics from Ireland, the perverted French guy, Fabian, and the German and Nigerian lesbian couple who were both 6'5". There were a couple of random professors, the Maestro, and then whatever young ladies Mullins was wooing at the time.

One dinner party I particularly remember was our March-Pre-Spring-Break-Post-Chinese New Year's-we-just-want-to-eat-some-good-food-and-drink-some-fine-wine party. You could also call it "Thursday." In any case, the invitations, as usual, invited guests to *The Lush Life at The Turf.*

*   *   *

Despite what you hear on TV, no one can predict the weather. Luckily, it doesn't usually matter, unless you're a farmer depending on the rains for your crops, or if you have a severe case of Seasonal Affectedness Disorder. This was not the case for any Lush Life attendees. We weren't farmers, or the children of New York psychologists. Sometimes though, the weather caught up with us. This particular night in March, for example, falling snow increased the length of our party to an all time high of fourteen hours.

It started like this: two days before, I had been practicing some Mingus bass solos in my room when Ellen and Mullins had appeared at my door. They waited patiently until I finished the phrase, for which I was grateful. Few people understand the annoyance of being interrupted while practicing. Especially if you are in the zone, it's like someone poking you in a deep sleep. Thus I had instructed them in the past to enter silently when I was practicing, and to listen humbly until I finished playing. They respected this wish, and after I paused, Mullins spoke quickly:

"Festivities in T minus two. 7:30 drinks. The usual number plus two of mine. You're on hors d'oevres, Moet, Shiraz, and Oz Chard, plus music, and oh, the plat de resistance is Filet de Flet a la Moutarde."

Surprised? A couple of college kids, and they didn't even have the courtesy to ask if I liked Australian Chardonnay with a mustard sauce! Imbeciles! Oh, but I loved them anyway. At least I got to pick the wine, and more importantly, the music. If Ellen had been in charge of the music, we'd have Sinatra until you were ready to shoot yourself right between your old blue eyes. Worse, if it were Prateek, we might have to suffer through the emotional slop of late Romanticism. Mullins was never put in charge of the music. He did not want to be drawn from the conversation.

Happy with my lot, I spent Thursday preparing for our feast. For hors d'oevres I made moules with a garlic and butter sauce and a pistachio dip to be served with crackers for the vegan of the week. You never knew who would be the vegan of the week, but there always was one. Most people in college go through ideals faster that a bottle of Moet and Chandon. Which is not to say that the fill-in-the-blank idea of the week isn't worthwhile. Only that it's not predictable.

After finishing my shopping and cooking, I spent Thursday afternoon trying to solve one of the great mysteries of my life: the squeak on the high G string of my bass. Now why would it squeak like that? There was no reason. In fact, I was becoming more and more sure that the bass was just getting back at me for smashing it into a New York subway door. Of course I had apologized to the bass after the incident, pointing out several times that it was the door's fault, and that I really had nothing to do with it. But for a hollow instrument, that bass was dense, and kept squeaking until I got it totally re-strung and re-varnished in May.

At 5 pm I decided to play along with some jazz CDs. I turned up the volume, blocking out the sounds of the apartment and my roommates' banter.

At 7:38 pm I exited my room to find three chefs in aprons dashing around in the kitchen, and two guests frightfully sipping champagne in the corner.

"La sauce!" I heard. "Where are my shallots!" An apron whipped past me. Then another: "This carrot peeler is as dull as my psychology class! And who stuffed the disposal with pastry dough?!"

Mullins was madly chopping spring onions. He looked up at me for an instant and kept chopping. "How do you suppose the dish 'Beef Chow Fun' got its name?" he asked. I told him I didn't know, so he offered to tell his guests and me the story. Luckily for those who didn't care, he was interrupted by the entrance of the Maestro, who ballet danced his way through the front door and around kitchen to the champagne bottle on Ken the Counter. This was quite a feat, considering he kept time with the Sinatra ballad blasting from the living room stereo. After draining two flutes in two twirls, he curtsied. Then he reached into his "warrior's sack" with two hands and pulled out a bottle of cognac and a small wooden box. "Blunts and booze for all!" he shouted.

The chefs stopped their bustling to cheer. The Maestro always brought classy gifts. One of Mullins' guests, a girl I didn't recognize, leaned over and asked me, "What's a blunt?"

Before I could answer, Mullins laughed loudly and told her that it was "a green cigar, organic, with natural ingredients," and that she wouldn't suffer from trying it. I was about to explain to her what it really was, but at that moment, the rest of our guests began to arrive. Tonight's invitees were Géorg and Frita, Mr. Pore and his girlfriend, the Maestro, Barry, and Mullins' two friends. I poured champagne and served my appetizers while the chefs finished their handiwork. Then I turned down the lights in the living room and lit the tea candles. As I placed them on the windowsill, I looked outside and saw light snow drifting toward the streets.

Our guests spread into the living room, and my hors d'oevres began to disappear. Earlier in the year Prateek would have suggested that everyone sit in a circle. But we learned that circles rarely stimulated conversation. Much more fruitful was the "nook group" (not to be confused with the "nookie group," another party phenomenon) which appeared spontaneously but often led to excellent conversations. As a host and the DJ, I didn't get to talk to everyone that evening, but I tried to stay aware of the group's energy and to adjust the music accordingly.

After replacing the Sinatra with Ella Fitzgerald, I stood in the kitchen and watched the partygoers in the living room. The Maestro sat silently on the couch, stroking his beardless chin. He eyed his fifth glasses of champagne, and then drank.

Barry began the evening's conversation by bemoaning the plight of the Franklin students graduating in just two months. It wasn't jobs, or their opportunities for success that he worried about—he just thought they were still fools and didn't deserve to leave yet.

"Idiots!" he muttered, talking to no one in particular and therefore implicating most of the party guests. "People want to move out of Philadelphia and get into the real world. They haven't even learned basic economics! They don't understand anything! I was talking to someone recently about tax theory, and he didn't care at all. I don't think he even *realized* that he was going to be paying taxes next year!"

"Who wants to pay taxes?" said Frita. "It sounds like Texas!" Géorg began to make horse noises. Then he told Frita and Barry that, "never paying a cent of taxes in her life, *or visiting Texas,* Catherine the Great died under a horse."

"What do you mean?" Barry asked seriously. "She was thrown off in battle?"

"Oh no," said Géorg, with a twinkle in his eye.

"No man could please her!" Frita giggled and bounced into the kitchen.

Barry continued to ask Géorg what had happened, trying in vain to comprehend the relationship between paying taxes, Texas, and dying under a horse.

In another corner, Mr. Pore and his girlfriend were talking to Mullins' two friends. They were good at meeting new people. Both were dorm advisors and experienced with unbalanced situations. Mr. Pore was talking about his latest research. I overheard that he was working on "new pathological understandings of split personality disorder."

"It's good fun" he told them, laughing, "although it can get confusing at times!" His girlfriend laughed too. All the while, Frita was bouncing around the room, introducing herself to people she already knew and repeating absurd stories of photographing transvestite nightclubs and Communist architecture in Eastern Europe.

Eventually Ellen, Prateek and Mullins came into the living room, each carrying multiple steaming plates. "Dinner is served." Ellen announced, to which the Maestro clapped slowly. She curtsied lightly and passed out the food.

Before they even ate, I knew that our guests would appreciate our cooking. Guaranteed. Not because we were superb chefs, but because "cooking" at all was a meritorious achievement in college. If you're a college kid who can throw something even barely edible on a plate and fold a napkin, you're a success. My dad told me he used to impress dates by serving ketchup-covered chicken breasts in tin foil. You can only imagine, then, the impact of a French menu on the same audience. Triomphe!

Before we started eating, Mullins introduced everyone to his two friends, Amador and Shane. Amador was half-Texan, and half-Filipino, and he admitted with a grin that he was going straight from business school to international wealth and fame. I don't know if he was as talented as he was ambitious, but he certainly played the part. He was tall, tanned, and neatly dressed, and I gathered that he was well-traveled and outgoing.

Mullins' other friend was Shane, a short blue-eyed girl from North Carolina with curly blond hair and conservative clothing. Shane was cute and spunky, but she flinched when anyone cursed and kept silent in any conversations mentioning sex.

We ate slowly, savoring our meal. Frita and Géorg led the conversation, their antics interlarded with a few Mullins tales and the requisite Barry objections. I didn't feel much like talking, so I sat next to the Maestro, who liked his peace. Meanwhile, Prateek and Ellen preyed on our unsuspecting guests, entertaining them with theories of all shapes and sizes.

As soon as we had finished the main meal, Ellen brought out the Takahashi-3000, which was subsequently loaded with the appropriate fuel and set alight. Our astonished new guests watched as a fiery flaming spectacle rose from the coffee table and magically lit the room. Everyone was stunned into silence. Then joy emerged from the corner of our lips. The absurdity of this machine (and our lives) was indeed blissful. As Ellen had mentioned again that evening, we really were living in a luxury hotel. We had few wants, and fewer needs. Almost all of them were satisfied quickly and without much work. We were sometimes stressed, but even that was nothing before the sacred flame of luxury.

Finally as the spectacle died down, bubbling, boiling delicious coffee was produced. To it we added whiskey or Baileys or Godiva white chocolate liqueur and Mullins' chocolate pastries. As the sugar, caffeine and alcohol took hold, we entered our favorite sated trance, a place where we needed nothing and were content just to be.

Actually, nobody was content just to be. Before I knew what was happening a Turf creation, the double Twister Board had appeared on the floor, and a self-selection of writhing bodies were struggling, laughing, sweating, and groaning to achieve outrageous contortions. Behind the Twister board, Shane was sitting sleepily in the wing-back. She kept nodding off, and then dragging her head up again. After a several valiant efforts, she lost to the Sandman. In another corner, Mullins was busily chatting to Ellen and Amador.

The Maestro was not much of a Twister player, and after a moment he came over to the jukebox where I was tending the tunes. He asked me about my thesis—we were the only two of our friends writing a senior paper. He was writing about music in 19th century Philadelphia bars, and I was writing about the jazz scene in Japan. Neither of us were working like crazy to get our papers finished, but we agreed that we were far ahead of most people we knew.

"I can't understand it, how are they going to finish on time?" I asked.

"I don't think they are," he said. "I don't think they care. I think we," he gestured around him, "are living in our own world."

"If I slacked on half of what I'm doing," I said, "I would be in a hole so deep I could dig my way to China with a dinner fork."

The Maestro nodded in agreement. We refilled our glasses of port, and Mullins joined us in the kitchen.

"Quite a game," he said, gesturing at the Twister board. Prateek's head was sticking out between somebody's legs, and he seemed to be screaming at Géorg about some point of the rules. No, that wasn't it—Frita had sat on Prateek's palm pilot. Barry, Mr. Pore, and his girlfriend were also entangled in the bunch, but they seemed to be having their own conversation. Shane was still asleep in the chair behind them, and Ellen and Amador were nowhere to be seen.

"Poppycock!" crowed Géorg. He raised his head and cawed. The game continued.

Mullins nodded his head at Shane. "What do you think?" he asked us.

I shook my head. "She's asleep," I noted. "At a dinner party with a Twister game."

"I don't know Mullins," the Maestro added, "haven't you had enough ladies for the moment?"

"What do you mean?" Mullins drank some port. "How can you have enough ladies?"

The Maestro shrugged his shoulders. "Well Mullins, weren't you just bitching last week and the week before and the week before that about the girls getting you down? I mean, you're always telling stories about these ladies you're after and how you're always getting screwed."

"It's the story of my life!" said Mullins. "It's the story of my life man!"

"Why don't you just chill out for a while. Get a new story."

"Oh, it's worth it to have a girlfriend. You know."

"Yeah," said the Maestro. "But listen, it's not everything, Mullins. You have to focus on yourself."

The music went off, so I changed the CD. I threw on some Medeski Martin, and Wood featuring John Scofield, and when I finished, the Maestro was telling Mullins how he was about to break up with his woman.

"I don't know," he said. "I just don't know. We get along really well. We respect each other completely. But I feel like I want to start over now. She's about what I was in college—she keeps me in that role."

"What, she doesn't respect your independence?" he asked. "She's playing you?"

"Nah. I can't really explain. It's just the cues. She's a cue for the way I was when I started dating her two years ago, and I don't want to be cued that way anymore."

"Listen, people are always going to cue you. No matter where you are. Shouldn't you just deal with that?"

"I don't know" said the Maestro. "But it seems like I have a choice here. I don't know." He looked uncomfortable, and I decided to change the subject back to Shane.

"Didn't you meet her at a party? Does she always sleep like that?" I asked Mullins.

"Oh, she's unique," he answered. "Keeps her own hours. Also, she only eats before noon. Did you notice her convenient lack of appetite? That's why I think the liquor really got her."

"Not a good sign," I told him. If she's anorexic she ought to see someone, and if he knew about it, he ought to help.

"She claims it's healthier," he said and shrugged. "She says she does it for 'a variety of moral, philosophical and religious reasons.' How are you going to argue with that? You can't argue with someone who believes something religiously."

I shook my head and poured everyone some more port.

"I agree with Aaron," said the Maestro.

"Maybe," Mullins continued. "It's funny, it reminds me of a time when I was in Prague with some friends. One of my friends wanted to hook up with this empty-headed crazy girl. Neither of them wanted a real relationship; they couldn't even talk to each other. But I guess they were horny. So when we got drunk together, he tried. And I don't know why I did it, but I interrupted them, I broke it up." Mullins finished his port.

"In retrospect, I probably should have let him hook up with her, but I guess at the time I had strong ideas, and I felt like I was doing the right thing. But now I wonder if I was right. I mean, he didn't feel any better for it, I don't think, and I don't think he ever felt like I did him a favor. For a while I thought I had done him a favor, and now I don't know what to believe. It just seemed like an immature thing for him to do. But on the other hand, was it just an immature thing for me to do? How do you know that shit? What the hell?"

I opened my mouth to answer but I didn't have anything to say. So we were silent. We listened to the groans of the twister game and drank some more.

"Well," said the Maestro, "nobody said it was easy."

"Yeah," I agreed. We sat down at the kitchen table, picking at what was left of the dessert.

After a moment or so, Shane came out of the living room bleary eyed. She tapped Mullins on the shoulder and said thank you and that she had to leave. Mullins was disappointed. "You don't want to stay and hang out?" he asked. "You probably won't even have class tomorrow you know."

She smiled and I could see why Mullins was attracted to her.

"Well," she said, "I go to church early every day, and then I have to work out, and then I have a lot of work to do."

"Are you sure?" he said. "Why don't you just chill and have some more dessert? Or, do you want me to walk you home?" The Maestro and I looked away, so as not to disturb the moment.

"That's nice of you," she replied, "but no thanks. Goodnight." And with that, she zipped up her coat, tossed her hair, smiled again, and left the premises.

"Oh well," Mullins grumbled as the door slammed. "It's just another one for my stories. I rack 'em up like empty bottles."

"Mullins, don't sweat it," I told him. "She might even like you; she's tired, and she just wants to go home."

"Why don't we go for a walk?" he suggested in response. I agreed, but the Maestro said he would stick around and work on his port.

I got my coat and my hat. Mullins put on a jacket, and we headed out the door. We hit the snowy night with our heads down and headed north on 18th Street. There was at least two inches on the ground and it was still falling fast. We walked in silence to Chestnut Street, turned right and continued without speaking down to 2nd Street. As we walked, we crunched our feet in the white powder and kicked it into the street. I tasted some on my tongue.

After a while, it occurred to me that Mullins, the talker, wasn't talking. I wasn't talking either. But that was on purpose. Mullins had suggested the walk, and as far as I was concerned, he could decide what kind of walk it was going to be. We turned right again on Spruce and headed up to Rittenhouse Square. We walked for about an hour without saying anything.

"You know" he told me as we walked through Rittenhouse, "I'm really confused about myself. Sometimes I think I'm smart, attractive, social, all of that. But other times I wonder if that's a total illusion, something I just imagine. Maybe I'm just a lonely fool, pretending he has character and charm. Maybe I don't have anything." He paused and took a deep breath. "It's not that I expect to know myself completely—it's just—my continuous failures with girls make me think…"

I looked at him through the falling snow. He didn't look back. "I just don't know…" he continued, "all these ups and downs, all these people moving through my life…" He walked around in small circles, kicking the snow with his boot. "It's like some kind of melodrama. Or maybe I'm just stupid to keep getting upset?"

I didn't know what to say. But, I didn't have to answer. Just as I was about to open my mouth, I saw a purple scarf flying at the end of the square and then heard "Guys!"

Ellen ran across the park toward us, and threw a snowball at me. When I blocked it she ran into me and pushed me into the snow. She sat on me, took off my hat, and rubbed snow in my hair. Then she made another snowball and threw it at Mullins. She hit him square in the chest. He stood still, and kept kicking the snow with his feet.

"What's up big guy?" she asked. She got up, ran over and began punching him playfully in the stomach. Mullins didn't respond. He looked up at the sky and smiled tightly. Ellen kept punching his stomach until he looked down at her. Then, she shoved a handful of snow down his pants.

"Agh!" he yelled, laughing and crying at once.

"That's what you get for doubting!" she said.

He tried to retaliate, and began gathering snow. But she was too quick, and jumped on his back, dumping them both into the white powder. She wrestled him onto his back and sat on his stomach. Then she leaned into his face "You don't get to be down," she said softly. He began to protest, and she shoved some snow-covered grass in his mouth and pointed at the clearing sky. "Where were you when the morning stars sang?" Then, she quickly jumped off him and started walking toward the Turf. As I got up and wiped the snow from my pants, I thought I heard her crying. "By the way" she said without looking back, "the kitchen burnt down."

*   *   *

We got up and ran after her.

"What!" I yelled.

"What happened?!" Mullins demanded. He groaned, trying to get the snow out of his pants.

The fire wasn't serious, she told us. Shortly after we left, the Maestro had a lit a third blunt for Prateek, who claimed that "two was for weenies." Subsequently, our rather intoxicated Higgins left his man-making cigar on the kitchen table and left to umpire a game of Twister.

No one noticed the table was burning until half of it was gone. Then, seeing the flames, Prateek reacted quickly, smashing the Maestro's bottle of cognac on what was left of the table.

Was anything wrong with what Prateek did? How he bravely tried to extinguish the flames? In fact, there were two small problems:

First, cognac is not easy to make. You start with fine wine from the Cognac region in France and then you distill it two times in copper pot stills. Then you take the product and pump it into French oak casks, where it ages for at least two and a half years. The best Cognacs are aged even twenty or thirty years before being blended for taste, bottled, and put on the market. Now, why would you ever want to pour cognac in a fire? Big mistake number one.

Mistake number two is that Prateek had dumped *alcohol* on a fire. Anything striking about that? Yes, well it struck the table. And then it struck the floor, and the cabinets, and the walls. Then, after a spectacle that topped even the Takahashi-3000, we lost the rest of our eating space before you could say "Chin chin." What can I say, the Senator believed in efficiency.

At this point, Ellen had apparently emerged from her room and called 911. After reporting our address and the nature of the fire, she ran around trying to find everyone and get them out of the apartment.

She had rounded up everyone she could, and then she tried to find us. She was angry, she told us, and then afraid, but finally the fire department showed up and put out the blaze and we weren't dead at all. In fact, there were no casualties except that

Prateek had a burned arm. If you ask me, he deserved much worse for destroying a perfectly good bottle of Cognac. The nerve.

When we got back, we found the kitchen in perfectly good shape, excepting the table, cabinets, counters, walls, and floors. Strangely, half of our guests were still playing Twister in the living room, and there was a CD of Vince Guaraldi's Charlie Brown tunes playing in the background. Ellen explained that under Géorg's leadership, they had banded together and protested that because they were wearing their finest, they were unable to return home in the snow, and so we would be stuck with them until it melted. I told her I didn't mind.

Now you might think that we would be worried about destroying the kitchen in a rented apartment. You might think we would have to pay for it. But if you did, you would not be using the logic of the Turf. You see, two days after our fire, a notice appeared on our front door alerting us that after a year of discussion, the landlords would be completely replacing our kitchen at the end of the week. We were instructed to remove and dispose of everything we could from the area.

Even before I knew about the kitchen replacement, I wasn't upset about the fire. I've always found myself nonchalant at the loss or destruction of material goods. There is something powerful, something zen, when they disappear. I always feel lighter.

Back in the apartment, Mullins and I studied what was burnt. Meanwhile, Prateek was on his hands and knees scrubbing the walls with rubber gloves. I told him he didn't have to feel guilty and that we wouldn't blame him for the kitchen, at least until the bill came.

"I don't care about the bill!" he yelled maniacally. "How can I live in this mess?"

Guests still twisting in the background, I conferred with Ellen and Mullins and we decided it would be inappropriate to go to bed. No one felt like sleeping. So we let ourselves into our neighbors apartment, used their supplies to cook some hot chocolate from scratch, and then put on some movies. We watched le Charme Discret de la Bourgeoisie, the Big Lebowski, and then Annie Hall, three Turf classics. We ignored the crazies playing Twister in the corner. Laughing on the couch, we didn't even hear them.

The snow was still falling outside at 8:30 am when Ellen announced she was ready for breakfast. And what had I been planning to cook, she inquired. Mullins and Prateek laughed. They knew that I was powerless to resist breakfast food (and the charming woman asking for it). I got my boots and coat on, and trekked to the 24-hour BABA not-so-quickie mart down the street. I found the omelet materials, the closest thing they had to fresh fruit, maple syrup and a Snickers bar. Then I got in line behind a guy paying for his cigarettes with pennies and nickels. After waiting so long I was sure the snow had melted outside, I returned to the Turf and used our neighbor's kitchen to cook blueberry-strawberry chocolate chip pancakes, individually tailored omelets, and a fruit salad. Returning to the Turf with the food, I graciously left a Snickers bar and an IOU sticky-note for the 402 pinochlers.

While I was gone, Prateek and Mullins had raided my citrus jar and made fresh squeezed orange-grapefruit juice with our juicer, saved from the blast since it lived in my room. Ellen defrosted some of her Molasses bread and prepared the spreads.

Since the twister crowd had fallen asleep on top of each other in the living room and the kitchen was non-existent, we went into my room to eat. I put on Mendelssohn's Octet, and we ate one bite at a time.

We didn't talk much, except for Prateek, who kept murmuring "take a little bite and chew chew chew," to himself. We just enjoyed our food, and the sunlight from my window. We ate, and ate, and ate some more, until we were full and bloated, and then we rolled off into bed.

*   *   *

After that evening, Ellen began disappearing from the Turf. We didn't know why, but over the next ten days we hardly saw her. She came in after we went to sleep and left before we got up. The following week was Spring Break, and I flew to Austin and then to Chicago to audition for two bass playing and three teaching jobs. Prateek was in New York to interview with banking firms, and Mullins stayed in Philadelphia to work and think about his future. Ellen was supposed to be going home, and she left the same day as I did. But she never arrived. Her parents phoned the apartment that evening to ask if she was there, and when Mullins went in her room to find her, he found a note instead:

```
Mullins,

When my parents ask, I am staying for
Break in Philadelphia. I'm not. But I'm
fine, don't worry.

Hugs!

Ellen
```

Mullins followed her instructions. He told her parents she was in Philadelphia, but was "currently indisposed" and would get in touch with them as soon as possible. She didn't. Nor did she get in touch with us. She didn't return from break when we did, not even five days later. When she wasn't back on Sunday we got worried and decided we would call the police if she didn't show up on Monday. She didn't show up on Monday. But we did get an email from her that evening, saying:

```
Guys,

Still fine.

Hugs,

Ellen
```

We stopped worrying about her until Wednesday, when Prateek realized someone could have kidnapped her and figured out how to hack her email. He got upset, and told us that if she wasn't back on Friday he was calling the Police, emails or not.

Wednesday and Thursday went by with no sign of Ellen. We only went out when we had to, in case she called or needed any help. On Friday morning around 10:30, Mullins, Prateek and I were sitting in the living room reading when we heard a knock at the door. I jumped up and rushed to get it. I opened the door and was surprised to find a highly tanned Amador wearing sunglasses, shorts, a t-shirt, and sandals. It was thirty-five degrees and raining outside. Amador was carrying an inflatable chair and two suitcases. He shrugged and smiled.

"She's coming right up," he said.

"What?!"

"Where is she!" demanded Prateek. "And what are you doing here?"

"Oh," said Amador. "We just got back from Puerto Rico this morning."

"You what?" exclaimed Mullins.

"Puerto Rico," Ellen shouted, running in the door to hug us. "Hey guys!"

I was shocked, but mostly glad to see Ellen alive.

"Honey, I'll just put our stuff in your room," said Amador. He kissed Ellen on the lips and took their luggage into her room.

"Well!" I managed to utter. Prateek, Mullins, and I looked at Ellen in total surprise. We didn't know what to say, and she didn't wait for us. She skipped over to the fridge and found her tofutti cheese.

Finally, Prateek spoke: "When did you and Amador start getting jiggy with it?"

"Prateek!" Ellen teased. I didn't say anything.

"Later," she told him. "I need to unpack and rest first." She smiled, took her fake cheese, went into her room, and closed the door.

*　　*　　*

We didn't see Ellen until that evening. Unfortunately though, we did hear her all afternoon. She and Amador were not quite as tired as she suggested. I knocked on the door and told them to keep it down, but they just laughed in response. So Prateek set up his enormous stereo on the new kitchen table, facing Ellen's room.

"Now then," he said. "What is the music they would not want to hear right now?"

"I know!" I said. I had a CD of music from rural West China which sounded like little cats being stabbed in a microwave. We put it on, and cranked it up.

Two minutes later, Ellen's door opened and a shoe flew out at us. It landed harmlessly on the counter, and we laughed. We did not adjust the music, and they did not adjust their behavior for at least ten minutes. Under the screeching, I yelled to Mullins and Prateek I would make some fruit smoothies for us, and they sat around the kitchen table looking at Ellen's door and grinning. When I was about half way through my fruit peeling, Ellen's door opened again. Prateek and Mullins scooted away from the center of the kitchen to avoid any flying projectiles, but no projectile appeared. Instead, Ellen and Amador emerged from the door, covered with a blue bed-sheet. The sheet was draped over their heads and bodies, and they had poked holes in front for their eyes to see. Giggling, they pranced to the bathroom like schoolchildren, where we heard them turn on the shower.

Prateek changed the orientation of the boom box toward the bathroom, but Ellen and Amador didn't seem to mind. They didn't come out of the bathroom for at least an hour, during which we had to listen to the entire painful CD and another CD of "Music from Star Trek" (one of Prateek's favorites).

Finally, we had had enough. Mullins and I decided to go out for lunch. We hit the noodle shop at the end of our street.

"I can't believe it! They just met!" he said.

"Yeah, did you even see them hanging out during the party?"

"Not really," he replied, "though now we know why Ellen was gone so much the week after."

"I thought she was doing a dance or something?"

"Dirty dancing, more like it. Well, good for her if she's in love or whatever."

"Yeah," I said. "I hope she is."

"It's funny though that she didn't talk about it at all to us. I mean, she always asks about the girls I'm going out with; she always wants to know everything."

"Yeah man, I know," I said. "I guess some people just don't talk about it."

We returned later that afternoon. Amador had gone home for dinner, and Ellen emerged from her room shining and refreshed. I was cooking a stir-fry for Prateek and Mullins.

"Do you have enough for four?" she asked.

"It comes with a muzzle," muttered Prateek from under his newspaper. He'd made the unfortunate decision to stay in the apartment the whole afternoon and he had a headache from all the loud music.

"Sorry guys," Ellen apologized. "You know, it happens."

"Right," said Mullins sardonically. "Whatever."

"Listen," she said. "You guys can't be upset about Amador. He's...fabulous."

"I'm not," I said. "I think it's great. I was just a little upset that you disappeared for two weeks, and then you got back and disappeared again. We were worried about you, you know."

"I wasn't worried!" Prateek insisted. "But it harms my credibility to have to lie to your parents."

"Well guys, you know, when you're in love..."

Ellen sat down at the table and gave us selected scenes from the past few weeks. Apparently, she made an immediate romantic connection with Amador at the dinner party and volunteered to help him with the Filipino dance festival, which he was coordinating. Over the course of the week, they had "become lovers" and had "revealed to each other their deepest secrets."

"I don't know what it is," said Ellen. "I've never told anyone what I told him, and he says the same thing. At first, neither of us were even sure if we wanted a relationship. Then, then it just happened."

"Why didn't you talk about it?" Mullins asked quietly. "I would have cheered you on."

"I know Mullins," she said sympathetically. "But I didn't want to work myself up. You know, if I started telling you my heart and my stories, well, I would have just worked myself up about him and made a bunch of decisions that I didn't have to make. I would have had all these expectations and then I would have had to confront Amador on them, and…it would have been a big mess."

"Right." He didn't understand. Prateek put some plates on the table, and I served the food.

"Eat up!" I said.

Ellen ate ravenously, and Mullins noted how sad it was that fake cheese hardly gave one enough energy for an afternoon of bedroom acrobatics.

"Don't worry," said Ellen. "We'll be at his place from now on."

"I should hope so!" said Prateek. "The impacts on my investing would be untenable! But actually, that's not true after today."

"Huh?" I said.

"I'm moving out," he announced.

"Higgins, what are you talking about?" Mullins asked.

"I got a room in the dorms," said Prateek.

"You what?" said Ellen. "Why would you want to live in the dorms instead of here?"

"I'll still keep my room," said Prateek. "But I'm just putting a few things in the dorm. My computer, a few books, et cetera. And I'll sleep there."

"Why?" said Mullins. "In the middle of your last semester?"

"And why didn't you tell us about this?" I asked him.

"It wasn't finalized. I hadn't signed the papers. Listen, the reason I'm moving out is so I can be more disciplined. I can't get things done in here. There're too many distractions."

"What do you mean?"

"All the books, all the stories, all the antics—this whole place is alive all the time, and you can't escape it. To think, or to change, whatever, it's too much."

"Prateek, I've never heard you say anything about this!" Ellen replied. "When did you start to feel this way?"

"I always have," he said. "But don't worry, it's not about you guys. I'll still get the rent paid, and I'll still be here a lot. But I need more discipline. I need to liberate myself so I can think about next year and start living a religious life."

"A what?" Mullins said. We had never heard Prateek talk about religion before.

"Religion is the most important thing in my life," he said calmly.

"Since when!" I countered.

"Oh, it's always been. I don't need to pray or anything to be religious. But the rigor, and the ideals—that's a solid enterprise. And I can't work on it from here. I can't improve. I need space for all of this. I need to clear up."

"Wow," I asked, "but do you have to move out?"

"Yeah," he told us. "I do. It's next weekend, and if you guys could help me that'd be good."

Over the next week we tried to understand why Prateek was leaving, what he meant by religion, and if it was possible to convince him to stay. We accomplished nothing. The Senator was always his own man, and he didn't really like people trying to understand him. So he stayed a couple of steps ahead, plotting and planning his next move, always ready with some reason or justification, even if it made no sense to us. I wasn't mad at him for leaving; but was just surprised that he hadn't said anything previously. Ellen, of course, had no grounds to complain, and she didn't notice much anyway. She spent most of her time with

Amador now. Even when she was at the Turf, her boyfriend came with her.

After he moved out, Prateek continued to stop by. He kept his food in our fridge, and most of his books in our bookshelves, and his new disciplined life still allowed for some social time.

But so far as the Turf went, the core was now Mullins and me. Sometimes it was lonely like that, and sad too, to see our community dissipate. I knew though, that I had to let go, and that I couldn't let my feelings overwhelm my daily living.

Chapter Nine

On those rare April days when Ellen wasn't with Amador, I tried to spend time with her. We played squash, or cooked, or took walks. We also liked to go out on the balcony and make splatter paintings. Our technique was to stand at each end and hurl paint at each other, knowing we would eventually hit the canvas.

But the product of our painting didn't really matter. We knew that. We weren't painters. We were painting. Not paintings, painting. That's what Ellen explained to me mid-April as we scrubbed ourselves with turpentine.

"You know what I just realized Aaron? We're painting. We can paint anything we want. So this is my new theory: we're not the painting. But we're the *painting*."

"What? What are you talking about? Of course we're painting. That's what we're doing."

"No, we are the *painting*-the painting process, not the canvass. That's why if we don't like what we paint we can change our technique or learn some new tricks. That's why we can transform ourselves. Don't you think?"

"I don't know what you're talking about," I said. "Can you give me a concrete example?"

"Look at Mullins," she suggested. "He's smart, talented, educated, and still depressed. What do you think is his problem?"

"Girls?"

"No!" she replied, laughing. "Girls have nothing to do with it."

"I don't know about that," I said. "I think they have everything to do with it."

"Ok. But he thinks he's the painting, not the *painting*."

"And he's a painter? Is that what you're saying?" I still wasn't following her.

"I'm saying he's confused himself with the canvass."

"What do you mean?" I said.

"Painting isn't easy," she replied, mostly to herself. She had given up trying to explain. "But you know, learn a little every day." We looked at our painting of the day. It was a white canvas covered with blue and green splotches. Two red lines of dots crossed the canvas, making a tee-pee, or an unfinished A. It didn't look like much. But, we were painting, and I guess that was something.

*　　*　　*

I can think of very few things for which I will interrupt the key hours of morning slumber. Since I realized the pleasure of getting up at 10:30 am, I rarely give it up. But some things are worth more even, than sleep. And one of those things is squash. You'll have to trust me on this if you don't know, but there are few pleasures like smashing that little rubber ball.

The game, the ball—they move fast. Most rallies last less than ten seconds, some less than five seconds. But no matter how far behind you are, you can always win. The trick is that you'll win if you're winning. It sounds stupid, I know, but the answer is in a little book that Ellen lent to me called *Zen and the Art of Archery*. You have to play your best without getting angry or losing your focus. In other words, you play what is *exactly that moment*.

Because Ellen spent most nights at Amador's, I started playing squash with Mullins. He was a reasonably athletic guy, and he grew to like the game as much as I did. He got pretty good pretty fast too, and after a month, I really had to work to win.

One Friday morning in April, I decided to skip my thesis class to play squash. I knocked on Mullins' door and asked if he was game. At first, he murmured:

"What? Where am I? Where am I?"

"Mullins," I repeated. "Do you want to play squash?"

"What? What? Where is this?"

"Squash!"

"Ok, squash, squash. Fifteen minutes."

We left at 9 and walked to the courts. The breeze was brisk as the sun rose, and we wore windbreakers and walked quietly with our hands in our pockets.

When we arrived at the squash courts, we pulled off our jackets and stretched for a few minutes. Then we warmed the ball up on the court and started to play.

"You wanna serve?" I asked Mullins.

"No, go ahead," he said, and I did. I served the first ball well, and he missed the return.

"Damn," he said. He smiled as we switched sides, and told me it was the last point I would score. "I just took a lesson with the best player at Franklin."

"Ok, Mullins, whatever you say." I served again, and he returned. We volleyed a few times, and I eventually scored the point.

"Huh?" He looked confused. "Don't worry," he told me, "I've been practicing a lot. As soon as I get warmed up, you're in for trouble."

We switched again, and I kept serving. I managed to keep in hitting sweet spots on my racket, and I kept winning the points. After each score, he would say, "I'm just not good at this today," or "I don't know what I'm doing." As the game went on, he would occasionally score a point, but as I got farther ahead, he stopped making eye-contact with me. Instead he would grunt and walk over to serve the ball.

It must have been a particularly good day for me, but it was also a bad day for Mullins. I managed to win the first game 9 to 3. The second game was much the same, except that Mullins got stiff. He began to hit the ball with all his force; it didn't matter where. He would scream "Ahh!" with each return, and if he missed, he would swing hard enough to almost knock himself over. He wasn't really focused though, and as I kept winning points, he kept getting more frustrated.

"I can't play this fucking game," he muttered.

"Come on, Mullins," I said. "Stay with it. This is game point." I served again, but he missed the ball and hit his racquet at full force against the wall.

"Shit!" he yelled.

"All right." I called for a water-break.

We left the court to re-hydrate and stretch. Mullins still wasn't looking me in the eye, and he kicked the wall a few times with the bottom of his shoe.

"Listen Mullins, cool it," I said. "This is a set of five, so you still have a chance to win if you pull off the next ones."

"Yeah," he muttered. We returned to the court and warmed up the ball silently. When I played with Ellen, and usually when I played with Mullins, we were rarely silent on the court. Since we weren't that serious, we usually had great chats about all sorts of things, which were only interrupted by a particularly hardy volley. Today though, Mullins wasn't in the mood. He served first and scored.

"Good shot," I said. He didn't respond but switched sides with me to serve again. I won the point and started a scoring streak. Mullins either missed the serve or messed up the return. He wasn't really playing. Instead, he was talking about himself.

"I just can't play right. I suck at this," he exclaimed. Between each point, he would comment on his poor skills or mutter an obscenity. Soon, the score was 8-1, and I was serving the match-point.

"Ready?" I asked, and looked at Mullins. He was facing the other wall and didn't answer me. The back of his neck was red and he was breathing heavily.

"Match point," I yelled. I served the ball. It went high, but he returned a low shot to the front corner. I ran to get it and hit a long shot back. He returned that ball as well, although he was slightly off balance when it hit, yelling "Ah!" and running lightly into the back wall. I was still at the front of the court, and when the ball came, I tapped it lightly so it would hit the front wall and fall nearby. I heard Mullins scream from the back of the court and start running toward the ball. He clomped across the space as fast as he could, yelling as if he were in battle. I turned and saw his face, so full of desire for the ball, so determined to force himself to it.

Mullins reached the ball before it bounced twice. But he was out of control. He hit the ball straight up and then ran into the front wall, his arms barely blocking his crash. Then everything went dark. Mullins had hit the ball straight up through the roof netting and smashed the court light bulb. A shower of glass fell towards the court, and I covered my head with my arms. Mullins was still crouching against the wall. Luckily, most of the glass fell behind us in center court. The ball stuck in the socket though, and it must have short-circuited the other courts too. I saw the lights in the courts next door to ours went off and heard our neighbors groaning as they finished their games.

In the semi-darkness, Mullins finally made eye-contact with me. His lips were bleeding and he was clutching his ankle, which he seemed to have sprained. Other than that he was ok, and I helped him get up.

"You went out hard," I said. "Good match."

He moaned "Oh man."

"Breakfast?" I suggested.

"Ok." He smiled weakly.

We left our court and Mullins went to the locker room to clean himself up. On our way out I told the guy at the front desk who we were, and that we would pay for the damage. Then we left the gym and walked back to the Turf.

When we got back, we found Ellen and Prateek eating in the living room. "How was your game?" Ellen yelled at us.

"Great!" Mullins yelled back. He laughed, limped into his room and shut the door.

"Yeah," I said. "Definitely full of excitement." I got some of the eggs and pancakes left in the kitchen and joined Ellen and Prateek in the living room.

"Hey" Ellen suggested, "why don't we go to Casablanca tonight?"

"I like it, I like it," said Prateek. "I need to get out of here!"

"Excellent" Ellen confirmed. "And let's invite one person each."

You had to go with a group to Casablanca. I yelled to Mullins, and he responded that he was game.

*   *   *

After breakfast I called and invited my friend Erik, a hard-core traveler with a penchant for free-style rapping. Erik rapped in the rhythms that James Brown, his "spiritual godfather," spoke. He had rapped on the streets of West Philly, in the villages of rural Indonesia, and through the towns of southern India.

Ellen invited the Maestro since Amador was away on a job interview, and Prateek brought his new friend Darcy. Darcy was Prateek's fiercest competitor for the elliptical machine at the gym, and his project partner in the international environmental studies class he was forced to take. Mullins invited Clive, but the baker called at the last minute to cancel. He told Mullins that he had mistakenly killed his mother.

Hey, it could have happened to anyone! Ellen, Mullins, and I all kept our mothers in the fridge and occasionally we would lose one. For an animal that doesn't do much, yeast is highly suicidal.

We all met in Rittenhouse Square that evening except for Erik, who was coming later. Prateek introduced us all to Darcy, a sporty girl wearing lycra pants and a hiking backpack. She was apparently from the West Coast and had taken two years off before college to work in Singapore and in Portugal teaching English. Now she was doing environmental studies at Franklin. The rest of us introduced ourselves, and then we walked slowly to Casablanca, on 5th and South Streets in an alley called Leithgow.

Casablanca is a Moroccan restaurant in Old City. There is no sign on the door. It is a simple brick building without windows at the corner of an alley. It has a black awning and a single spotlight shining on a thin green door. The door has no handle. You have to ring the bell to be admitted.

When you walk inside, you feel like you're to about enter Narnia, or a Kubrick orgy. But you don't. When you enter, you're crunched into a tiny entrance hall, and you feel instead that you would like your table to be ready soon. The lighting is by candlelight, the walls are covered with dark colored draperies, and the floor with oriental carpets. When you get to your "table," you sit on circular cushioned benches with pillows in deep colors: red, blue, and green. Between the cushioned benches, there is a round wooden table which looks like a broad stool, and that's where the big plates of food are placed for you to eat with your hands. Everyone eats from the same plate, and you usually eat until the food is gone. Then the next course appears and the feast begins anew.

A few minutes after we arrived, Erik came in wearing a red fez. I asked how he was doing.

"Chillen like a villain. You like my threads?" He pointed to his hat.

"Yeah man," I said. I introduced him to rest of the group. A waiter took our coats, and led us to our table. Ellen sat at one end. Then there was Erik, the Maestro, Prateek, Me, Darcy, and Mullins. As we washed our hands in a bowl passed by the waiter, Ellen and Erik began to tell Darcy about the terrific art exhibition they had seen at the Philadelphia Art Museum. Meanwhile Prateek, the Maestro, Mullins, and I talked about the idiocy in our country's foreign policy.

"You know what the president ought to do," advised Prateek, "He should declare a world-wide free trade regime and enforce it with our army!"

"That's a scary thought," said the Maestro. "Talk about amoral!"

Mullins changed the subject to another international topic. He told us about a party he had attended the previous night at the Franklin International House. There were apparently Saudi Arabians, Japanese, Koreans, French, and Zimbabweans, and they had apparently formed some "international relations" before the night was out.

"Our food is arriving!" Erik announced. We all watched as the waiter brought our first plate of the evening, a salad plate. We were starving, and ate quickly. We finished soon and another plate appeared. We kept eating and each empty plate was quickly replaced by the next course. First was chicken with prunes and almonds on a bed of couscous, then Kefta with poached eggs and a tomato sauce, then mixed kabobs with onions and peppers, and then a vegetable plate with potatoes, carrots, walnuts, raisins, celery and other cooked vegetables. We ordered four bottles of red wine and drank them for thirst. Everyone ate ravenously except Darcy, who took a lot of salad and afterwards ate slowly and not very much.

As we were finishing the main courses, Erik piped up. "Can I make a toast?" he said, holding up his kabob stick. "Can I make a toast?" he repeated.

"Sure," said Mullins. Erik stood and raised his glass.

"With this glass of wine," he said, "I'd like to bust a rhyme. I'd like to celebrate, the peeps and the plates, the rhythms and the beats, the moments and the honey, a life off the streets. I wanna shout yo for the words that I find; I wanna shout louder, so you don't give no mind to the bull, S.H.I., R.I.P., longer-play, the business of the choosin of your every single day, and your every single pay if you're sitting or you're eating, or you're hyping or you're griping, or you're fighting or you're reading. If you're gonna singe your own shizzie, don't singe mine. I'm gonna keep myself going, I'm taking my time, off, scoff in the face to the "meaning-ride", and gimme the strength, to put up a side, you know to that ol' ad-vice, that ol' fool-spice, that ol' play-nice, that ol' brain lice. It won't get me sub-cu-ta-ne-ous, it won't get an ear and it won't get fuss. Cause I'm living day to day, and I don't need no more; I keep my homies close and their foot in my door. To them I toast, in the hot and the chilly; for them I pray, be it anywhere and Philly!"

We clapped and Erik guzzled his wine. Soon afterwards, dessert arrived. It was an enormous plate of baklava, sesame seed pastries and glasses of sweet mint tea. As we ate, Mullins entertained everyone with his tales of college adventures. Apparently, he and his friends had made frequent trips to the local breweries, and come back to campus drunk, trying to pick up girls.

"How successful was that enterprise?" Prateek inquired.

"Yeah, you know that's not really my thing," said Mullins. "I don't really do too well with the ladies."

"Are you gay?" asked Darcy.

"No," said Mullins. "Just haven't figured out women yet." We finished our dessert and Prateek told Ellen, Erik, and the Maestro about his investment performance over the last quarter. Apparently he would soon be able to afford a white BMW 7-series, if he sold his assets.

"When are you going to be fiscally responsible enough to join my fund?" he asked and laughed, "Ha ha ha."

They laughed back. No time soon.

On my left, I heard Darcy speak to Mullins. "I wish I were a gay man," she said.

"And why," he answered, "would you want to be a gay man?" He looked at her with bemused fascination. "Not that I'm homophobic or anything, but it's one of the most discriminated against groups there is."

"I don't know, I just do," she said, cocking her head shyly. She knew she was beautiful.

"That's big talk," added Erik, who was not really listening to Prateek.

"Oh!" said Darcy. She pouted and hung her head.

"What?" said Mullins.

"I'm not a very good person." She twitched her nose.

"Compared to whom?" Mullins asked.

"I don't know. Anybody. My sisters are much better people than I am."

"What does that mean? Of course you're a good person."

"No," she said. "What do you do? Are you a student?"

"I am, but not in school currently. I graduated two years ago."

"So how are you a student?"

"Well, I'm following Mark Twain's advice. He said: never let school get in the way of your education. There's all sorts of things to learn about in this world."

"Specifically?"

"I'm learning the good life. And I'm trying to pick a career for next year."

"A career for next year," Erik chimed, "Get in line!"

"That's not what I asked you," said Darcy to Mullins. "What do you do during the day?"

"Not much," he replied. "I'm a part-time librarian, I do some audio work, and at night I'm a baker."

"You bake? What?"

"Oh, all sorts of pastries, breads, cakes, you name it. You should come in and have a free sample sometime."

"Thank you, but I don't eat baked goods."

"What do you mean you don't eat baked goods?"

"I don't eat them. I don't eat any foods with butter, salt, sugar, or oil in them unless I absolutely have to."

"Oh. But didn't you eat them tonight?"

"No, I didn't. I only had some of the salad."

"Oh, I see."

"No you don't," she told him. "Or you wouldn't be baking."

"Fine," he said, not really understanding. "So what do you do in your spare time?"

"I like to walk around the city, go jogging, biking, hiking, all that kind of stuff."

"Wow you're really heath conscious."

"No. But if I don't exercise, I feel horrible."

"Who do you go biking and hiking and jogging with? The outdoors club at Franklin?"

"No, I go by myself. I need to spend time on my own."

"Why, do you live in a crazy dorm or something?"

"No, I live by myself."

"And you just like being on your own?"

"No, I need time on my own."

"Ok,"

There was a pause in their conversation. Then Mullins spoke.

"Do you know what you're doing after you graduate?"

"No, I don't like to think that far ahead."

"Well, do you want to work for an environmental company or something?"

"No, I don't think so. Maybe the government, but I'm not sure."

"To do environmental policy?"

"No. But I'm not sure what I would do."

"Well, you'll figure something out."

"No, I don't think so," she said. "I'm not capable of figuring it out. But eventually I'll have to make a choice. Then I'll live it."

"Ok!" said Mullins, not so sure it was. "You know, I've had a lot of career ideas this year too. You wanna know about them?"

"It can't hurt too much," said Darcy.

"What are you guys talking about so seriously?" interrupted Ellen.

Mullins laughed. "This and that."

"Listen," she said. "We have to pay the bill and get out of here. The Maestro is going to a concert, and Erik has to go to a poetry slam."

Darcy looked at her watch.

"Oh!" she said to Ellen. "I have to go too! Sorry!"

"Where are you off to?" Mullins asked. "Big party?"

"No," she said. "I have to go to the library."

"On Friday night?"

"It can't hurt." She pouted again.

"I don't know," said Mullins. "You don't think you might be missing something? How about you come out with Aaron and Ellen and I. We're going salsa dancing." This was news to me, but I let it slide.

"Can't," Darcy responded. "I have lots to do. Have fun though." She took her wallet out of her back-pack, dropped a twenty on the table, and put the wallet back. Then she got up, said goodbye, and thanked Prateek for inviting her. She found her coat by the door and left.

"Did she say goodbye?" Mullins asked. He leaned over to me. "She smelled like lavender," he whispered.

After paying the bill, we left Casablanca and went back to the Turf for port and chocolate. Prateek supplied the port from his personal collection, saying he was no longer interested in twelve year old port, and from now on only drank ports aged more than fifteen years.

"If you know what you're drinking, the younger stuff is just crap," he explained. Mind you, this was Prateek's first bottle of port ever. Still, he refused a glass of his "pitiable" twelve year liquor and was content to eat a few chocolates with some grapefruit juice. "This juice is superb," he said. "Superb."

*   *   *

The next day was Saturday, and, true to his parents wish, Mullins and I met with an alumnus of Franklin who was a lawyer. After I had suggested it to him twice, Mullins had arranged to have an "informational interview." Of course, the chances of me, a bass player, becoming a lawyer were slim, but Mullins convinced me to come along because he needed someone to listen in case he got distracted.

"Distracted with what?"

"You know, when people talk, I just start coming up with ideas in my head, and I forget everything. Now since I might want to be a lawyer, this guy might have something important to say and I can't miss it!"

I told him to take Prateek or Ellen, but he told me that since I trained my ears all day long I was thusly the best listener for the job. I couldn't argue with that.

Since it was raining and we had dressed up, Mullins convinced me that we should cab it over to 15th and Arch for the meeting. We did, and soon found ourselves in the impressive offices of Steven J. Biliamoria, Attorney at Law. The back wall of the office was an enormous book case stuffed with law books and an impressive looking stereo. In front of it was an enormous desk made entirely out of glass, a huge leather chair, and on our side of the desk, two stools with a coffee table in between.

A tall, clean shaven man in his fifties let us into the office. "Call me Steven," he told us. His voice was deep and he spoke fast. He was wearing black slip-on shoes, suit pants, a blue shirt with a white color, red-suspenders, and a tie with pictures of nude female breasts. He noticed us noticing his tie and laughed.

"This is my weekend tie. You have to have some fun when you work on Saturdays."

"You work every Saturday?" Mullins asked.

"I wouldn't call it "work" exactly because it's pro-bono. What do you boys study?" We told him. "And you're interested in the law?" We nodded. "The law is a great career," he said, "if you know what you're getting into. But a lot of lawyers hate their lives."

"Oh?" said Mullins.

"They do, they do. But they got into it for the wrong reasons. Money, you know, or because they didn't know what else to do. Bad reasons to do anything."

"Agreed," I said.

"What are the right reasons to become a lawyer?" asked Mullins.

"Because you love the law. Because you love our justice system. Because you're good at arguing and writing and speaking persuasively. But you better beware: the hours are long, and the work is tough, the competition is slick, and there is no room for fuck-ups." Steven folded his arms. "What I'm saying is, if you want to be a happy lawyer, you better have a damn good reason why you're here. Even a nice office looks like a prison if you're stuck there all day and night."

Steven answered a few more of our questions and then we left.

"Wow," said Mullins cynically. "I'm not sure if even a boob tie is a good trade for your weekends." The rain had stopped, and we were walking back to the Turf.

"A boob tie? Maybe he had a secretary in there too and we didn't know it," I joked.

"You know, I don't think I have any reason to be a lawyer," said Mullins, who hadn't really heard me.

"But isn't that exactly what you do in your storytelling, Mullins? Just like being a lawyer?"

"Maybe."

"You'd be good at it, at arguing and everything."

"At the risk of being arrogant," he said, "I think I could be good at a lot of things. It's more about how I want to spend my life." He looked at me.

"Well, I don't have it figured out, so don't look at me," I told him.

"Don't worry," he grinned. "Listen I'm going to see Drew this afternoon for some advice. I have one more interview with this Franklin group, and I want to stop at the library first to pick up some more CDs. So I'll go right on Chestnut."

That was fine with me, as I had an audition for the Philly Orchestra that afternoon. We split at Chestnut St. and I headed back to the Turf. When I got back to the apartment, it was empty. After a quick audition in the afternoon, I spent the rest of the day reading Nabokov's short stories and listening to Getz/Gilberto featuring Antonio Carlos Jobim. In the evening I went out to dinner with the Maestro who told me about his latest compositions and cigar acquisitions.

The apartment was still empty when I returned from dinner. I sat in the living room thinking for a while about nothing in particular. I don't know if I drifted off or what happened, but when I next checked my watch it was midnight, and time for me to go to bed. I could usually hear 18th Street from my room, but that evening the street and the apartment were especially quiet. I got into bed and listened to my breath until I fell asleep.

*   *   *

April 11th, Saturday, 10:13 am

Darcy,

Hi, this is Mullins. Do you remember me? It was nice to meet you on Friday at Casablanca, and it'd be great to continue our conversation. Would you by any chance be interested in having lunch Tuesday?

Yours,
Mullins

*   *   *

April 13th, Monday, 3:32 pm

Mullins—

Nice to meet you too. Lunch is fine
Tuesday. Where do you want to go?

*Darcy

                  *   *   *

April 13th, Monday, 4:46 pm

Dear Darcy,

I'm open to anything, as long as it
involves deliciousness. Here are three
suggestions: go to a food truck and eat in
the park; eat at the Blue Line Café; or,
have a refined lunch at L'Arbre—the French
restaurant in Old City. Just let me know
what's good for you, and when you're free.
I can make reservations if we need them.

Yours,
Mullins

                  *   *   *

April 14th, Tuesday, 7:46 pm

Mullins—

How about the Blue Line Café at noon? I
haven't been there. Where is it?

*Darcy

                  *   *   *

April 14th, Tuesday, 10:35 am

Dear Darcy,

It's on 46th and Spruce. I'll look forward
to seeing you at noon!

Yours,
Mullins

*   *   *

April 18th, Friday, 11:55 pm

Dear Darcy,

Thank you so much for having lunch with
me. I really had a fabulous time. How'd
your week go? How are you? Did your tests
and paper work out? I suspect they did,
considering most of the kids around here
don't have a clue what's going on. So,
even if you are the "horrible student" you
claim to be, you're still better than most
people, who I don't think can be called
students at all.
I'm doing really well. Since I last saw
you, I ran twenty miles, played three games
of squash, and re-shelved all the books at
the brail library. I also baked a lot of
pastries, but unfortunately, your dogmatic
insistence on "unclogged arteries" will
prevent you from enjoying them.
I was thinking: would you like to come
downtown this coming Monday or Tuesday
nights? Maybe we could catch dinner, and
also a concert if you're interested.
Let me know.

Yours truly,
Mullins

*   *   *

April 20th, Sunday, 2:31 pm

Mullins:

Thanks for lunch. Next time it's on me!
My tests were ok; at least they're over.
I'm glad to hear you are staying active.
Thanks for the invite, but I don't go out
during the week because I have too many
things to do. Maybe another time.

*Darcy

* * *

April 20th, Sunday, 3:35 pm

Dear Darcy,

I'm so glad you can't go out this week!
I can't either, what with Mary ill and
another child on the way. And this winter
was so rough, well I don't know if we'll
be able to afford the plantings for spring,
or scurvy medicine for young Jonathan. To
be frank with you, it'll be a miracle if
his mother, my beautiful wife, survives
through Thursday.

But Friday, well Friday is another story
altogether. I should be a free man Friday.
You too maybe?

Mullins

* * *

April 23, Wednesday, 4:45 pm

Mr. Mullins,

That's some story—you have quite an
imagination! Friday is ok for me, (if I

don't die of scurvy first) but I won't be
free until later because I'm going with a
friend to the art museum.

  *Darcy

                *   *   *

April 23, Wednesday, 6:04 pm

Darcy Dear,

Why don't we go to a jazz club near
Broad Street? Aaron tells me someone good
is playing. He also said the food is decent.
I'll come and pick you up at 39th and Locust,
near the post box, at 8 pm. If it's bad
weather, we can take a cab or something.

  Looking forward to seeing you,
  Mullins

                *   *   *

April 24, Thursday, 7:47 pm

Mullins,

That's fine with me. I don't know anything
about jazz though. By the way, my cell
phone number just in case is 215-287-7868.

  See you Friday.

  *Darcy

                *   *   *

When I asked Mullins about his lunch with Darcy, he
wouldn't say much. He told me he was adopting Ellen's strategy
for luck and that he would be thinking about it on his own. He

did, however, make me his strategic email consultant for the final stages of wooing his latest woman. I helped him with his wording and restaurant strategy. With our combined smarts, we figured, Darcy would be pulled in like a junk-yard car to an electric-magnet crane.

Otherwise, I didn't see Mullins much that week. On Tuesday evening he jogged over the bridge to Delaware and back. On Wednesday he played half the squash ladder and won most of his matches. On Thursday he worked in the library and baked all night.

*   *   *

While Mullins was looking up, Prateek was looking around. He'd just been rejected from several major investment companies in New York, and he wasn't sure where to go next. On Wednesday evening we met with Ellen at the Blue Fog, as he plotted his next move.

"I'm impressed Prateek," I told him. "You don't seem upset at all."

"Upset?" he asked. "Why would I be upset?"

"No return on your investments," Ellen joked, "I mean, in New York."

"Ha ha ha. Nope. I don't worry about that. I've invoked the Chestnut Doctrine."

"The Chestnut Doctrine," I said, "what's that?"

"You guys don't know about the Chestnut Doctrine? Oh yeah, I forgot. It's proprietary."

"What?" I said.

"Proprietary Aaron, that's…oh never mind," he said. "The Chestnut Doctrine's a policy position I researched and tested over the last three years and then patented. After proving extremely efficacious and worthwhile, I began using it full time in October."

"What's the doctrine?" Ellen demanded. "What's the Chestnut Doctrine?"

"Ha ha ha," Prateek responded. "You may know it already, although not by its proper name, the Chestnut Doctrine. Now I've patented it though, so you better consider the royalties before you use it."

"Ok fine," I said, "so what is it?"

"The Chestnut Doctrine is a long and dense philosophic argument which uses a number of classic paradigms and epistemological pathways to reveal a rule of life."

"And that rule is?"

"That rule is…" Prateek started.

"Yes?" I said.

"Fuck that shit!" he said, louder than he should have in the Blue Fog piano room.

"Huh? That's it?"

"Oh yes," said Prateek. "And there ain't nothing better. Ha ha ha."

"I like it," said Ellen.

"Yeah," Prateek responded. "I came up with the initial idea Freshman year, after I concluded that the opinions of most people were completely worthless."

Prateek was righteous. But what was wrong with applying an absurd formula to justify his indignation with an absurd world?

"That's funny." Ellen took out her notebook. "I'm going to use that."

"Oh yes," Prateek instructed. "It works for understanding most situations. But you can only use it when you can say it with genuine joy, that's the only rule. Because that's when you know you're right."

"You know Prateek, you weren't the only one of us to come up with a doctrine," I told him.

"But I bet I'm the only one of us to patent it," he responded.

"Fine," I said. "Mine is called the 34th Street rule."

"The 34th Street rule? What happened on 34th street?" Ellen asked.

"Oh you don't want to know," I responded. "The important thing is, like the Chestnut Doctrine, the 34th Street rule is based on lots of experience and thinking, and it's good to use in many situations, as long as you have your inner joy."

"And what sayeth the 34th Street rule, then?" Prateek asked.

"Bitch!" I yelled, louder than I should have in the Blue Fog piano room. "Now you have to understand," I continued. "You can't use this rule to hate anybody. Only to understand them."

"Brilliant," said Ellen sarcastically.

"No, no, this is good stuff," I told her. "The profundities of my education summed up in one word."

"Yeah," she taunted. "We have to wonder about that, don't we?"

"To which you may apply another fine application of the Chestnut Doctrine," said Prateek. "So long as you recognize its founder. Checks and credit cards accepted."

Chapter Ten

On the last Friday in April, Mullins sat tall at the breakfast table. He was pleasant and charming, and he seemed ready for anything. The apartment smelled like the cool turpentine I had spilled on the floor. But the morning light was warm and painted the kitchen orange. Mullins sat across from Prateek, silent and smiling. It was unusual for him to be noiseless now; normally he blathered on while the rest of us went about our morning business. In fact, the mornings were his favorite time to explicate this or that baking method or to pontificate about the origin of certain Japanese verbs. Sometimes he even would talk to us in Japanese, in a sort of violent way. I never knew why, but he seemed to think it was funny.

This Friday morning, he didn't blab and he didn't speak Japanese. He sat peacefully, eating slowly, and grinning to himself. As I cleaned up the turpentine, I noticed that he looked proud, even powerful. He was sitting straighter than normal, with relaxed shoulders and ankles crossed under his chair. He was savoring each bite of oatmeal. And when he spoke, he spoke slowly, in a calm and controlled voice.

"How IS everyone this morning?"

Prateek looked up from the pink pages of the Financial Times. "I'm getting fucked in the market," he answered, "but I might have a job offer for next year."

"Hey, congratulations," Mullins said, without a hint of envy.

"Yup. I'm going to go to NYC today to pick up the offer letter and to decide if I want the job."

"Awesome!" Ellen tussled his hair. "We'll be crashing at your place next year."

"No prob," said Prateek, who continued reading the editorial page.

"In return we'll take you out to the opera and to dinner," she said. "Oh wait, you'll be at the office all night every night. Never mind. We'll send you a frozen pizza."

Prateek rolled his eyes.

"And how are you today Ellen?" Mullins asked slowly.

"Oh, ship-shape and peachy," she said, tossing her hair. "This morning between 6 and 8 am I wrote four essays, re-catalogued my library, synthesized three of my to-do lists, and made your breakfast. And, I cancelled classes today because I'm going to the Morris Arboretum."

"What are you going to do at the Arboretum?"

"Research," she answered. "I have decided that next year, I will grow all my own spices and herbs."

Mullins chuckled slowly. "A spice dream?"

"You bet. Then I'm going to the art museum," she continued—"to see the Degas exhibition."

"A Degas exhibition? I didn't know about that."

"Oh yes, lots of dancers—fat ones, thin ones, and nude ones."

"Cheeky," said Prateek.

"Indeed." Mullins stretched out his back. "And you?" He looked at me. "How did you sleep?"

I told him I was fine. I was spending the day at a bass lesson, conducting class and, as usual, in the practice room. I was still working on Bach's cello suites and trying to put some pieces together for my recital. Then I was going to a jazz band rehearsal at the Annenberg center. The Franklin University band, I told him, had a few musicians and a lot of holes. They were paying me to sit in on a few tunes.

"Nice!" he responded.

"And you, Mullins, you seem on top of things today," Ellen remarked.

"Do I?" he asked. "Am I not on top of things everyday?"

"Um…" said Prateek, not looking up from his paper.

"It's funny," said Mullins, "I can't imagine feeling any other way than I feel right now."

"You always say that," said Ellen. "What are you up to today?"

"This and that," he said with a smirk. "This and that."

"Yeees?" she pried.

"Oh, some baking, and you know, I'll probably read something nice, maybe listen to some music, take a stroll, eat something…" His voice faded and he finished his last bites of oatmeal. "Breakfast was great," he thanked her. "Delicious as usual."

Shortly thereafter we took our showers and got dressed. Ellen found her bus to the Arboretum, Prateek found his train to New York City, and I found my cab to my bass lesson.

And Mullins? Mullins floated off to work.

"Aaron, I'll see you later," he said to me, as my cab pulled to the sidewalk. He swaggered off, shoulders back and arms swinging. His bag seemed unusually small, and his upper body moved back and forth as he walked. Right before he turned the corner onto Walnut, he raised his hand to wave, without turning around. I knew he was smiling, and I waved back.

*   *   *

Ellen had suggested eating dinner at the Banana Leaf to hear about Prateek's trip to New York, but there was a freak hailstorm just as we were about to leave, so we stayed in and cooked seasoned chicken breasts on the George Forman Grill. We cooked an extra one for Mullins, but when he didn't arrive, we devoured it ourselves. Actually, we knew that he was going out with Darcy that night. Well, Ellen knew. I had forgotten about the emails and failed to notice such things as: cologne, a haircut, new clothes, shined shoes, and a ring.

"Are you blind?" she asked. Apparently I was, but I reminded her that blind people have excellent ears for music. Not distracted by superficialities of dress or scent, we focus on the profound melodies of life.

Ellen nodded 'yes' and then said: "B.S."

Ok, she was right. But more important, I asked her, what did she think about Mullins' chances? Wasn't she excited for him? And Prateek, he was friends with Darcy, what had she been telling him?

"No idea," said Prateek, "she hasn't said anything to me." Ellen nodded in agreement.

"Well," I responded, "after such a long time, he's got to get a break in his luck at some point."

Then we talked about moving out, and who would be taking on the Turf next year. We would start interviewing candidates soon, as not just anyone was acceptable to carry our mantle.

After we finished dinner, we cleaned the kitchen and looked at the weather outside. The sky seemed to have cleared, so we decided to take a nighttime stroll around the park.

When we got outside, we found the air moist and warm, even as the remnants of the hail lay dissipating on the street. As we left our building, I suddenly felt the same freedom I had felt at the beginning of the year, even though I didn't have a job or know where I would be in a few months. It didn't matter what the future was: I loved Philadelphia, and I loved that moment. Prateek and Ellen were next to me, and though I can't say for sure, I think they were feeling the same thing.

As we walked around the west side of Rittenhouse Square, Ellen said "I've caved in. It's too good." She laughed self-consciously.

"You're going to Paris?" Prateek asked. Ellen had recently applied to teach English there. She would have minimal commitments and maximum time to enjoy herself. I had actually suggested the idea to her earlier in the year, but she had derided it as unproductive in her quest to solve the world's education problems. She seemed to have changed her mind.

"How can I not?" she answered. "Have you ever stood at Trocadero at night and watched the lights of the Eiffel tower?"

"If I remember correctly," Prateek replied, "that was Hitler's favorite spot in Paris."

I punched Prateek in the shoulder. He laughed: "Ha ha ha."

"It was!" he insisted, "he was going to build his palace there." I punched him again. "But," he conceeded, "I'm sure you'd make a great dictator."

"It just seems perfect." Day-dreaming aloud, Ellen had not really heard him. "It's a year for me to catch up with my reading, to make contacts, and to eat and drink like ze French do. I'll only have to work for twelve hours a week; the rest will be mine to prepare so I can come back and start schools."

And the moral side of it, I asked. That was what worried her before? Was she wasting a year in which she could be learning about education elsewhere?

"I don't know" she added. "I can't know. All I can hope is that this year will be a chance to reflect and get my ideas in order, which will help me when I really get started."

"Besides," I said, "when else will you have a chance to spend free time living in Paris?"

"Are you kidding?" she retorted. "I plan to spend at least half of my life there doing nothing except enjoying art and that city. An education reformer needs constant inspiration."

Prateek shook his head. "Well! We'll see who eats better!"

"What's this!" said Ellen, and gave him a big hug. "Are you taking that job in New York?! Are you living on Fifth Avenue and running fast with the fifteen dollar martini crowd?"

"Sort of."

I asked him what he meant. For some reason, I was nervous.

"The guys in New York gave me an offer," he said, "but it wasn't for New York."

"What was it?" Ellen asked "What was it for?"

"Saaaaan Francisco!" he yelled. Ellen and I were shocked into silence for a second, and then we burst in congratulations. He accepted these with a typical smirk, as he had planned it all along. Then he explained:

"Apparently the company had already accepted enough people for their New York office in the traditional interview cycle. But they still had some spots left in their new San Fran office. Since I'm on the West Coast, I'll have fewer long days, and I'll get to really take advantage of the city."

"Prateek that is incredible!" said Ellen. "We will definitely be crashing at your place for eats and arts and opera." He could count me in too, I said.

I was happy for my friends, but I couldn't conceive that they were both moving thousands of miles in opposite directions from the Turf. Still, I would be excited to be able to visit two of my favorite cities when I could. After more discussion of Prateek's new job, Ellen asked me about my possibilities. I didn't have anything solid yet, I told her.

We made a left turn down Locust, and strolled almost a mile to Independence Hall. Prateek and Ellen talked about finding housing and meeting people in their new cities. I listened to them, and to the city, wondering where I would end up and what I would do there.

We sat on benches outside Independence Hall and enjoyed the evening. We didn't talk much. We just sat in the breeze. I won't say I didn't get the urge to talk. I did. But I ignored it, and kept things for myself.

Eventually we got tired and decided to go back. Prateek and I each took one of Ellen's arms, and we waltzed up Walnut Street, past the dark areas around Jefferson, past the glamour of Broad Street, past the fancy restaurants and exclusive clubs on the way to Rittenhouse, and finally into Rittenhouse itself. It was Philadelphia at night, and in that moment, it was my entire world.

As we ambled around the square, the wind puffed the trees and the leaves that had survived the storm. By this time, most of the lights in the buildings around the square had faded. The night hung low in Philadelphia and the moon lit our path. As we walked the last few blocks, we could hear only our steps, a few passing cars, and the sound of each other's breathing.

*   *   *

I went to bed, but only for two hours. At around quarter of four, I was woken by a light thumping on the apartment door. Eventually it stopped and the door opened. But I was too tired to care, and I went back to sleep.

About ten minutes later I heard another thump and then a loud crack. It sounded like someone had knocked the table over and then stepped on a bunch of peanut shells. But I didn't care; I was still too tired.

I went to sleep again, but I was awoken shortly afterwards by moaning outside my room. At first I thought it was part of my dream. Eventually I realized it wasn't.

I got up. Maybe it was a robber, I thought. I grabbed my squash racquet and unzipped the case. Brandishing my weapon, I crept to the door and reached for the knob. I paused for a minute and listened for the intruder. I didn't hear anything.

I opened the door, and starting to walk into the dark kitchen. But I didn't get far before I ran into Mullins.

He was lying face down in front of a toppled kitchen table.

What happened?! Was he ok?! I reached down slowly, and touched his sides. He moaned.

"Aghh!" he said, weakly.

He was alive, but he seemed to be in bad shape. Then I noticed he was missing a shoulder. Instead there was a huge bump in his back. His arm was behind his back! I had to take him to Franklin Hospital. It was just across the bridge. I yelled for Ellen and Prateek who quickly came out of their rooms. Luckily, Prateek had stayed over because our walk ended late.

Ellen screamed: "Mullins!" Seeing him on the floor, she ran over to him, hysterical. I turned to Prateek and told him to grab her. He picked up the table first, then he did.

With some difficulty, I picked Mullins up and put him on the table on his stomach. He was holding onto his left elbow with his right arm. But his left arm was totally out of place and there was something wrong with his back. Picking him up, I also noticed that he was freezing cold, that his clothes were drenched with water, and that his body was mostly limp.

Ellen broke free of Prateek, grabbed some paper towels and pressed them to Mullins' face. Then she hugged him, trying to give him some warmth. Prateek ran and got a towel from the bathroom. He said we should get Mullins' clothes off. But I didn't want to mess with the arm, especially if we were going out again.

I told them I was going to the hospital with Mullins. I told Prateek to put Mullins on my back. I knew I could make it there. I had been carrying a contrabass on my back all across the country. But first I ran to my room and threw on some clothes from the floor. I grabbed my coat and threw it over Mullins.

NOW, I told them. They got him on my back, piggyback style. I got my hands under his legs and we went.

They followed me out the door. We looked for a cab, but the cabs were full, or else they didn't want to stop for a broken kid.

So we ran, the three of us, Mullins on my back, across the

Walnut Street bridge. I couldn't see Ellen behind me, but I heard her bathrobe fluttering in the wind and her slippers rubbing on the pavement. Nor could I see Prateek, but I heard him struggling to run in his flip-flops. He kept losing one or the other flip-flop, and each he time would curse, find it, and run even faster to catch up. It was almost funny, but I didn't laugh.

Halfway over the bridge I stopped hearing. I saw only the lights of Chestnut Street bridge and the Market Street bridge reflecting beautifully in the water. I saw the Post-office and I saw Thirtieth Street Station gleaming from the West bank. I saw the river running, and the stars in the sky. And I saw that cast-iron bridge in front of me, that railroad bridge painted red and blue, painted before anyone could remember.

Everything was silent until the bridge. But as I ran underneath, all the speakers blasted, full force. I heard the train, I heard Mullins yelling, I heard my breath, I heard Prateek, I heard Ellen, and I heard what I thought were Cathedral bells. At four in the morning?

I made it to 34th Street and to the hospital. At first the receptionist tried to make fuss about Mullins not having health care. Prateek would hear none of it, and taking out his massive wallet of credit cards, he tossed it at the receptionist like a baseball.

Just before Mullins was admitted, he whispered to me that it was completely unfair for this to have happened to him, and then gave me a faint smile. At that time, I was too worried about him even to listen, and I shushed him until the nurses came with the stretcher. After we sent him off, Ellen, Prateek, and I collapsed onto the uncomfortable and squeaky waiting room chairs. We didn't talk. Ellen was sobbing, and I took her in my arms. I don't remember much else except that the TV blared in the background, and we hid ourselves from it and closed our eyes.

*   *   *

About thirty minutes later, a tall African-American woman came out of the ER and found the three of us in a heap. She asked for me, and I got up to talk to her.

"I'm Dr. Hartmann. Mr. Mullins would like to see you," she said.

I asked her if everything was all right. She said Mullins would live, but that she didn't know what would happen with his arm. "Mullins has to be awake for the procedure, so try to distract him a little bit. Now put these on." She gave me some scrubs. As I put them on, I told Ellen and Prateek that they had better go back to the Turf and call Mullins' parents.

"We don't want to leave," Ellen pleaded. But there was nothing they could do, I told them. I would call as soon as I had news.

I followed the doctor into the emergency room. To my surprise, it wasn't one room. It was really a series of small radiating chapels around a huge central nave. In the central room was a group of nurses' desks, and a bunch of machinery you hoped to never need. The doctor led me around the corner and past a curtain into Mullins' room.

He didn't have much privacy or coziness. The walls were curtains. The bed was white, and the nurse in the corner was dressed in white too.

Mullins was sitting up, and he looked terrible. He had a couple of tubes sticking out of his right arm, and a huge brace holding the left part of his back away from the bed. His shirt had been cut off, and his left shoulder was gone. And Mr. Mullins, I should say, had a huge grin on his face.

I told the doctor she had to give him credit for smiling.

"Honey" she said to me, "we got so many drugs in him he doesn't know where his mouth is."

I asked how I was supposed to talk to him.

"You're not supposed to talk to him," she said. "You're supposed to keep him together when we put his arm back."

So be it. I sat on his right side and grabbed his good hand.

He looked at me and squeezed. I squeezed back. He was going to be all right, I told him, but they had to fix his arm.

He tried to answer, but he couldn't seem to make his mouth move properly. "Quiet," I told him, "just concentrate on your breathing."

After a minute or so, four burly guys in white pants, white shirts, and white shoes came into the room. Two moved to each side of the bed, and I saw the doctor rolling up her sleeves and putting on gloves. This, I thought, is going to hurt. Mullins must have thought so too, but he only managed to spit. The nurse didn't clean it up.

The doctor walked over to the left side of the bed and gave me a look.

"Look at me!" I yelled to him. He did, and we made fierce eye contact. Just then the orderlies pressed down on his body and the doctor grabbed his arm.

"Keep looking!" I said, and squeezed his hand harder. He kept looking. At first his eyes burned with fire, then they welled with tears. But he kept looking, and he didn't blink. After a moment the tears left his eyes, and I saw the fire again, which the tears had not extinguished. And then it was over, and Mullins closed his eyes.

*   *   *

"We are," Ellen once prophesied, "the architects of our own lives. We build the types of rooms we want, and decide who gets to join us there." Ellen was half-right. You can open the door for another person, but you can't make them walk through it.

Mullins had to stay in bed for a few days after he returned from the hospital. Ellen and I made his meals while he was home, and served them to him. At lunchtime on the second day he was back, I went into his room to join him while he ate. As I was handing him his tray, he threw Madame Bovary at his desk. He had finally finished it that morning.

I put La Boheme on the stereo, and then I sat down in his chair to talk. Before I could say anything, the phone rang. I answered it, and it was for Mullins. I handed the receiver to him in his bed, and stayed in his room in case he wanted to hang up soon. He listened for a minute, said yes, that's wonderful thank you very much, that he was currently a little out-of-it but that he would be in touch. He handed the phone back to me to hang up.

"What was that?" I asked. "Parents?"

He smiled with half his mouth.

"What?" I almost asked again, and then I stopped myself. I didn't want to pry too much. Mullins hadn't yet talked about his experience, and we hadn't wanted to bring it up either.

He took a deep breath. "I just won a scholarship to travel the world for two years learning about stories and storytelling. All expenses paid." My jaw dropped in awe, and I heard a scream from the kitchen behind me. Ellen had overheard and she immediately alerted Prateek.

Ellen and the Senator came in Mullins' room and cheered for about ten minutes. "You're golden," Prateek kept yelling, "Golden!"

Mullins didn't move very much, but he cracked a smile with half his mouth.

"We should all drink to celebrate Mullins!" said Prateek.

"Love to," Mullins croaked, "but I'm not supposed have alcohol for a while. Why don't you guys go have one on me at the Blue Fog." Ellen and Prateek protested, saying they wanted to stay and drink with Mullins, but he insisted they go out and celebrate. "Someone should," he told them, and so they went. They weren't being frivolous; we all knew they would discuss Mullins' future in depth. We also knew that at this moment Mullins needed rest and peace.

When they left, I told Mullins my congratulations. I told him he had done it. Then I gave him a hug. That was a bad idea. He screeched in pain. But when I stood up, he smiled.

"It's amazing," he said. "Never, never would I have thought, or hoped…I mean, I had no ambitions, no idea that I would get this…at the interview I didn't even care because there was no hope. You remember—that was the day we talked to the lawyer."

"Yeah," I said. "Funny, that."

Mullins looked at me for a moment, and then, to my surprise, he began to cry. He kept his gaze straight on me, as tear after tear ran down his face. Then the stream increased, and his head began to jerk forward in short bursts. I got up and gave him the tissue box from his desk. He tried to talk, but his words were lost in his emotions.

Eventually he got his voice back. It took him a few tries, but finally he spoke to me:

"Aw man, it's good to have you guys. You can't imagine how I fucked it up this past week, and I mean, I might be dead if it wasn't…"

I looked at him, arm in cast and sling, drugs by his bedside. I smiled and told him he could buy me a drink later.

He laughed, but with tears in eyes. "You know what I realized, Aaron," he said. "I had no idea what I was doing."

I didn't say anything. I didn't know what to say.

He looked at the wall and continued. "I worked myself up about Darcy, to a place where I had no right to go. During that week, I was so glad to imagine her that I became another person." He looked at me. "Did you know?"

Sort of, I told him. But I didn't think it was serious.

"It was," he said. "In my head. And that's where it came apart."

I wanted to be as sympathetic as possible. I told him it could happen to anyone. Not knowing what "it" was, this was a risky statement.

"I don't know," he answered. I saw his right hand draw into a fist, not in a threatening way, but revealing his pain. After a few seconds, he took a deep breath and let his hand loose.

"Do you know what happened?" he asked. "How could you!" he continued and then unthinkingly tried to scratch his nose with his left arm. He couldn't, and only yelped in pain. I laughed.

"Well, you know," he remarked "we were supposed to meet, Darcy and I, at 39th and Locust Walk. You remember the emails. Anyway, I had been looking forward to it my whole week. Fuck, I had been looking forward to it my whole life."

He paused, and took a breath.

"It's just, this whole year…and I thought I deserved it! If anyone! God, it sounds horrible, but it was so fucking unfair!" He was protesting to the whole world. But there was only me, sitting next to his bed, listening.

"On paper, on paper I thought, I look so fucking good! I swear to you. You know it!" He began to cry again, and I got him some more tissues.

"Calm down," I told him. "You're OK now."

Slowly, he relaxed. Actually I think he *wanted* to be worked up in anger, to expend his frustration. But we'd had enough pain. Just then the sun broke through the clouds and shone on him through the window, which helped. It's hard to be angry in the warm afternoon sunlight.

"So I did it, you know," he told me, as a matter of fact. "I was so psyched for this date. I got a haircut, clothes, everything. I even got cologne. I never wear cologne. So I got dressed up, and I felt so nice. I felt handsome, or whatever, and I was really ready. I was confident that it would be great, that she would see how great I was, and that there would be love." He exhaled. "I know it sounds incredibly stupid, trite even."

"It doesn't matter," I said, "it's your story."

"It was hailing that evening, you know," he continued. "Really hailing. But I didn't even notice. I felt like the sun was following me around all day. Even when the bitch who asks me to take the raisins out of the pain aux raisins came into the shop, I just smiled and took every single one out. She was flabbergasted." Mullins laughed. "I told Clive I needed to leave a little early, and he told me I could go whenever I wanted. I always listen to what he tells me, but I don't even think I heard his answer. In fact, the whole day I was just in my own world, with Darcy." He grimaced.

"Darcy. So I walked after work to 39th and Locust. Oh yeah, I forgot, I went out during lunch and bought flowers, actually roses for her. She studies the environment, right, I thought she would like flowers. Hmm, it didn't seem cheesy at the time. So I walked with the flowers from work, really slowly. Each step was like walking through a cloud. I saw a couple of people I knew, and when they said 'hi' and waved, I smiled at them and nodded my head. I was full, completely full. I thought: oh those people waving to me, they can feel my happiness even across the street. I knew they could." Mullins stopped to wipe his chin. I looked out the window for a moment, just to slow things down. It was a lot to say all at once.

"I got there a little early," he continued. I looked back to Mullins, who was staring at the wall behind me. "Even though I thought I was walking slow, I was probably walking fast, and I had given myself plenty of time. There was no way in hell I would be late for something like that. I thought it would be a critical moment in my life, where every thing would change, and be completely different from then on." He laughed. "My problems with girls were over, and I would be able to become my best self, love the whole world, all that. I was exploding, and I thought it was only a matter of time before I became the god inside me."

I didn't understand. "Was it love?" I asked him. "Did you think it was?"

"It was, but how could it have been!" he almost shouted. "I didn't know her at all. She hadn't told me anything to make me think she cared for me. She hadn't even told me anything to make me think I was a great guy." He smiled at me. "She was right about one thing though," he added sheepishly. "I have a good imagination."

That, he did, I agreed. That, he certainly did.

He smiled with half his mouth. But then he pushed his cheeks up, to squeeze a few tears from his eyes. He went on with his story:

"The sun was out when I left work. But I guess sometime during sunset, it must have disappeared. I was skipping in the clouds, so I didn't even pay attention. I assumed the sun was following at its own pace. It wasn't. In place of the sun, dark clouds rolled over me. I didn't even notice. Maybe I just thought it was nighttime.

"I got to 39th and Locust early because I'm always early, and I like being early. I was probably ten minutes early. So I waited patiently. At first I sung a song. Then I thought it wouldn't be so cool if she arrived and found me singing in the middle of the city. So I whistled for a while, you know, some Nat King Cole tunes, and some Louis Armstrong. That stuff is *the* love music, I don't care what anyone else says," he chuckled, somewhat heavily.

"I was still floating, and I didn't really notice when eight o'clock passed. And I hardly noticed at 8:05 when it started to rain. At 8:10 I checked my watch and saw that she was a little late. Also, I was starting to get pretty wet and a little cold, but I didn't mind. I thought: we'll just take a cab down to the club instead of walking. Everything was fine."

He laughed and then shook his head violently.

"At quarter past, I started to wonder what was happening. Surely she would show up, I thought. Maybe something terrible had happened to her! That's how naïve I was, I started to really worry about her safety! At 8:20 I called her on her cell phone. Her phone rang and rang, so I knew it was on. But she didn't pick up, and it went to her voicemail." Mullins sped up. He was talking fast now, and his eyes were moving back and forth, no longer looking at me. I noticed his right hand and saw that it was again clenched around his blanket.

"I left her a message. I must have sounded like a complete idiot. I said something like: 'Hi Darcy, this is Mullins. It's a little after we were supposed to meet, and I don't see you here, so I just wanted to make sure you're ok, and that nothing happened to you. Just give me a call when you get this. I'll wait though, right here.' That's what I said. What an idiot. 'I'll wait,' God damn. So I waited. I waited in the middle of a terrifying storm. The thunder cracked and the hail beat me on the head. But I kept looking around, turning to see if she was coming from any direction. If anybody was walking up the street I ran to see if it was her, or if she was behind them. Seeing this drenched guy with drooping flowers must have freaked them out, and they shied away from me. But I couldn't get shelter, you know. There's a small park at that corner, and there's nowhere to escape getting wet. By around 8:30, I was soaking wet. My coat was wool, and it seemed to have soaked up ten gallons of water. My shoes were full of water too, and my hair was plastered to my head. I started shivering, but I didn't even notice because my mind was racing and worrying about Darcy.

"Then I called the Turf, to see if you guys were at home, or if you had heard from her. I talked to Ellen, and she said she had run into Darcy and Erik the rapper at the art museum earlier that evening, but that she hadn't heard from her since. Maybe, I thought, maybe she forgot and just went straight to the jazz club. Was that what the email had said? I couldn't remember! Maybe her phone had died, and she just went straight to the jazz club. Oh shit, I thought, I've really screwed up! She's waiting for me, and she's been waiting for half an hour! Oh shit Oh shit! So what did I do, I ran down to Chestnut Street to try to get a cab." He shook his head.

"And of course, it's the same shit. You can never find a cab when you need one."

I knew it, I told him, and I laughed.

"So I ran around trying to find a cab. I ran like a madman, flopping around in my wet shoes and my wet coat. Hell, if I'd been a cab driver, I wouldn't have picked me up either, except if I saw the look on my face. You can't imagine how I felt.

"Since I couldn't find a cab, I decided to run, to run down Chestnut Street until one passed me. So I started running, as fast as I could. In the hail, I was running in my good coat and my good shoes, no longer good. God I must have looked like a fool. I kept checking my phone, and I called again a few times to see if she would answer. She didn't, and I kept running. Around 31st street, under the railroad bridge, I finally got a cab. I told him to drive me to the Chameleon Jazz Café as fast as possible. He complied, but he probably would have driven recklessly fast anyway. I didn't care. I didn't care about anything, except getting there. My heart was pounding so hard I thought it would come out of my chest, and my stomach seemed to have leaped into my neck. Eventually he let me off on Broad Street, and I threw a ten dollar bill at him and ran off. I found the alley of the Chameleon, and I ran down the street so fast that I splashed in all the puddles and got myself even dirtier and wetter. My new clothes were ruined I knew, but I didn't care."

Mullins had risen in his bed, and now he was sitting straight up, staring without blinking. I'm not sure at this point whether he knew I was there. He had picked up more and more speed, and now there was tremendous emotion in his voice.

"Finally, finally, finally I reached the club. I was ready to see her standing there, to run up and tell her I was so sorry, that I had screwed, but at least now we could be together and…all that." Mullins stopped talking. He was choked up, and he was crying again.

"She wasn't there," he managed to get out. "The Café was closed for construction." Then he was crying again, and he hit the wall so hard with his right hand that I thought he would break his fingers.

"Aghhhh!" he yelled, enraged.

"Calm!" I told him. "Breath! You can't afford to hurt yourself any more. You're made out of gold now!"

He looked at me without blinking. "I was standing in the hail, but I didn't notice," he said. She hadn't called me. I couldn't

reach her. I tried again. Finally I called the Franklin directory
and got Erik's number. He told me that Darcy had gone home
a few hours ago, and that she had said she was going to sleep.
I hung up. I couldn't talk. I couldn't move. The hail was in my
clothes now, but I still didn't notice it. I couldn't imagine what
had happened. I must have stood there for an hour."

"Jesus," I said. "Why didn't you come back?"

"I did. I walked back to the Turf. But I couldn't go in. I
couldn't stand the thought of it. So I kept walking. I walked all
the way into West Philadelphia in the hail, all the way to the
park and that statue of Dickens. I sat there for a while, and then
I took the subway downtown. I was still too wet to go inside
anywhere but I wandered around Penn's Landing like a drunk
fool, alone and freezing. Eventually I got really cold. I couldn't
feel my legs, and I knew I had to go back. Somehow I stumbled
back to the Turf. That must have been around three something.
God, I had been wandering around all night. I was mindless and
out of control."

"Damn!"

"When I got back, I couldn't go in my room. I just walked
around the apartment in a mindless stupor, bumping into walls
and tables. I was thinking, but I wasn't. At some point, and I
don't remember why, I got up on the kitchen table. I walked on
top of it thinking my life is shit because God or whoever cursed
me. Why did he screw me like that?"

"Yeah?" I said.

"And then...and then...I don't remember anything after
that." Mullins stopped talking. His head slumped. The sun had
gone behind a cloud, and it was almost dark in his room.

*　　*　　*

Prateek and Ellen came back for dinner and we spent the
whole evening with Mullins. I told him about opening my door,
and about taking him to the hospital. He thanked us again, and

said he couldn't even tell us how grateful he felt. Around eight, we left Mullins to go to sleep. But as I walked through the door, he told me to leave his light on. Prateek went home and Ellen went to Amador's. I stayed around to read, in case he needed me. But he didn't, and I went to sleep around midnight.

The next morning, I knocked on his door to see if he needed anything, and when I walked in the room, his light was still on. I don't think he had slept. I helped him get to the bathroom and made him some breakfast. Then I opened his window and we sat in his room. While we were eating he said to me,

"I did a lot of thinking last night."

"Oh yeah?"

"Yeah."

"Just about Darcy or what?"

"It's not about Darcy. Darcy was nothing. She didn't matter at all."

"She didn't?"

"No. It wasn't Darcy." He took a deep breath. "What she did was extremely fucking rude, but I should have been able to deal with it. I shouldn't have gone crazy. That's what I thought about last night. This year—all the girls—it was me. Me. I know it sounds ridiculous, Aaron, but I think I had no idea what I was doing to myself until this happened."

"Yeah?"

"Yeah. I mean, I think you guys told me: you're not going to get anywhere by dramatizing. All my storytelling was bullshit."

"That's not true Mullins, you're a great story teller, and everybody always loved it."

"At my own fucking expense! Aaron, I built fantasy worlds that entertained everyone, but I had to live in them!"

"You did?"

"All the stories were about *me!*" he said. "They were about what had happened to me, but they were also about how I was telling the story! I was making my story as I was telling them. I was making my life. But I didn't realize it."

"Yeah?"

"I never thought what happened would have happened. Never. But it's because during all that storytelling, all of that drama—I never once listened to myself."

"Yeah?"

"My expectations were way out of line. The world is upside-down sometimes, and you can't fight it. You have to keep on choogling, and sometimes you even have to live upside-down for a while."

"Yeah."

He took the stuffed Watch Owl from behind his bed, opened the window with his right arm, and threw the bird into the street.

*　　*　　*

Mullins knew more now. He had learned from hurting himself. But did he believe what he was saying? Did he believe it enough to see who he really was? Would he live what he had learned?

I don't know. That story is yet to be told. But as I write these final words, I realize that I have my own story to worry about. What's written here isn't just about Mullins—no, Mullins is just an actor in the drama. It's Aaron Richards now, his story that is hiding in the weave of my words. I've made my memory, and I have to live it, even if it's upside-down. So I'm going to read over what I've written. I'm going to learn what I can. It's Spring in Philadelphia, and it's my story now.

Epilogue

"All right man!" Drew told me. "I haven't felt like that since Rocky III."

"You pulled it off," Prateek nodded solemnly. "Honestly, I didn't think you had a chance."

"Thanks Prateek," I said, "It's always nice to know I had your vote of confidence."

"Finally!" said Ellen. "It's over!"

"Thanks Ellen."

"I didn't even help you this time." Mullins hugged me with one arm. Then he cleared his throat and said to everyone: "three cheers for Aaron: even if he never achieves fame or fortune, he will always be loved by his friends. And that," he said, "is more than we can ever ask."

We all cheered and drank champagne. I had just joined my buddies at the Blue Fog for a celebratory lunch. That morning I had performed an intense program of Brahms, Beethoven, and Bach at my graduation recital, and everyone seemed to have been inspired. Actually, the Maestro was slightly offended that I didn't include any of his music, but I couldn't please everyone. What I had done made me happy, and anyway it was over.

We ate lunch slowly, but it wasn't slowly enough. Too soon we found ourselves ambling around Philadelphia, going to a Bar-B-Q and outdoor concert at Franklin, eating dinner at the

Banana Leaf, and catching a late film at the Fitz. The weather was perfect and that night we opened the windows at the Turf and drank champagne until dawn. It was our last night together. The next day was the Franklin graduation and the dreaded move-out. Our sub-letters were taking over the apartment and we were spreading around the city to stay with friends for the next few days.

*   *   *

Graduation day was sunny and hot. Mullins and I sat in the stands with binoculars trying to spot Ellen, Prateek, and our other friends.

"I think I see Erik," he said. "He's standing up and he seems to be rapping to the people in his aisle. They look scared."

I laughed. "Look," I pointed, "there's Maestro and the Bop on the stage. But I can't see Ellen and Prateek," I said.

Just then a waft of cigar smoke rose from field. When it cleared, I saw my friends. Amador, Ellen, and Prateek were sitting together with the Veterinary students, despite the fact that none of them were in the veterinary school. Amador and Prateek were smoking cigars, and they seemed to have acquired an enormous toothbrush balloon.

The band marched in, and everyone stood for the national anthem. Then, after a few trite speeches and some honorary awards, the students were declared graduated. They whooped and cheered, and Prateek accidentally burst the balloon, which shot right up to the stage into the face of the Provost, who was not well-liked. Everyone laughed, and cheered some more, and then the band marched the students off the field and into the rest of their lives.

*   *   *

We made the most of our last few days in Philly. On the last evening, with the aid of the Maestro and his lock-picking skills, Ellen, Prateek and I climbed to the roof of the Franklin college building to watch the sun set on our city, and on our last year living together. We brought a bright-colored Mexican blanket and a selection of chilled beers from the subcontinent.

The blanket was only to sit on. It was May and the evening was warm. But the beers were for drinking. And that's what we did, laughing at our memories, our futures, and each other. At one point, Prateek got fairly intoxicated and announced he had always planned to run for president. At another, Ellen revealed that her greatest earthly fear was indoor swimming pools. She didn't say why.

We watched Philadelphia turn all colors. I don't know if it was the pollution, but the sky became the most wonderful pinks, purples, oranges, and greens before the sun disappeared from the horizon.

As the last light faded, we heard a yell from the ground, about two-hundred feet below us.

"Hey! Hey guys!"

I ran down the stairs let to Mullins in and helped him get to our strategic enjoyment position on the roof.

In the month since he hurt himself, Mullins hadn't told many stories. In fact, he hadn't talked much at all. I don't know what was going on inside his head. I think he wanted to figure it out on his own. He spent a lot of time alone, researching where he would travel, reading, and for the first time that I know of, he started a diary.

Occasionally I would see him downtown walking around aimlessly. He seemed lost in his thoughts, entirely distracted from the world around him. But there was something new in his walk; each step seemed to be directed toward a solid spot on the ground.

"Hey Mullins, where have you been man?" Prateek asked.

"Oh, you know Prateek, doing drugs. You?"

"Hey, that's my line man. My line."

"Patent it and come talk to me." Mullins laughed.

"How's the research on the travels going?" Ellen inquired.

"Great," he said. "Great." He took a swig of beer. "What do you guys think about Antarctica?"

"It's one of the continents," I said. "But not on my list of vacation resorts."

"Aw man!" he replied, "It's gonna be fantastic. And I bet the guys down there will have amazing survival stories."

"If you want to hear a survival story," Prateek said, "there's a guy I'm working with next year who used to run this mutual fund..."

Ellen spilled the last of her beer on his head. Everyone laughed, and the sun dropped under the sky.

"Yeah," said Mullins, "I'll sure have plenty of stories of the Turf to tell them too."

"Oh yeah?" said Ellen. "Like how to live in an apartment where the bathroom never gets cleaned?" She looked at me and smiled, but I thought: Chestnut Doctrine, because she never cleaned the bathroom either.

"Yeah," he said. "You know, despite everything I've been saying all year, I'm not sure what my story of this year is yet."

"The returns, you're saying?" Prateek asked, "or what happened to you, or what?"

"All of that, I think."

"We're behind you," Ellen said, and then she smiled her beautiful smile.

"I know," said Mullins slowly. He looked at each of us for a second, and then he looked at the sparkling city and drank his beer.

We sat in silence for a while, in the cool night air, and watched Philadelphia light the dark.

When I close my eyes, I am still there, sitting between Ellen and Mullins, listening to Prateek opening his next beer and curse as it fizzes all over his lap.

*   *   *

July 6
San Francisco

Hi Aaron,

I bought a hat, and a white convertible
with white leather seats. Driving out here
is like Mary Poppins on crack; you fly over
these hills and just hope your underwear
doesn't show. (I got four tickets last
month, but they are really teaching me how
to drive!)

Work pleases me. I'm getting good returns
at the moment, and avoiding the shit jobs.
Most of the people here don't know what
they're talking about, and once they figure
out that I've got it by the balls, things
will be easier.

I eat in the nicest restaurants in the
city, all on the business. I haven't met a
lot of people I like yet, but there's a lot
to explore so I'm never bored.

By the way, don't forget to submit your
latest wine reviews to the Turf website.

What the hell's going on with you?

Tootles,
Prateek

*   *   *

August 10

Lima, Peru

Hola senior,

How are you?! Peru is amazing! I'm
learning so much about South America, and
living is cheap and good. Best of all,
I'm cooking the local delicacies with my
roommate Gastón, like cibiche (raw fish in

lime juice), and squash with hot peppers.
I don't always cook though--some of the
restaurants have unbeatable atmospheres,
and we go out a lot. You'll be happy to
know that I've finally taken some salsa
lessons and got to dance with some hombres
calientes! Amador is so jealous!

It's funny, Paris seemed so right, but
being here has been unbelievable. Also,
the group I'm working with is a fantastic
bunch. You'll have to meet them all at some
point.

By the way, I'm coming to visit you
next week. The tickets are purchased, and
I don't wanna hear no lip. You better have
ALL your stories ready for me.

    Hugs,
    Ellen

                  *   *   *

September 24
Accra, Ghana

Yo Aaron!

What's up, man? From my end, world
travel isn't so bad! I'm in Ghana now,
which has a real mix of modern development
and traditional living. I'm taking a lot of
pictures, and I'll send you copies when I
get them developed.

You would really enjoy the music here.
People play and dance and sing until they
drop! None of that stolid keep-your-mouth-
shut-and-your-feet-on-the-floor classical
bullshit. You have to move, you have to!
So, most of the storytelling I'm doing and
learning here is with music. It's amazing—
the guys here—they remember so many stories,
so much history, and when they talk,

everyone listens. We need more respect for
our storytellers in the US! I'm going to
write to my congressman about that.

It's sometimes lonely on the road. But
I meet people I like each day, and I'm
writing a lot in my journal and thinking
about things. Recently I've been traveling
with a Kenyan girl who's teaching me a lot
about how to live in Africa without getting
stressed out. She's doing a tour of the
West Africa before she settles down.

I miss everyone. When's our first Turf
reunion? Also, how's everything going with
you? Did I hear you were working on a book?
What's it about?

Keep it real,
Mullins

*   *   *

As for me, I got the job with the Philly Orchestra, and I wrote
down this story between my rehearsals. I'm the only one from
those years at the Turf who's still here, and I'm proud to be the
Philadelphia branch of the family.

It seems so rich when I look back. With the right music on,
and the right ambiance, the memories take charge, and the
colors are more real than what's in front of me. The shapes find
their perfect form, and the people and stories spin together like
an old film reel.

Drew once told me that the funny thing about young people
is that they think their life is a movie. Maybe that's true, and
maybe when I tell you about it, the whole thing seems cinematic
or artificial. Or maybe Drew's wrong. Maybe young people
aren't funny at all, but the filmmakers who remind the rest of us
where life's drama begins.